MW01128617

FURY UNLEASHED

WES LOWE

Copyright © 2020 by Wes Lowe

All rights reserved.

No part of this book may be reproduced in any form or by any electronic or mechanical means, including information storage and retrieval systems, without written permission from the author, except for the use of brief quotations in a book review.

CONNECT

Join our Action Thriller Readers Group and get two action thriller novellas from our two best-selling series. They are not available for sale and are **EXCLUSIVE TO OUR SUBSCRIBERS.** To join, visit:

www.wesleyrobertlowe.com

All warfare is based on deception: When attacking, seem unable; when using force, seem inactive; when near, make the enemy believe you are far away; when far away, make him believe you are near

SUN TZU, *The Art of War*, c. 500 BC

The Lord is a warrior; *Yahweh* is his name. When you go to battle your enemies, and see horses and chariots *and* people more numerous than you, do not be afraid; for the Lord your God *is* with you.

MOSES, *The Old Testament,* c. 1400 BC

PART I

PROLOGUE - EVIL DAWNS

BETRAYED

Forty-three-year-old lawyer Garret Southam, gazed pensively out the window of the Hong Kong Business Aviation Centre, a small airfield that catered to an exclusive clientele where private planes could get in and out discreetly and efficiently. Standing erect in his perfectly tailored blue suit that could not mask his powerful physique, he resembled that quintessential James Bond in his prime: Sean Connery. Physically and financially, he was a distant cry from the unkempt, scrawny broke teenager that arrived at the British colony decades ago.

His concentration was broken up by a sudden tug on the arm by his daughter. "Is that the one, Daddy?" asked the eleven-year-old, broomstick blonde Olivia excitedly, pointing to a plane taxiing on the runway toward them.

"No, not that one. But it will be soon," replied Garret in a warm sonorous baritone that still contained a small vestige of his British accent.

From down the hall, a young Chinese girl squealed in a familiar voice, "Olivia, Olivia! What are you doing here?"

Garret and Olivia pivoted to see ten-year-old Abby Sung

scrambling toward them. Waddling behind was her rotund and bling-adorned father, Tommy.

Abby was the Chinese version of Olivia. Both girls were jailbait and, in a few years, Garret and Tommy would need baseball bats to fend off all the hormone-crazed guys that would be chasing their daughters.

Olivia hugged Abby. "I'm here to see my mommy."

"Me, too!" cried Abby.

Narrowing his grey blue eyes, Garret's face tilted up to the cloudless sky. "Well, we won't have to wait too long. I'm pretty sure that's her plane landing over there."

He cocked his head to Tommy and said in a hushed voice, "I thought Jocelyn was coming in tomorrow."

Tommy shrugged. "Chin pulled a rabbit out of his hat. This flight was fully booked, but somehow he got her on board."

Garret squeezed a fist to mask his sudden chill. "I wish our wives would stop trying to save the world. Going to Thailand right after a tsunami was hardly a smart idea. They could have had a building fall on them or gotten typhoid."

"Would you rather they stayed home and played mahjong?" Tommy grinned. "Besides, what's the point of having a trophy wife if you can't show her off? Having them do charity work is good for business."

Even Garret had to snicker. It was impossible to stay serious with always happy and gregarious Tommy around. "You're incorrigible, Tommy."

"As if I knew what that meant, Mr. Fancy Pants Lawyer," snorted the high-school dropout Tommy.

"It means..." But, before Garret could finish, Olivia and Abby began waving and jumping in delight as the plane taxied closer to the arrival bay.

"Hi, Mommy. Hi! Welcome back," shrieked the excited girls in their high-pitched penetrating voices.

"It's about time," muttered Garret. "We have some things to discuss."

He frowned in Tommy's direction, whose head bobbed solemnly in agreement, muttering as if he were speaking to a clandestine operative. "Yes, we do. Does Mary know?"

"She will soon. How about Jocelyn?"

"Same here. She'll love it, though. We're moving to Los Angeles. Disneyland, here we come!" Tommy danced a little two-step. "Are you sure you want to move back to London?"

"Can't stand the beastly Americans. Never could."

"The plane's coming. It's almost here," shouted Abby.

They all spun around to focus on the plane crawling down the runway toward them. It seemed like an eternity to the young, screaming girls who hadn't seen their mothers for seventeen days.

Suddenly, disaster.

BOOM! BOOM! The plane exploded! Instead of a plane on the tarmac, a long cylindrical inferno was burning out of control. Flames shot thirty feet in the air and, even through the large glass window, cries of anguish sounded briefly before being snuffed out by the sprouting billows of black smoke and conflagration.

Nobody could survive the fiery apocalypse. Pandemonium erupted inside and outside the terminal.

As Garret held her close to his chest to prevent her from running outside, Olivia pelted her father, crying hysterically, "Mommy! Mommy!"

Abby dove into Tommy's arms, sobbing. "No, that's not Mommy. It's not Mommy! That's the wrong plane."

BOOM! The plane split in half.

BOOM! The plane exploded into smithereens.

All jolliness and decorum disappeared. Devastated eyes of Garret and Tommy bore grimly into each other, suspicious and afraid beyond human belief. They knew it was not the wrong plane. It was exactly the right one.

They both knew it, and they both knew they were responsible, but damned if they would or could admit anything to anybody at any time...especially their daughters.

An explosion of this magnitude had likely destroyed everything, including the supposedly indestructible black box. But, even if the flight data recorder survived, it would never be found.

DESPERATION

HONG KONG - FIFTEEN YEARS AGO

W ith Tommy quaking beside him in the shabby hall of a fifth floor tenement in Hong Kong's poverty-stricken Shan Shui Po District, Garret pounded on the simple plaque on the door that announced the existence of the Good Shepherd School.

A slight man in his early thirties, George Reid, opened the door and arched a startled eyebrow at the sight of the odd couple: an immaculately clad businessman and a portly wanna-be Casanova.

George and Sarah Reid, husband-and-wife missionary teachers, operated the small private English language school out of their apartment. While they could make a lot more money by teaching in one of the expat schools, both of them had a burden to care for Hong Kong's poverty-stricken and underprivileged. None of their thirty-two students had much money and none was demanded or even requested. Tuition was "free" or by "freewill offering," which could mean a bag of oranges or a cooked chicken or, on rare occasions, a thousand dollars from an occasional benefactor. George and Sarah had always operated on the principle that, "The Lord will provide" and, somehow, at the end of the month, the rent was paid, their bellies were full, and they had enough to make sure the students had adequate school supplies.

The Reids were previously in a rural area close to Shanghai where George's father and grandfather had also been missionaries. They loved the small village but the Tiananmen Square Massacre in Beijing by the Chinese government on June 4 and 5, 1989, as well as rising oppression against Christians, made them realize that China had become too dangerous. So they packed up their few belongings and their two-year-old son Noah and moved to Hong Kong, which was still under British control.

The move also allowed the Reids to include a greater Christian component in their teaching curriculum, something they were afraid to do in China. This was not for their own sakes, but they were deeply concerned for their students. There had been stories of Christians being jailed or sent to disappear in anonymous labor camps and the Reids didn't want to risk the futures of their pupils.

Without adequate funds to have a separate space for a school, the Good Shepherd School was integrated into their fifth-floor elevatorless apartment. With an open door policy, they never knew who would should up. It might be grimy illegals, dope addicts, or working girls trying to get out of the life. Or, as happened almost every day, some of the grateful denizens of the area would drop off some fresh veggies, a chicken, or some still-warm baked pastries.

But this odd pair of middle-aged men, one in a tailored suit, one looking like a peacock pimp, was a first.

Not that that would influence or fluster George. Without a hint of surprise at seeing the new arrivals, George inquired pleasantly, "You look a bit lost. May I help you?"

"We'd like to speak to Master Wu, please," said Garret. "I'm Garret Southam and this is Tommy Sung. We are friends of his."

If you are friends of the sifu, you certainly haven't come from around here. George noticed the urgency in Garret's voice and responded, "He's meditating. Please come in and have some tea. He'll be awake within an hour."

"It's imperative that we speak to him now. In private," Garret said, failing unsuccessfully to mask the urgency in his voice.

"We need his help," pleaded Tommy. "Please, please, please."

George scanned the duo with fresh eyes. The tone in Tommy's voice revealed a disturbance and, even though the staid Brit tried to mask his emotions in front of the American, Garret's troubled eyes and tense posture impressed upon George a severity and desperation.

"I understand. Please come in."

INSIDE THE CLOSED BEDROOM, MASTER WU, GARRET AND Tommy sat cross-legged on the floor. While Master Wu's face remained emotionless as Garret and Tommy poured out the painful story, inwardly, his heart was breaking. The story had unfolded beyond his worst fears.

Twenty years ago, Garret, Tommy and Chin Chee Fok were Master Wu's prize students. However, Chin, seduced by visions of opulent grandeur, formed the Golden Tiger Triad. Master Wu tried to dissuade Garret and Tommy from joining, but the allure of easy prosperity was too much.

Only when Garret and Tommy got married and had Olivia and Abby did their consciences change. Even so, it took years before they had the guts to leave Chin. Surprisingly, when told of their plans, Chin was most understanding. They would leave when their wives returned from Thailand.

How gullible could they be...

"We should have listened to you," confessed Garret.

"We want to go after Chin, and we need you to help us," Tommy stated emphatically. "Now."

Master Wu's brow furrowed. Even though it had been years since he had seen them, they were still his students and he would never abandon them. Master was still master, and disciple was still disciple. Inhaling, he said quietly, "Chin has poured gasoline on your hearts and the fire within you rages. But are you ready to wage war with the Tiger Master?"

It was a rhetorical question. Garret and Tommy both knew that they could never match Chin's resources.

"But we can't let him get away with it," burst out Tommy.

"You and Garret will be almost immediate casualties. Your daughters need you. Who will take care of them if you are dead?"

"When then, Master Wu?" asked Garret.

Master Wu was firm. "Not until your daughters are fully grown."

The two men knew why the master had chosen that time far into the future. Other than siring children, normal relationships with women had little interest for Chin. Forbidden fruit was his sexual preference. Master Wu was telling them that they had to wait until Olivia and Abby would no longer be attractive to Chin.

A bitter, but wise pill.

"Yes, Master."

"But there is something more. The two of you must go back to work for Chin."

"What?" exploded Garret.

"That's crazy," said Tommy.

"All warfare is based on deception," said Master Wu simply. It was a quote from General Sun Tzu's "Art of War," the ancient Chinese military treatise that was foundational to Master Wu's teaching.

Garret and Tommy resisted the urge to walk out. They had rejected the master's advice before and their wives had paid the price.

"We can send Abby and Olivia away for schooling but what do we do for fifteen years until they are grown?" asked Garret.

"You train."

"Won't work for me. If I go back, eating and drinking is about all I do," said Tommy.

"How about you, Garret?"

Garret's voice hardened. "I could make time if that's what it takes. But by the time the girls grow up, I'll be well over fifty. I couldn't keep up with Chin. He hasn't let up, and I'll never catch up."

"Not you," said Master Wu. "I have someone else in mind."

They heard the slamming of a door closing on the outside of the bedroom.

"Noah, what happened to you?" they heard a woman scream in worry and frustration.

They heard a boy brag, "You shoulda seen the other guys. Bam. Bam. Bam!"

"Fighting's not excusable, son," said his father sternly.

Master Wu, Garret, and Tommy stood up. Master Wu

opened the door and the three saw a scrawny thirteen-year-old boy with one helluva shiner lying on the couch.

Sarah, carrying an ice pack, shook her head. "Master Wu, what am I going to do with Noah? He's getting into all kinds of trouble with the things you teach him." She put the cold, plastic sac on Noah's bruised eye.

"I promise, Master Wu, I didn't start it. Honest. They were stealing Jenny's buns, you know the lady with the cart down the street. You know how hard she works. I couldn't let them get away with it. Right? Right?"

"Not exactly right, but it's a start." Master Wu glanced at Garret and Tommy. He saw Garret's breaths quickening and could sense Tommy's body stiffening.

His dark hazel eyes flashed a clear message. *Noah is the one.... Trust me.*

THE ABYSS

Noah was exhausted. That day's workout with Master Wu was a killer. Today was his eighteenth birthday so, for a present, the sifu gave him the most grueling workout he ever experienced—every muscle in his body begged for more oxygen.

As he limped painfully down the hall to the family apartment, all Noah wanted was a long hot shower and his mom's promised home-cooked prime rib dinner, a rare and costly treat in Hong Kong.

He opened the door. "NO!" he screamed.

Three dead bodies were sprawled on the floor lying in their own pools of blood. His mother, his father, and Kai, a serious drug addict that Noah's parents wanted to rehabilitate.

Knife wounds were on his parents' faces and gashes split their bloodied clothing.

There was no evidence of foul play anywhere on Kai's body, save for a blood-stained knife imbedded into his chest right above the heart.

It was clear what had happened. The narcotic-addled

substance abuser had pillaged the apartment looking for cash to feed his addiction. When George and Sarah returned home from their shopping expedition, Kai, as if some demon had possessed his soul, pivoted on them, hoping to rip away whatever funds they had.

When Kai discovered they had none, he grasped the carving knife from the counter that was going to be used to carve the roast. He slaughtered Noah's parents, then turned the knife on himself.

Noah crawled to the cabinet that held school supplies... and a half bottle of his father's scotch, or 'holy water' as George liked to call it. Noah stumbled backward, then slumped silently cross-legged on the floor and polished it off.

His eyes glazed, his world began spinning, and then he passed out, throwing himself over his mother's body.

"Hey, bro, happy birthday!" called Chad from the door.

Chad Huang was Noah's roommate. Years ago, he had started off as a student at the family's school but, when Noah's parents discovered he was an orphan, they insisted he stay with them. He and Noah had a rough start but now, they were like real brothers.

"Holy shit!" yelled Chad when he entered and saw the bloody havoc.

He dashed to the neighbors and banged on the door. When Mrs. Wong answered, he cried, "Call the police and get Master Wu here as fast as possible."

Chad ran back to the Reids and gently lifted Noah's blood-soaked body off his mother's. Chad cradled his unconscious bro' in his arms, murmuring "Noah, we're gonna get through this. You can't let the bad guys win."

IT WAS A TIME OF BEGINNING, AND IT WAS A TIME OF END.

This tiny Protestant church with a seating capacity of one hundred had been a mainstay of Hong Kong since the 1850s. Its rough wooden pews, twelve-foot tall wooden cross at the front and a large unfurled rice paper scroll with the words "Jesus Saves" written in Chinese calligraphy were all over a century old. It was the church where the Reids had worshiped since emigrating from Shanghai, and now it was the church that would send George and Sarah home.

At the front were two plain wooden coffins. Noah covered his mother's, Chad over Noah's father's. Master Wu knelt between the two of them, his arm around Noah's back.

"Why? Why? Why?" cried the teenager. "Mom and Dad never hurt anyone. All they ever did was help everybody they could. They never took anything for themselves. How could a good God allow this to happen?"

It was the question that had troubled or stumped every spiritual person regardless of faith since the beginning of time. For most, there had never been a completely satisfactory answer. Master Wu's answer from his Buddhist/Taoist background was as good as any.

"Don't look at the immediate, Noah. Think a year, a decade, a century ahead. No one knows the mind of the gods...of God. This may be the turning point, no, this is the defining moment of your life."

"I couldn't care less. Kai, the bastard...he stabbed them a hundred times each. For what? We have nothing. I'd kill him except the coward stuck a knife into his own heart first."

"If there is a hell, you can rest assured that's where his soul is."

Chad went to Noah and cradled his arm over his shoulder. "I don't give a crap about where Kai is," he blurted.

"That doesn't help Mom and Dad. They didn't deserve this. That doesn't help Noah or me."

"I know. I know." So much to say, so few words of genuine comfort. Master Wu pulled the weeping boys to his chest. "Your parents were the finest people I ever met."

Noah replied bitterly, "And look where that got them..."

"NOAH, YOU MUST QUIT DRINKING NOW," CHASTISED MASTER Wu in the foyer of his martial arts studio.

"Who are you? My mother? It's legal. It's in the Bible," slurred Noah as he chugged down a quarter of a bottle of the cheap firewater. "Or do you think you're too pure to have booze in 'Master Wu's Kung Fu Palace and Pie Shop.'"

Master Wu grabbed the bottle from Noah and heaved it against the wall. The glass shattered into fragments and the tan liquid spread out over the floor.

"What the hell you do that for? That cost me good money," cried the despairing Noah as he drunkenly pounded on Master Wu.

Master Wu did not put up any resistance and allowed Noah to strike him for as long and with as much strength as he could muster until the young man hadn't a shred of energy to punch anymore.

"Are you giving up on me, too?" cried Noah in despair.

"Hit me some more, Noah. Hit me until the pain stops, never to return again."

Noah took a wild, inebriated roundhouse at Master Wu. Completely missing his target, he stumbled to the floor and started vomiting.

PART II

DARKNESS DESCENDS

1

GRADUATION

N oah, now twenty-eight, stood in the wings of the Henry Wilson Hall's stage, waiting for his name to be called. Even though he wore the same regalia as the other Northern Summit Law School graduates, the loose-fitting gown could not completely hide his lithe, athletic build and definitely not his leading man good looks.

Noah's sharp blue eyes glinted as they patiently searched the eight hundred happy seated faces in the audience, wondering whether a special person had shown up. He started at the back of the auditorium and slowly worked his way toward the front.

There he was! Sifu Wu was seated in the eighth row in seat eight.

Noah chuckled to himself. *I should have figured that out. Typical Chinese. Lucky number eight.* Master Wu had taught him that eight was a lucky number because, in Chinese, the word for 'eight' rhymed with the word for 'luck.'

Unlike the gowns and suits worn by everyone else in the room, Wu stood out, appearing every bit the grandmaster of

Hung Gar Shaolin martial arts that he was. He wore an orange traditional uniform: loose-fitting trousers and a jacket with his Chinese surname embroidered in a small, single gold letter over his heart.

Although Master Wu had on his usual stoic face, Noah thought he detected a hint of pride sneaking through. Since the death of his parents, Master Wu was not only his *sifu*, but his mother, father, and teacher.

With incredible sensitivity, he nurtured Noah not only back to an acceptance of life's circumstances, but an expectation of what he might be capable of. Without Master Wu's patience, prodding, and understanding, Noah too might have fallen permanently off the rails. Deeply spiritual, Wu taught Noah about the "Dao," or the "Way," the ancient Chinese philosophical view of living in harmony with the sources, patterns, and substances of everything that existed.

During his journey to healing, Master Wu encouraged the poverty-stricken Noah to explore every avenue to finance his dream of going to an American school and getting a law degree. Noah felt it was hopeless but obediently went through the motions.

Eight Years Ago

Noah did a flying handstand and landed in front of Master Wu. "I got it! I got it! I got a scholarship. Los Angeles, here I come!"

"And you didn't think you'd get in anywhere. I'm proud of you."

Noah whipped a sheet of paper out of his shirt pocket and waved it in front of his sifu.

"Can you believe that? I got a 'special university scholarship.' All I have to do is teach three martial arts classes a week: beginner, intermediate and advanced. A one in a million chance at getting something this good."

Master Wu beamed at Noah, hiding the truth behind his smile. *No, it is a one hundred percent chance when you talk to the right people. And in a few years, you will get another 'special scholarship' for law school, again to teach martial arts classes...That's the only way we can be sure you will keep your training up.*

"Hey, you've got to come visit me. Check out Disneyland, Knott's Berry Farm, Hollywood," said the beaming scholarship winner. He knew that his sifu had absolutely no interest in anything like that, and that was assuming he knew of their existence.

"I don't even own a television. And besides, I hate flying. You've got to come back to me."

"Someday, Master Wu. Someday."

Present Day

"Noah Reid." The clear voice of the president of the Northern Summit Law School knocked Noah out of his reverie and back to reality.

Noah proudly stepped forward, received his diploma, and shook the president's hand.

"Congratulations, Noah. Now your life begins."

Although the president would say that two hundred times that day, Noah did not feel he was mouthing a cookie-cutter platitude.

Noah's life *would* begin today.

～

"DIDN'T THINK YOU'D MAKE IT. THOUGHT YOU HATED

airplanes," joked Noah to Master Wu at the garden reception.

"Coming here was my first time on a metal bird and going back will be my last. I head back to the airport in fifteen minutes."

"Don't you want to see Hollywood? Or the La Brea Tar Pits? Or Knott's Berry Farm? Or the Getty Museum?"

"I came here to see you graduate and now that I have confirmed that you actually did, I have no other reason to be here."

"I'll go with you to the airport. Give me a few minutes to say goodbye."

"Noah, stay and celebrate with your friends. They're your family, too."

Noah knew better than to argue with his sifu—he would never win. And he was ready to party hearty.

"See you back in Hong Kong then."

Young man and old bowed deeply to each other. Noah returned to the reception while Master Wu stepped to the entrance.

Enjoy yourself while you can, Noah, because the day I have been preparing you for is coming soon. Your destiny with Tiger Master Chin is upon us... and I pray I guessed right.

A FITFUL RIDE

SOMEWHERE OVER THE PACIFIC - SUNDAY

T hree non-stop days of partying with all the other Northern Summit law school graduates later, a conked-out Noah bounced up and down in a wide-body Boeing 747 airliner. He had drunk so much that he was oblivious to the turbulence in the darkened passenger cabin.

Dressed casually in jeans and a wrinkled linen shirt, Noah slept cramped in a fetal position in an economy window seat.

A frightened five-year-old girl sitting beside him, wearing glasses with Coke bottle lenses, poked her index finger repeatedly into Noah's side, whispering, "Mister? Mister?"

However, Noah remained lifeless to the world as the restless girl kept stabbing her agitated finger into him. "Hello? Mister?"

When Noah's lack of response continued, the girl unbuckled her seat belt, climbed and pulled back his arms that were wrapped around his knees. She then clambered onto his lap and boxed his cheeks with her fists. Noah

finally awakened to discover the young Shirley Temple
sitting on him.

Noah resisted his urge to throttle her and instead willed
a friendly smile. With an alcohol-impaired hoarse voice and
a breath that smelled like a cheap winery, he uttered, "Hi,
cutie. I'm Noah. What's your name?"

"Cassie."

"Well, what can I do for you, Miss Cassie?"

Throwing her arms around Noah's neck and gripping
tightly, she whimpered, "I'm scared, Noah. It's really
bumpy."

A sudden drop in altitude freaked everyone on board.
Cassie whimpered, "Please save me."

"As long as you are with me, I will make sure nothing
happens to you," burped Noah.

Cassie's wide eyes glistened as she snuggled into Noah's
chest. "I love you."

The young girl's affection came from out of the blue.
Seeing the apprehension on Cassie's pale face, Noah knew
there was a little more than a bumpy ride on her mind.
Pointing to the out-of-shape slob sleeping in the aisle seat
with more than a few empty little bottles of brandy rolling
around on his passenger tray, Noah asked gently, "Is that
your father?"

Cassie held back a tear as her little head nodded. "Yes.
Mommy ran away...Daddy's having a rough time."

Noah's heart caught in his throat. This was so unfair to
Cassie...and he felt utterly helpless.

Cassie hugged Noah even harder. "Mommy says Daddy
is a loser. But I..."

Cassie's words died in the air as a nerve-racking series of
bounces rocked the plane. It was probably the first time in

history that every white-knuckled passenger had obeyed the "Use the seat belt sign."

Trying to soothe the young girl's pounding heart, Noah whispered in her ear, "My mom used to say, 'Whenever there's a storm, it gets a whole lot worse before it gets better.'"

And then an indistinct but chilling deep and prolonged crying came from the wind, some terrified passenger or possibly the sound of some animal howling?

The girl screamed with primal terror. "That! Did you hear that? Someone's trying to kill a bear!"

"Hey, Cassie. Don't worry," Noah reassured her. "He'll have to eat me first and then he'll be too full to eat you."

The spooked cherub pointed out the window. In the far distance was the faint glimmer of lights from another plane. "I think the bear is over there."

Noah squinted in the direction of Cassie's pointing finger. "There aren't any bears flying out there. They are afraid of heights."

"If it's not a bear, it's a tiger."

"You might be right. Good thing we're here and the tiger's over there."

Then, just as suddenly as the violent masses of air movement began, calm arrived. Oblivion was averted, replaced by an oasis of tranquility.

"Now weren't you silly to be afraid, Cassie?"

"Noah, there's always something to be afraid about. And don't you forget that."

"Yes, ma'am."

THE LIGHTS CASSIE SPOTTED IN THE DISTANCE BELONGED TO A

Cessna Super Cargomaster EX. Its seasoned crew wasn't concerned about the air turbulence; that happened on virtually every flight. Not to the degree they had just experienced, but keeping their seat belts fastened allowed them to keep confidently focused.

That feeling of assurance did not extend to its passengers, especially one inside its four hundred and twenty-seven cubic feet of cargo hold. In the moody shadows created by the pallets of goods, boxes and crates, a Bengal tiger was imprisoned in an iron cage. Deep indentations of bite marks on the iron bars showed the cat's desperate struggle to be unleashed.

The powerful, endangered golden feline with the ink-black stripes was in pain, caused when one of its long upper canine teeth broke off. The tooth was lodged in the door's keyhole, broken off when the animal hoped to break free from its prison by biting on the cage's lock.

A sudden, brutal turbulence caused the turboprop to rock furiously and cargo toppled against the feline's cage. The big cat pounced to its feet, exploding with a roar that permeated the air.

THE WIDE-BODIED COMMERCIAL AIRLINER FLOATED ONTO THE tarmac in the growing darkness at the Hong Kong International Airport. Flanked by glowing red lights, the metal behemoth ambled down the runway like a giant sloth, slowing gradually until it reached the arrival gate.

Cassie's father gently lifted his sleeping daughter from Noah. "Sorry about that, man. Things have been kind of rough but I'm going to make it up to her."

The father watched as Noah reached into his pocket and

pulled out his wallet. He removed a fifty-dollar bill and tucked it into Cassie's pocket. "Buy something nice for her. And tell her it was from you."

Cassie's father's hand trembled as he removed the bill from Cassie and gave the money back to Noah. "I'll buy something nice but will tell Cassie it was from you. I wasn't passed out. I heard everything. I...I...I'm going to try harder. You're a good, decent guy, Noah. Thanks."

"No worries."

The two men fist-bumped.

AT ANOTHER PART OF THE AIRPORT, UNLOADING THE SPECIAL caged cargo off the Cessna Cargomaster was not going smoothly.

Four husky men, wearing thick Kevlar-reinforced gloves and jackets, gingerly carried the increasingly hostile tiger off the plane.

A foul-smelling piece of shit slithered out of the iron pen and onto the ground.

Too late to prevent his foot from landing on the crap, a handler slipped on the slimy poop, releasing his hold on the cage to break his fall. "Aah!"

The other men steeled their grips, struggling to keep the iron-barred box from crashing.

The mishap made the men more careful, especially as the now fully awake feline thrashed about even more.

3

THE TIGER MASTER

HONG KONG - SUNDAY NIGHT

I nside the Hong Kong terminal, the tension that knotted Noah's being vanished—he was home. After clearing customs and collecting the huge duffel bag that contained all his possessions, he exited the sliding glass doors, then went to catch a cab.

Ouch! There was a lineup of twenty fares ahead of him in the taxi queue. Sighing in resignation, he shook his head, eyes wandering throughout the airport.

And then, a jaw-dropping sight: four hardened toughs with ravaged faces and battle-scarred forearms rode on a flatbed truck carefully holding onto a cage that contained a livid, thrashing Bengal tiger. Even more astounding was the person standing erect on top of the truck's cab overseeing the proceedings: a superbly conditioned Chinese man in his fifties, wearing an impeccably tailored navy blue Chinese suit, looking larger than life...invincible. If martial arts superstar Bruce Lee had lived to his fifties, this is what he would have looked like.

Noah didn't know it but this was Chin Chee Fok, the source of Garret and Tommy's downfall so many years ago.

Noah stood transfixed, watching the surly feline pace and gnash at the cautious and fearful handlers.

"Hey, Boss! Rajiv, at your service. You coming in or not?" shouted a voice speaking with a strong Indian accent.

Noah twisted his head to see a turbaned young man holding the door open to an old Yellow Cab.

"Sorry about that. Can I sit in the front? I like to see where I'm going."

"Sure." The cabbie stuffed Noah's duffel bag in the back seat while Noah climbed into the passenger seat. "Where you going, Boss?"

Before Noah could answer, mayhem erupted right in front of them.

The driver of the flatbed carrying the tiger struck a rare pothole, knocking the cage off balance. To keep it from tipping, a handler grabbed one of the iron bars. That split second was all the tiger needed. With one swift bite, the tiger chomped through the man's Kevlar glove, severing several of his fingers.

The victim screamed, releasing his hold on the barred prison. Reacting, the driver slammed on the brakes. With acrobatic agility, Chin remained on top of the cab, but the forward momentum carried the cage forward, smacking the other handlers. The freaked unfortunates frantically pushed the cage off their bodies.

That was a mistake.

The tiger's attempts to bite its way free from the cage were partially successful—the lock had been broken with one of the animal's bone-crunching chomps. However, the broken tooth stuck in the keyhole had kept the door closed.

Until now.

One handler yanked on the cage's door when he tried to

steady himself. The tooth in the lock loosened and dropped to the ground.

The gentle sound of enamel hitting asphalt thundered a toll of catastrophe.

The prison's door burst open.

The beast surged out, teeth bared. It chomped the arm of one of the hapless minions, severing it, then made an electrifying bolt to freedom. The handlers and onlookers shrieked and screamed as they haphazardly scattered in all directions, trying to evade the striped fury.

Chin's reaction was completely opposite. His face steeled, transforming from respectable Chinese mandarin to mammalian stalker. He leapt from the top of the cab to the ground and chased the raging beast down the walkway of the airport terminal, weaving around all the bystanders.

"Follow them," shouted Noah, pointing at Chin and the tiger.

"That's a plan!" yelled Rajiv as he stepped on the gas.

The cat was fast, but its hunter, blazing like a world-class sprinter, matched the tiger stride for stride.

With Chin gradually gaining ground, the feline terror's innate jungle survival instinct kicked in. It sprang from the sidewalk to the top of a passing station wagon.

The vehicle's panicked passengers squalled white-knuckled fright as the cat's paws slashed downward, trying to break the window. Picking up the pace, the driver swerved frenetically, trying to dislodge the unwanted passenger.

Chin was relentless in the pursuit of his savage prey. He effortlessly sprang onto the roof of a passing SUV, then leapfrogged from vehicle to faster vehicle to keep up with the tiger.

He was almost there when the animal vaulted to the top

of a hundred-foot-long van that rumbled by the station wagon.

With a superhuman leap, Chin followed suit, bounding and then landing at the opposite end of the van from the tiger.

Tiger and man, both on top of a moving truck, with nowhere else to go except the inevitable destination: each other. The two locked eyes—hatred flared in the feline's and confidence emanated from the human's.

The two charged, taking less than two seconds before the battle's next phase. The beast, gnashing its razor teeth, leapt at Chin. Simultaneously, Chin, combining grace with power, sprang to meet his foe.

Noah gasped in horrified wonder as man and beast collided in midair. The tiger tried furiously to sink its teeth into his captor, but Chin restrained it by adeptly grasping the feline's nape. Crooking his forearm under the animal's neck, he applied viselike pressure to choke the animal.

It seemed an unfair battle. The tiger had the strength to bring down an animal eight times its size, and its bite could decapitate a deer. As formidable as Chin was, he was no match for an infuriated tiger, and the tiger broke free.

Chin lunged after the beast and leapt onto it. He maintained a viselike grip and the two rolled off the van's roof. As they plummeted, Chin positioned himself on top. The beast was his cushion when they slammed the ground.

The beast thundered in excruciating pain. With its back now badly injured, the tiger struggled to writhe free, but Chin locked the animal's head and secured its body with his legs, preventing its escape.

"C'mon, boy, you can do it. You can do it," whispered Noah, hoping against hope that there was a miracle in the feline's future.

Chin began grinding his knuckles into the tiger's temples. The beast tried to bite its way to freedom, but it was too weak to withstand Chin's relentless assault. If the animal could speak, it would communicate how the ceiling was spinning, how its aching skull fought with confusion, how its brain was on fire. But instead, it sagged, unconscious.

Chin stood victoriously and stepped aside as the handlers arrived and threw a mesh net over the insensate animal.

Rajiv inched his cab slowly by the victor and his booty. "You ever see anything like that?"

"Never. That was one crazy, scary mother."

"Who? The ninja or the tiger?" swallowed Rajiv.

Noah's eyes flicked back for a final glimpse. Chin's hard angled face with unwavering eyes seemed to penetrate his soul. "My mistake. Those are two crazy, scary mothers that I would never want to mess with."

"Be careful what you don't wish for. Brahma has a habit of humbling us."

"Well, my karma's good."

"Right." Seeing Rajiv's troubled eyes reflecting in the rearview mirror revealed to Noah, that the cabbie was unconvinced.

And neither was Noah.

4

DANNY BOY

HONG KONG - SUNDAY NIGHT

I n a circular driveway in front of his gargantuan mansion in the ritzy Victoria Peak area, now fifty-something Tommy parked his metallic blue Mercedes Roadster alongside his BMW, Land Rover and Caddy. Stepping out of the car, he did something he had never done before—spend a moment to appreciate his home.

Obviously, something was on his mind as his eyes wandered from the pool to the fortified fence to the tennis court to his custom-built eight thousand square-foot mansion.

Tommy hadn't changed much over the years. Still dressing flamboyantly, still wearing too much bling, still eating way too much. Except now, his hair had thinned. He was ridiculous with his comb over, but there wasn't anyone that would dare mention that to him.

He climbed the six granite steps to the front door. Before he could get the house key from his pocket, the oversized wooden door swung open.

"Hi, Daddy," greeted now twenty-seven-year-old daughter, Abby.

"Love you, babe," beamed Tommy as Abby pecked him on both cheeks.

"I've got something special for you," winked Abby as the two stepped onto the entrance's marble floor. She pointed to Olivia, sitting on the piano bench in front of the eight-foot Steinway grand piano in the living room.

"Olivia, you're finally back," called Tommy, waddling like a penguin up to her where he got his second smooch in one minute.

"Yes, I am, Uncle Tommy," confessed Olivia.

Noting she couldn't hide a bit of bitterness, Tommy offered, "Do you want a drink? We have..."

"No, no, no. Abby and I have been practicing."

"Sit down, Daddy," ordered Abby, leading her father to the oversized maroon leather sofa.

"Yes, ma'am."

Abby stepped over and stood beside the piano as Olivia seated herself on the piano bench. Abby pointed a finger to commence and Olivia's fingers began caressing the keyboard.

Abby's luscious, soulful voice crooned:

> Oh Danny boy, the pipes, the pipes are
>   calling
> From glen to glen, and down the
>   mountainside.
> The summer's gone, and all the flowers are
>   dying.
> 'Tis you, 'tis you must go, and I must bide.

Tommy's eyes misted. It was his favorite song. At the same time, he hated it because it always reminded him of the past...it had been Jocelyn's favorite song too.

Tommy gazed wistfully at the innocent performers. Abby and Olivia had lived up to the potential they exhibited as kids—they could be heartbreakers or home wreckers.

With her slim, supple body, makeup that highlighted her large sensual eyes and short elegantly coiffed hair, Olivia had her mother's classic beauty of a sandy-blonde Audrey Hepburn.

Abby didn't resemble either Tommy or Jocelyn. She was more like a contemporary Chinese movie star, with luscious lips, long wavy ebony hair and sumptuous hazel eyes.

Tommy's reverie was interrupted by his vibrating cell phone—it was from Garret, the only person he would have taken a call from. He answered in hushed tones and stifled consternation from showing up on his face.

With the girls coming to the end of their performance, Tommy quickly and discreetly hung up and composed himself. Wrapped up in their music, Abby and Olivia did not notice he was wound with the tension of a coiled spring.

Tommy jumped to his feet for a standing ovation, applauding vigorously. "Bravo! Bravo! You must have sung that song a thousand times for me, and every time it gets better."

Abby opened appreciative eyes. "Thanks, Daddy."

Dancing with the moves of a 1960's Doo Wop dancer, Tommy joked, "So that's what the two of you do in New York. You're keeping all the jazz clubs there in business."

The girls joined him and pulled him down on the sofa.

"Hey, don't you like my moves?" protested Tommy as he squeezed beside his daughter.

"No," giggled Abby as she leaned over to the coffee table and shut off her iPad, which had recorded the performance.

Olivia feigned indignity. "Uncle Tommy, please. Abby and I were extremely diligent in our studies."

Tommy cracked up. "Yeah, yeah, yeah. You took courses at every bar, watering hole and club in town. Birdland, Iridium, Village Vanguard or whatever they have there now." He wagged his finger in mock accusation. "Don't try to hide it because I have the credit card statements to prove it."

"That's called research," protested the petulant songstress.

"Of course. And I'm Santa Claus."

"I'm serious. Daddy, it's a genuine fusion of international cultures coming together. Irish, Asian, American..."

"Spare me the philosophy." Tommy got up and stretched out the stiffness from his inner turmoil. "I have to go out now to earn some cash to pay for your Irish-Asian-American singing lessons."

"But you just got here," complained Abby. "Just stay for one drink."

Tommy kissed his daughter on the forehead. "Save it for me. Bye."

As Olivia lounged back on the ultra-comfortable sofa, Abby carefully poured two glasses of merlot from the crystal decanter. She handed a glass of the ten-year-old red French liquid to Olivia.

Olivia raised her glass. "Your dad left in an awful hurry."

Abby shook her head. "He's got the craziest schedule. I've only been back a few days but we haven't had a chance yet to sit and talk for more than fifteen minutes. And all of it is chit chat."

Olivia took a slow sip, pensively swirling the liquid in her mouth before swallowing. "That sucks. Especially when you're going back to New York...I wish I could join you. I hate the idea of starting work."

Abby's voice dropped as she let out a bombshell. "Actually, I've decided to stay and help Daddy with the company. I haven't let him know that yet. I'll never hear the end of it if I do."

Olivia made the cuckoo sign, twirling her finger at her temple. "Are you nuts, girlfriend? You're an artist, not a businesswoman. I'll drive you to the airport myself. Juilliard Jazz Studies program is where you must be."

Abby took stock of Olivia's comment, rubbing her index finger over the rim of her glass. "Daddy needs me."

"Men don't need anybody," snapped Olivia with more than a touch of bitterness.

"Stop bringing your father into everything, Olivia."

Olivia made a nasty face at Abby, then exhaled. "It's not just Dad. It's just that I hate...I hate lawyers. All they want to talk about is sports and the law. On the rare occasion when they want to talk about something else, it's anatomy. My anatomy. 'You've got a nice tush,' or 'Are those for real?'...I hate it. I want someone who will talk to me about Igor Stravinsky or debate with me about Pascal or have an intelligent dialogue about the films of Kurosawa."

Abby giggled. "I'll be thrilled if he just talks...with his hands in his pockets."

"Boy, do I ever know where you're coming from...You really staying, Abby?"

"Yes."

They lifted their glasses in a toast. Their shared horrific memory tried to surface, but the girls willed themselves to ignore their tortured memories.

5

THE TAXI

HONG KONG - SUNDAY NIGHT

J et lag and a crazy schedule finally caught up with Noah. He fought to keep his eyes open, staring through the window with fascination and anticipation at old memories and new wonders as Rajiv guided his vehicle through Hong Kong Island toward its destination.

Through his parents and Master Wu, Noah had a unique firsthand understanding of China.

Noah's own family experience dated back to the 1930's when his great-grandfather, a former coal miner, got religion and moved his family to rural Shanghai. His grandfather originally hated China and became a medical doctor in the United States but, when he was stationed in China during WWII, he discovered that his heart yearned for the Chinese, and he became a medical missionary in the same village as his father. Noah's father, George, had the same missionary zeal for China, and had it not been for the growing religious intolerance and civil unrest caused by the Communist Party, he would gladly have stayed in the same small village.

But that was not to be and, with a heavy heart, he moved the family to Hong Kong for a new beginning.

Through Master Wu, Noah developed an understanding of Chinese culture and how it came to be. Steeped in Chinese philosophy, culture and history, the sifu loved to teach Noah about China's multi-faceted heritage. Of Hong Kong's transformation from fishing village to thriving metropolis, how her original inhabitants came from neighboring Guangdong province and then of the British imperialistic influence that continued until 1997 when the British Crown Colony's ownership reverted to China. All the positives and negatives of China started infiltrating Hong Kong. Everything from dialect of Chinese spoken to having to a greater influence of the state on lifestyle.

The turmoil made many Hong Kong residents, including students of the Reids and Master Wu who had risen to financial independence during the boom, flee to North America and Australia, worrying that the Communists would confiscate their property and force them to work in the fields. After all, many of them, or at least their parents, had memories of what Chairman Mao had done under the Cultural Revolution when the state tried to eliminate anyone who opposed Communism or Socialism.

These fears proved baseless. Hong Kong not only maintained its reputation as a major financial center, but also advanced and evolved to a powerhouse. Like Shanghai and Beijing, Hong Kong's horizon was full of new modern skyscrapers and mega-shopping complexes with ultra-high-end designer labels everywhere in this monument of material indulgence. With more high-end luxury boutiques than New York, London or Paris, women and men were more fashionably dressed than in any other city in the Eastern or Western Hemisphere...except maybe for Shanghai or Tokyo.

Many of Master Wu's, and George and Sarah's, students returned to the 'Pearl of the Orient,' or at least, to visit. Like Tony Bennett who crooned about leaving his heart in San Francisco, they had left theirs in Hong Kong. Despite the myriad changes, the old heart of Hong Kong was still very much alive. Co-existing with the new, they wanted to be part of the change.

And so did Noah.

Now, as an adult, as a lawyer, he was no longer content to be an onlooker but wanted to be not only part of the transformation, but the preservation of Hong Kong's rich heritage. Alongside, or close to, the modern structures, he felt the vibrancy and charm in the older street markets, one-hundred-year-old tenement buildings, and hole-in-the-wall restaurants and shops.

LIKE EVERY CABBIE IN THE WORLD, NOAH'S HOPED A LITTLE conversation might bring a bigger tip. "So I, Rajiv, am the finest taxi driver in Hong Kong. What brings you to Hong Kong, boss?"

Face still glued to the window, Noah ignored Rajiv's self-aggrandizing and replied, "Hong Kong is home. And I am not a boss. Just plain, simple Noah. Noah Reid."

"Where you come from, Noah Reid?"

"LA. Just finished school."

"Oh, you one of those rich international students then. Direct flight. Zoom. Zoom. Fifteen hours nonstop."

"I wish I was that lucky. To get the cheapest flight, I had to take this berserk route. And then there were problems with the plane. And then there were problems with the weather. I went from LA to Nagano to Seoul to Delhi before coming here. Not to mention mindless layovers for hours in each place wondering if and when we would get going again. My head hurts just thinking about it... But it's all good. I'm back. Even if it's three days late."

"Your parents will be glad to see you back. They pay for you?"

"You gotta be kidding, right? They were missionaries."

"Oh, they rich like Benny Hinn or Joel Osteen?"

"I wish. Poor like Mother Teresa. I was born in Shanghai in the *Hua Dong* Hospital to missionaries and moved here when I was a toddler when my parents decided to start up the Good Shepherd School. Not much money in a mission school."

"No matter. Rich or poor, Daddy and Mommy always want to see kid. Right?"

Noah stiffened. The painful memory was something he hated to discuss, but Rajiv's question demanded an answer. "Not anytime soon. They were, um...killed. Killed at home."

Rajiv inconsiderately blabbed on. "No, that's not good. Why your God so mean? They nice to people, and they get dead."

"For them, it was the journey. They died doing what they loved. Helping people."

"Better than dying doing something you hate."

Seeing his hoped-for gratuity drown in negativity, Rajiv lightened the conversation. "So why you come back, boss? Are you crazy? Everyone wants to live in America. New York Yankees, Hollywood, Statue of Liberty and my favorite, the Green Bay Packers!"

Rajiv reached down under his seat and took out a foam Cheesehead that he placed on his head. "Like it? This is real. From America."

Noah glanced at the cabbie. Rajiv looked ridiculous. "Hate to tell you, buddy, but I bet it's made in China."

Rajiv refused to be discouraged. "Nothing wrong with that. That means it's cheaper. Right, boss?"

"Whatever."

"So back to my question. Why you come back? I've been trying for forever to get out of Hong Kong. Nobody wants me," grumbled Rajiv.

"Hong Kong needs you," yawned Noah, tiredness starting to attack. "It needs all of us. I couldn't wait to finish school so I could come back. I start work tomorrow."

"What kind of job? "

"I'm a lawyer."

Rajiv's face lit up—lawyers were big tippers. "Driving cab is dangerous. Maybe you give me a discount on my will."

"Sure. But then you have to give me one for the taxi fare."

"You're too tough, boss."

"Life's a cutthroat business, Rajiv."

Noah and Rajiv shared a chuckle, and then Noah couldn't fight nature anymore. Exhaustion was the victor. He leaned his head on the taxi's window, using it as a pillow. Sleep descended on the young buck.

BUTTERFLIES RUMBLED IN RAJIV'S STOMACH AS HE TRAVELED through this grungier part of town. Had it not been for the fact that he was a lazy cabbie who didn't know the city as well as he should have, he would have turned the fare down. The streets here were narrow, and most of the tenement buildings were more than a century old and in bad need of repair. Some didn't have running water, witness the public toilets and communal sinks housed in little buildings outside the apartment entrances.

Rajiv groaned. All the signs were in Chinese, and very few buildings had numbers on them. Of the buildings that did, most were faded beyond recognition. Not much British or modern Chinese influence here.

Uncertain, he shouted to wake Noah up. "Hey, boss man, where are we? There's no sign or number or anything here."

"Who needs numbers? You go by feel," croaked Noah with the raspy voice of the newly awakened. He shook his head to clear his bleary head and saw the old rundown buildings. "Hey, I'm home. Don't you just love it?"

"I love to stay alive, and I'm not sure I will be here," moaned the cab driver.

"You have no worries. Chinese don't like to eat browns," laughed Noah. "Just kidding. They haven't eaten anybody here since the war."

Rajiv quivered in response. "What war?"

"Duh." Noah tapped Rajiv on the shoulder and pointed to a dilapidated old building in a street full of dilapidated old buildings. "Slow down. That's the one. This is where I get off. Thanks, man."

Rajiv pulled to the side. As Noah got out of the taxi, two toughs appeared from behind a building. One had a knife and the other wielded a baseball bat.

Rajiv stepped on the accelerator but the taxi barely moved before the hoodlum with the knife stooped and rammed the blade into its front passenger tire.

The car spun out of control toward a streetlamp but Noah raced to the taxi and with Herculean strength pushed it out of harm's way.

"Tough white boy," sneered the guy with the baseball bat. He began swinging at Noah.

Noah ducked the stroke coming at his head, then sent a roundhouse kick to his enemy's mid-section.

The guy had abs of steel and Noah's foot did nothing.

"Prick!" the gangster swore as he raised the bat over his head, then came down with full force at Noah's.

This time, Noah stood his ground, reached up and grabbed the tough's wrists, halting the descent of the wooden club. It was a stalemate battle of force and wills.

While the maple cylinder stayed in the air, Noah and the tough exchanged kicks to butts and thighs.

Meanwhile, the other hooligan pulled his knife out of the tire. He launched the blade at Noah.

Noah twisted his body and the knife lodged into the side of the bat-holding thug.

"Ow!" screamed the goon as he released the bat and buckled.

Noah elbowed his opponent in the head and it was lights out for him. He stomped toward the other goon but he'd had enough. He swiveled and tore back into the darkness behind a building.

Noah walked over to Rajiv.

"You do this all the time?" shivered the cab driver.

"That was easy. They were just young punks," shrugged Noah.

"Punks?" Rajiv narrowed his brow for a moment, then flashed his teeth with a broad grin as he handed Noah a business card. "Call me anytime. I drive you anywhere."

6

HOME

HONG KONG - SUNDAY NIGHT

N oah felt something he hadn't felt in a long time as stepped through the door of Master Wu's studio —he was home.

Tension lifting, Noah savored the sight of the familiar time-tested martial arts weapons, including the *Chine*, or "the Gentleman of Weapons," with their double-sided straight swords and colorful tassels attached to their hilts. *Ch'iang*, or "the King of Weapons"—tufted spears that were used for centuries on the Chinese battlefield; *Kan*, or "the Grandfather of All Weapons"—long, tall, straight iron bar staffs; and the *Dao*, or "the General of All Weapons"— single-edged swords used for slashing and slicing.

While each weapon was more than a century old, they were not artifacts in a museum. Their easy access showed that these were tools for everyday use.

But it wasn't these incredible artifacts that Noah was here for.

It was Master Wu, who meditated in the lotus position in the middle of the room. With catlike silence, Noah put his bag down and donned his martial arts uniform. It was identical to Master Wu's, except his bore the Chinese character for *Shaolin* on the left breast.

He turned to the wall behind Master Wu. His eyes fixed on a watercolor of a tiger entwined with a crane. Noah painted it when he was eight as a gift to his sifu. Although it was crude and childish, Master Wu cherished it as his prize possession.

Noah crossed to join his sifu. He crouched and assumed the same position as his aged master, something he had done more than ten thousand times in his life.

Wu, with his eyes remaining closed, growled in a low voice, "Stop slouching, Noah."

"Yes, Sifu." Noah straightened obediently. He must have heard that a few thousand times, too.

They kept this position for another ten minutes, an eternity for Noah. This was so far removed from the fast pace of a law school in a big American city, and yet he knew this forced time of physical inactivity was something he not only missed, but needed.

One reason he didn't attend any of the martial arts schools in Los Angeles was that he felt they were all too commercial, even industrialized. Everything was about rank, position, what color belt you had, what degree of belt you had and what title you had.

And little attention was paid to the inner self.

That was so entirely unlike the teaching he received from Master Wu. The sifu just *did it* without care of status for his students or himself. He didn't care whether he was called *Sifu,* which means teacher, or *Sigong*, which means teacher of masters, or Grandmaster or whatever. To Noah, ever since he was a little boy, Grandmaster Wu was simply *Sifu* or Master Wu.

As if reading his mind, Master Wu spoke. "Like a river

gaining strength on its journey, dynamic tension increases the flow of the *Qi*, energy throughout body and soul."

Master Wu lifted himself from the floor and stood erect. Noah followed. The teacher began a series of smooth, elegant movements. *Tai chi quan*. Loosely translated, it meant supreme ultimate boxing, or Boundless Fists. It was a surprising name for these exercises as there were no signs of their warrior origins; there was no quick action and fighting. Master and disciple synchronized their slow, graceful movements of arms and body.

Master Wu droned calmly, smoothly, as their bodies flowed in unison. "Meditation is the core of the Shaolin, but today no one has the discipline for three days or even three hours. Now, boys who dream of being Jackie Chan or Bruce Lee populate the schools run by opportunists or fools who are only interested in fighting for fighting's sake. They had lost the *art* of martial arts...Once I sat for three months meditating by a courtyard wall."

This was too much for Noah. Try as he might, he couldn't maintain his composure. His serene disposition erupted into laughter. "Sifu, I'd rather be Bruce Lee any day than sit by a damned wall doing nothing."

The pupil hugged his master. "I really appreciate your coming to my graduation."

Not reciprocating Noah's affection, Master Wu waited until Noah pulled his arms away before flashing a wisp of contentment. "I wouldn't have missed it for anything. It is good to see you at home again."

Noah rolled his eyes. "Yeah, well, if the last half hour is any indication, it's like I never left."

Master Wu frowned. "You've only been here fifteen minutes."

"Yeah, I know." A yawn escaped Noah's mouth. "I'm bagged and I gotta get to work by eight tomorrow."

Without warning, Master Wu's right leg flew out toward Noah, landing it in Noah's chest and effortlessly knocking him back.

Noah surged to attack while Wu's leg hung in the air, but the old man snatched Noah's foot and with an effortless push shoved the new lawyer to the floor.

"Focus, Noah. Focus."

Noah rose and advanced cautiously. Circling...circling...

He adopted the position of a snarling tiger as if to hypnotize Master Wu.

Undaunted and uncompromising, Wu glared back at Noah and countered with his own tiger stance. Right foot ahead of left, weight primarily on the back foot with a slight amount on the balls of the front. Both arms raised, one a few inches higher than the other. Readying for attack, Noah spread his fingers open and formed them into tiger claws.

Noah struck at Wu's back flank, but before Noah connected, the master wheeled around at light speed. He easily knocked Noah to the ground.

As Noah attempted to get up, Master Wu pivoted and dropped Noah again.

Noah leapt to his feet, then stepped backward.

Master Wu's palms touched together as if praying, and then his hands sprang out, pushing Noah, tripping him with his leg, sending Noah to the floor.

Noah was panting now, but Wu's breathing remained calm and relaxed as he resumed the ready position.

As Noah lifted himself, a swirling, spinning Master Wu propelled his legs into Noah with a rapid combination of left and right, sending him colliding with the floor.

Noah, lying on his backside, gasped for breath. "I never saw that before. Where did that come from?"

"Did you think I took up knitting while you were gone? I created that. Thinking keeps you young. You should try that sometime."

"I could never do that, no matter how much I thought or practiced."

Wu took Noah's hand and pulled his young protégé to his feet. "A sapling grows into a tree with deep roots and a thick trunk."

"I doubt it. I'm going nowhere."

"You did much better than I expected. Did you find someone to work out with in Los Angeles?"

"Nope. My routine every morning before brushing my teeth, taking a shower or going to pee was to spend half an hour on the drills you taught me. Same deal every day, sickness or in health, rain or shine, exam or holiday. Only when I taught classes did I do anything connected to martial arts."

"That was better than nothing."

"Yeah, but I didn't improve. I just stayed static."

Master Wu tapped his fingers in thoughtful recognition. "You know the moves but lacked the need. However, when the time comes, you will release your inner tiger."

"Not likely. I just had an old geezer spank my ass."

Ignoring Noah's disrespectful comment, Master Wu snorted. "It's the heart. Not the muscle, not the age."

"I'm soft. It's in my genes. Blame Mom and Dad."

Master Wu whipped his arms and put Noah into a head-lock, applying bone-crushing pressure, firmly chastising his disciple. "You can call me whatever you want but do not dishonor your parents."

Noah flailed away but was unable to free himself. "It was a joke."

The sifu applied more pressure, squeezing until Noah's eyes felt they might pop out of his head.

"Not funny."

"Master Wu, you're killing me," rasped the new lawyer.

"Good." Master Wu then released Noah, who stepped back to rub his temples, trying to restore some circulation back into his brain.

"Your heart is what will give you strength when the time comes. And you will attack because you are a warrior."

"Sifu, I'm about to become a professional paper pusher. I'm no hero, no warrior. No Dwayne Johnson. No Jet Li. No Chuck Norris. No Jason Statham. No Rambo. No eye of the tiger."

Wu's eyes bored into Noah.

"You don't need to be. You are Noah Reid." He handed an envelope to his disciple. Noah opened the thin paper package. Inside was fifteen hundred bucks. He opened his mouth to protest but Master Wu spoke first.

"You just got off the plane and came directly here. There's no banks open and I'm sure you didn't change money before you left LA."

7

UNCERTAIN

Despite the hour, Noah was not Master Wu's final visitor that night.

Tommy had come earlier but when he saw Noah with the master, he exited the building and enjoyed a bowl of spicy pork noodles from a food cart. When he spotted Noah leaving, he waited until the new lawyer was out of sight, then slipped into the building.

Tommy stepped to the upper floor of the studio where the aging sifu resided.

Not elaborate or ostentatious, the living quarters were simple. A photo of a young Noah and Master Wu in martial arts garb hung on the otherwise plain walls. There was no furniture save a thirty-foot-long rosewood table with a huge tiger carved into the wood on one half and an equally large crane carved into the other half. The tiger and crane were symbols of *Hung Gar*, Master Wu's style of Shaolin martial arts.

Chairs were unnecessary because, at a height of only fifteen inches, the table was so low that one had to sit cross-legged on the floor to use it. In other words, it seemed to be a simple Shaolin monk's quarters matching the lifestyle of its owner.

That was unless one examined for details carefully. The magnificent tabletop was seamless in its grain, meaning that it was cut from a single tree, making it rare and even more valuable. Because they were carved directly into the wood, the details of the tiger and crane were not immediately obvious. Close examination showed the fine attention of a master craftsman—every feather of the bird was unique as was each whisker of the tiger. Rather than the ordinary depth of an eighth of an inch, the depth of carving was almost half an inch, giving a multi-dimensional quality to the animals.

The tea set was another understated marvel, a gift from Tommy, who knew how much the master appreciated fine tea. From the Yixing region of China, it was made of rare purple clay from the Yellow Dragon Cave and dated back almost three centuries. There was no design or writing engraved on the teapot and, to the uninitiated, it was not useful—it was too small—and definitely not worth showing to anyone because it was so plain. To those who knew, however, this set was a tea connoisseur's dream. The pot had been aged and coated so that tea served had maximum flavor and color retention.

Tommy knew Master Wu could never afford these treasures. He knew that the sifu had never turned away a student and never charged any that came, not even a cent. But he could have charged a fortune. He himself was trained at one of the great centers of the Shaolin, the legendary and mystical monastery, *Heaven*. He was there for two decades and not only learned technique, but also the history, the *raison d'être*.

By the time he left, Wu's knowledge of Hung Gar was

nonpareil. Just as the monks of Heaven never charged him, Wu promised he would never turn away any student because of finances.

This was not exactly the best business model in the world, but Wu lived by it. While most students simply took advantage of Wu's generosity, others shared their own good fortune with their sifu, especially Tommy and Garret.

They had quietly and discreetly provided this building for Master Wu, taking personal responsibility for its design and furnishings. Tommy and Garret made frequent but secret visits, feeling more at home in Wu's humble environs than their own homes built on the backs of human misery.

Tommy sat at the long table and handed the seated Master Wu a plain-wrapped parcel, about the size of a dinner plate and about an inch or thirty millimeters thick. "A going-away present."

Master Wu unwrapped the simple wrapping. Inside was a compressed cake of *pu-erh* black tea leaves. He tore off a small chunk and rubbed it in his palms.

After the leaves separated, he placed them into a small unadorned brown ceramic teapot and poured hot water onto them. He quickly swirled the pot to rinse the leaves, then discarded the water onto a tray.

Master Wu contemplated a moment. He realized that this tea was the rarest of the rare and easily cost over ten thousand dollars per kilo.

Filling the pot with hot water again, the master chided, "You should save your money."

Tommy's voice was somber but matter of fact. "I don't need money where I am going."

Master Wu silently poured tea into two tiny cups and handed one to Tommy.

Tommy took a sip. His voice dipped to a murmur.

"Freedom has been elusive. It has always been just another step away...and then another...and another."

Wu studied Tommy sadly. "We make our own prisons, but we can always escape if we truly want to."

"Would the honorable man do that?" questioned Tommy. "I chose the road I traveled. I chose my traveling companions. And we failed you and failed The Way."

Wu intoned, "The river always flows to its destiny, to its freedom."

"Sifu, you know I am right."

"It is not your fault. It is mine. I taught you improperly."

Tommy shook his head. "You taught us well. It was we who were wrong. There must be justice."

"Yes, I know but..."

Tommy interrupted. "You know this has to be the final step, but I have a concern. Noah. I have doubts. That the fire will devour him."

Wu nodded. "That could happen to anyone. You. Garret. Chin."

Tommy sensed a faint concern. "What's wrong, Sifu?"

Wu looked down at the table. Just as he had done with Noah, the fingertips of each hand tapped the corresponding fingertips of the other. "Noah got soft in America. He has lost his edge. When we sparred, I could have beaten him blindfolded. And he disrespected me... and his parents."

Tommy's brow furrowed. "Then you're not sure too. Is he the one?"

Wu took a long thoughtful breath. "I anguish over all my students. Noah? I have known and trained him since he was a child, preparing him for this moment. Does he have the potential? Absolutely. Does he have the skills? Without doubt. Does he have the heart?"

Tommy stated pointedly, "That's not the answer to my question. Is he the one?"

Master Wu measured his words carefully. "I can see no other choice...and yes, I believe that, when the time comes, the real Noah will emerge and unleash the fury."

That was not exactly a reassuring answer.

8

IT'S ALL GOOD

HONG KONG - MONDAY 12:30 AM

Tommy strutted with Garret down a bustling, neon-filled narrow street. The odd couple of *garish gigolo* and *consummately conservative* had traveled the lively chaotic block thousands of times during their forty-year association and had long stopped really seeing any of the locals or their activities, so familiar were they with the neighborhood.

But not today...especially Tommy.

He waved at Susan Mah hanging her laundry on a balcony clothesline amidst her clutter of clay pots and cans of orchids and fresh herbs. Seeing her son hawking pirated DVDs, he bought fifty of them. Over the years, he had purchased more than five thousand of them and he had never watched a single one—just threw or gave them away. From another sidewalk vendor, he purchased six bags of Chinese deep-fried dumplings. From another, five pounds of charcoal-roasted chestnuts.

He and Garret paused at the end of a block and began handing out their loot to the delight of the mystified street people..., kids and families.

Popping one of the chestnuts into his mouth, Garret spoke with grim lucidity. "This is the crossroads, Tommy. You realize that if we keep going, there is no return."

"Stop asking. I've told you a thousand times I'm all in...Are you having doubts?"

Garret shook his head. "Of course not. We have waited fifteen years to take our revenge on Chin...It's torn my soul and our relationship apart, especially not being able to share it with Olivia."

Tommy inhaled deeply then blew out a long gasp of air. "Our girls. That's the only worry I have. What will Chin do to them?"

"We've gone through that, Tommy. We kept them out of Hong Kong long enough...they're now too old for Chin to want to have any interest in them and if we're dead...they are useless to him."

"Do you think Noah can pull it off?" asked Tommy, tapping his heart.

Garret pulled away Tommy's tapping hand, turning his friend to face him. "I don't know how many times you and I have gone over this, but the bottom line? It doesn't matter what I think. We put our eggs in Master Wu's basket and he is the only one we have ever been able to count on."

"But this is different. And a hell of lot bigger and more dangerous."

There was no disagreement from Garret. The lawyer murmured, "Que sera, sera."

What will be, will be. The next few days would unfold the culmination of years of planning and deception.

There would be no more living a lie.

~

AFTER ANOTHER HALF-BLOCK, THEY STOPPED AT ONE OF THOSE buildings that seem to exist everywhere in the world. Nondescript in nature, there was always a queue of at least an hour for decked-out young studs, sexed-up sirens, and tourists with bulging tummies in their sweaty T-shirts and shorts.

Garret and Tommy shook hands. This was hard. Both knew this was the last time they would share a solemn moment together, except... at the end.

"Goodbye, my friend."

"Goodbye, Garret. Take care of Abby."

"Will do." Garret turned and disappeared into the crowd as Tommy arrogantly pushed his way to the head of the line. The beast of a bouncer recognized him and immediately opened the door to let him in.

"Good evening, Tommy. Glad to see you again."

"You're glad; I'm glad. It's all good, *paisano.* All good." Tommy handed the bouncer a hundred-dollar bill and gave him a knowing wink as he entered.

9

BIG MOUNTAIN TIME

HONG KONG - MONDAY EARLY AM

This gambling establishment was luxury exemplified. Not at all like the cavernous garish mega-casinos found in neighboring Macau or on the strip in Las Vegas where everything was *faux*, this place was the real deal: crystal chandeliers from Italy, genuine antiques from the Incas, the Tang Dynasty and Egypt and the *piece de resistance,* an original Picasso surrounded by other paintings from the Cubist era.

It was Tommy's idea to keep the building's shabby exterior. Part of it was that gambling joints were illegal in Hong Kong but a bigger motivation was to create buzz, that elusive ingredient that would mark a place as special. He wanted there to be the aura of mystique, of something taboo, a place for insiders only...The stark contrast between the outer appearance and inner luxury helped accomplish this.

Amy Peng, the proprietor, greeted Tommy with a kiss and a playful spank on the bum. Forty-two but with the figure of a girl less than half her age, she was ravishing in her long, red-silk *cheongsam,* the body-hugging one-piece dress of Chinese socialites.

"You haven't been here for two days. Amy no like you, naughty boy. You better not have found someone else." She spanked him again, then nibbled on his ear.

"If I did, I'd never tell you," joked Tommy as she escorted him to a private craps room.

"Now you have to make me some money."

"Always." Tommy took out five hundred dollars and lifted the slit in Amy's dress. She had legs for days, and his fingers danced up them. He deposited the money into her panties and his eyes sparkled lecherously.

"I'll find you later, you dirty old man," purred Amy.

She left Tommy in the room with other high-end punters.

He inhaled the familiar smell of Cuban cigars and expensive alcohol. Normally, his drink of choice was Hennessy Paradis, but tonight he ordered a bottle of Louis XIII Special Edition Rare Cask. At over $20,000 per bottle, he impressed even the most jaded gambling staff, a hard task to accomplish when they were accustomed to servicing the extreme whims of the most pampered wealthy.

Tommy's eyes explored the room as he remembered the first time he stepped into the room more than twenty years ago. Back then, it was a piece of crap—just like the rundown neighborhood outside. But, he felt it had potential and he was right. As business and the size of the pocketbooks of patrons grew, he decided to keep the grungy appearance outside, while enhancing the appeal of the interior.

As an added touch of mystique, he also never gave this gambling den a name. You had to be in the know to come here.

A ballroom-gown-wearing hostess showing her more-than-ample cleavage poured the French elixir into a tulip glass. Tommy gulped it down, then drew out a thick wad of bills.

He handed it to the dealer. The slight Chinese man returned to Tommy several large stacks of chips.

"Nice," chortled Tommy. He pushed $10,000 worth of chips onto the Pass Line and the tuxedoed Boxman handed him a new set of genuine ivory dice.

Swiveling his hips and shaking the dice high above his head, Tommy's excitement was infectious. "Owoo!" he howled.

"Owoo!" joined the other patrons, infected with the gambling disease that affected so many Chinese. From kids betting milk money on video games to high rollers who owned private jets willing to ferry them to Monte Carlo, Las Vegas or Macau, gambling was an irresistible addiction.

Tommy blew on the ivories, then encouraged them loudly, "Come on, little babies. You can do it."

An onlooker, infected with Tommy's surge of frenzied excitement, joined in. "Lucky, lucky, lucky!"

Tommy flung the dice. Boxcars. Two sixes. A loser.

"That's good. That's good!" cried Tommy.

"Why is that good?" asked the curious spectator as the stickman pushed the dice back to Tommy.

Tommy guffawed as he scooped up the dice and started shaking again. "You don't know nothing about craps, do you? One loss means that I'm that much closer to winning. You cannot lose forever. And when you win big, it is big, big, big!"

The stickman had barely taken away his last bet of chips before Tommy shoved another stack onto the Pass Line—this time, he doubled his bet—twenty thousand U.S. dollars.

Now things were getting interesting, taking the breath of

other gamblers away. "Big mountain time. Time for the big mountain!"

The hostess reached into her bosom and pulled out a pair of dice and handed them to Tommy. "I have been warming them up for you. Treat them nice, and I'll treat you nice."

"Always and forever and tonight!" He eagerly stuffed a two-hundred-dollar tip between her breasts.

Pulse now pounding like a jackhammer, Tommy barked out, "Come on, baby, come on. Boat's coming in. Mountain man's gonna climb all the way to the top. Boat's just waiting to dock. Lucky, baby, luck."

Tommy's thrill was infectious, and the other gamblers joined in the shouting as Tommy kept shaking the dice.

"Easy street coming," and "Lucky charms, lucky titties," and "Rocks are gonna roll."

Tommy feathered the dice onto the table. Unbelievable. Another pair of sixes.

"Yes! Yes!" shouted Tommy, pumping his fist into the air. "Now it's going to go my way!" Automatically, Tommy pushed $20,000 of chips onto the Pass Line and rolled again.

Six and one.

"Didn't I tell you? Didn't I tell you?" barked Tommy, waving his finger at the excited group gathering around as a dealer pushed a stack of chips to cover Tommy's winnings in front of him. Tommy pushed all the chips onto the Pass Line.

Tommy, wiggling and jiggling, now took the dice and shook them above his head, then to his left, then to his right.

He rolled—a pair of deuces on the dice-hard 4.

"Omigod. Omigod. This is so good."

The point was 4 and Tommy pushed $88,000 of chips on

the table as his odds and commanded, "$88,000 on 10. Split it up for all the hard ways!" In Chinese, he proclaimed, "*Baht baht. Faht faht.*" *Baht* was Chinese for the number eight and *Faht* was the Chinese word for lucky. Double eights meant double luck.

Now others were joining in—hey, you got to ride a winner when he's hot.

"Yes! Yes!" Tommy made eye contact with every rapt gambler around the table and saw greed in the eyes of the other players as they urged him on.

Tommy stopped shaking and all eyes converged on him. *What the heck?*

"Give me 6 and 8 for another $176,000."

Now everyone got the itch. Around the table, the onlookers yelled as they placed their own side bets, "Hard 4! Let's see them deuces! C'mon, Tommy. Do it!"

Tommy rolled the dice—he hit a 5!

"Great! Great! Nobody hurt, right?" Tommy pushed another $176,000 in chips to the Boxman. "5 and 9. 5 and 9. All the numbers! I can't lose!"

Tommy rolled an 11. He threw down another $288,000 in chips. "Press all my numbers!"

"Big time, big baby, big pay!"

"Rocket's landing and we're gonna ride!"

"Mo-ney, mo-ney, mo-ney, mo-ney. MONEY."

A frenzy of gamblers just threw money on any numbers. There was now over a million dollars of chips on the table.

"Tom-my. Tom-my!" chanted the crazy crowd of gamblers. Tommy lifted his hand with the shaking dice, allowing anyone that wanted to blow on his hand.

Meanwhile, another half million in bets showed up on the table.

Tommy shook the dice like a miniature dervish. He blew

on them and released. The dice rolled fatefully down the table.

Tommy rolled a four and three.

Stunned silence.

Everything was lost.

Tommy glumly took his remaining few hundred dollars and gave it to the croupier. "Down payment for tomorrow."

Tommy turned to leave and bumped into Chin. Chin clamped a steely hand on the portly man's shoulder.

10

SUCKERS

Dressed in a black silk Chinese jacket, the Tiger Master exuded sinister, tough confidence.

Tommy stuttered, "I...I...Welcome back, Chin. I didn't expect to see you back for a week."

"Hunting was very good. I finished early," stated Chin in a cold, emotionless voice. Without a flicker of a smile, he continued, "Now I am hunting for money. My money."

His sober countenance betraying nothing, Chin's impassive attitude unnerved Tommy. "What are you saying?"

"If tonight is an example of what is happening to my funds, there needs to be some additional explanation."

Tommy wiped the sweat off his brow. "Additional explanation?"

Although Tommy was easily fifty pounds heavier than Chin, with one hand the Tiger Master picked the gambler up off the floor as if he were a loaf of bread. In a single motion, he threw Tommy against the wall, in the process, knocking over the bottle of Louis XIII cognac.

"At least five hundred million dollars is unaccounted for, so there is a discrepancy. I want a proper accounting tomorrow. With or without you, I will proceed, and I am happy to go solo."

"It's all good, Chin. No problem. Everything's okay."

"I'm glad to hear that," scorned Chin. He did a rapid about-face and strode out the entryway.

Nerves on edge with emerging wary fear, everyone trembled as they gaped at Tommy. He had dodged a bullet but the thrill was gone from the room.

Clearing his throat, Tommy straightened himself out, brushing the wrinkles off his sleeves.

"Hey, no worries. Time for some fun." He took out a new wad of bills and threw it on the table. "Let's go. Go. Go!"

Instantly, the dealer took the money and gave Tommy another mountainous pile of chips. Tommy pushed a hundred grand's worth on the Pass Line.

The patrons gawked. How could he continue after threats like that? Was he crazy?

No one from the group uttered a sound—but they still wanted to watch.

Tommy reached in through the hostess's top and yanked a new set of dice from her cleavage, and in the same motion tossed them onto the table—a six and a five.

A winner.

The Boxman grinned and chortled, "Lady Luck's back, Tommy."

Tommy raised his arms in victory and gloated, "She never left. She never left."

Shouts of "I'm in!" and "Me, too!" rang through the air and, unbelievably, there were more dollars at stake now than before. Everybody wanted to join the party, and greed-fueled adrenaline once again coursed through the room.

What none of the rest of the patrons knew was that Chin was the real owner of this gambling joint and Tommy was just the front. Every cent Tommy lost was going to him anyway. Furthermore, Tommy and Chin had played a variation of this little game of dangerous odds for years with always the same result. Sometimes the amount Chin said was missing was one million. Other times twenty million.

It didn't matter. It was the show that counted. All the new patrons, blissfully unaware of what really went on, participated in what they thought was their turn of the Goddess of Luck shining on their fortune.

11

YOUTHFUL DREAMS

HONG KONG - FORTY-FIVE YEARS AGO

W hen Master Wu left Heaven, the mountain monastery in China where he learned *The Way,* to come to Hong Kong, Garret, Chin and Tommy were among his first pupils.

In addition to being discipled in Hung Gar martial arts by Master Wu, Garret taught them how to speak English. In turn, they tutored the Brit on how to read and speak Mandarin and Cantonese.

Chin, Tommy and Garret were inseparable. They lived and breathed Hung Gar Shaolin Martial Arts. They also dove into the Scripture study and meditated for hours. Master Wu didn't believe in dreaming, but even he had visions of creating a new Heaven in Hong Kong.

The group was broke, though, and living hand to mouth was a constant challenge. That didn't matter too much at first. After all, becoming Shaolin masters was the aim of them all, but young people being young people...well, things changed.

Master Wu watched the triumvirate grow increasingly restless. It was all well and good to be in a small studio and to learn, but that was not progress. They wanted to spread the "good news" of Hung Gar to the universe. Chin was the most enthusiastic, and he often went out into the streets to perform "tricks" for the gawkers. Earning a few bucks didn't hurt either.

Sometimes Garret and Tommy joined Chin, and this became a real event. Groups gathered in the parks and squares to see the three break boards with their heads and hands or spar with each other. The poses were fearful, and the action was ferocious.

They launched Chinese daggers at each other. However, just before the *dao* entered their hearts, it was snatched away by a lightning hand or kicked into the air by a speeding foot.

Sometimes they performed handsprings a dozen feet into the air in tandem. At the apex, they clapped each other's hands or had feet touch feet before dropping to the ground and standing upright.

Master Wu did not appreciate having his beloved and sacred Shaolin made into a spectacle, but Chin, Tommy, and Garret convinced him that this was "progress," the way of the future. Besides, they argued that Master Wu had done the same thing many years ago with Jingsha when the two brought showmanship into the sacred confines of Heaven.

It was all true and Master Wu reluctantly gave the trio his approval. After all, everything the three did was based on his teaching. When he saw their incredible acrobatic ability combined with a martial arts component, even he had to admit they had raised the bar, setting themselves apart from the myriad of other martial artists.

The razzle dazzle and an increased promotion of the Master Wu brand worked. New students flocked to the master so a bigger studio was needed. It was not even two months before that was outgrown as well. The only real solution was to add more studios. In fairly short order, Master Wu's name was on five Hung Gar Shaolin Martial Arts Centers with three more in planning.

Master Wu, while knowledgeable in martial arts, didn't understand or care to learn about financial structures or companies or anything related to business. He was glad to let Chin take control. Because the future looked so rosy, banks were willing to lend him the money to finance expansion.

EVEN MORE MONEY BECAME AVAILABLE WHEN CHIN discovered that nobody at the bank checked the figures they presented. On one loan application, Chin accidentally over-stated the income by five hundred dollars. No one at the bank noticed. Chin would not have noticed either except that Garret, who normally did the deposits, pointed out the error.

Feeling the flush of success—and deceit—Chin grew bolder. From that day on, Chin falsified income statements to help finance even further growth. He would have gotten away with it except for one thing: business started to tank. While others in his situation might have panicked, Chin remained unperturbed...at least for the moment. The important thing was to adapt and change.

Chin saw that donations for lessons were dropping. While some complained that it was because business was down everywhere, Chin felt it was due to Master Wu's voluntary payment policy. Against Master Wu's objections, Chin began charging for the lessons and housing. The strategy backfired. Rather than pay for what they used to get for free, students stopped coming.

An even bigger issue was Bruce Lee. Everyone everywhere was so enamored of him that anyone thinking about martial arts wanted to be just like this shrieking movie star chick magnet. Instead of Master Wu's strict, integrated discipline of meditation, Scripture study and martial arts, Chin saw students flocking to teachers of Bruce Lee's looser styles of martial arts, *Jeet Kune Do* and *Wing Chun.*

No boring stuff. All action. Kicking and punching and yelling and leaping like madmen. Chin could see the appeal. Secretly, he himself was bored with study and meditation.

Chin made a serious effort to persuade Master Wu to follow suit, but this was one area Master Wu refused to budge on: Shaolin was spiritual as well as physical.

With this impasse on direction, it was inevitable that Master Wu's empire would crumble. Over the next six months, huge debt accumulated, more students dropped out. Seriously diminished income, falling reputation, empty studios. No amount of marketing or branding could save a product nobody wanted.

And then...hell.

ONE MORNING, MASTER WU DISCOVERED THREE OF HIS remaining students dead at the doorstep of the flagship studio/temple.

He was beside himself. He cried, he rent his clothes, he flagellated himself but, of course, that did diddly squat. He suspected what had happened and confronted the three ringleaders, Chin, Garret and Tommy. Garret and Tommy were ignorant, but Chin defiantly confessed.

"I did this for you; I did this for us. Because you refused to change and wouldn't accept what I tried to tell you to do, I had to go out and find another way," snarled Chin.

"There is only one way, *the* Way," cried Master Wu.

"You are so pigheaded. Of course, there are other ways. I borrowed money."

"More money than we borrowed from the banks?" exclaimed Master Wu.

"Of course."

Garret and Tommy were dumbstruck. Although Chin did not state so directly, he didn't need to. Master Wu, Garret, and Tommy knew that Chin had borrowed money from the Triads, those monstrous, historic, violent criminal organizations that controlled so much of Asia's under- ground. When he didn't pay back, retribution was swift.

"And, if you don't start changing now, old man, things will get even worse. You have to do what I say."

A line in the sand had been crossed. Let alone the deception, no one had ever insulted Master Wu. Master Wu cared little about the personal attack but the honor of the Shaolin was at stake.

"That is totally against everything I stand for, everything I have taught you."

"You said you wanted to reach out to the world. That is what I have done. This is the way of the future."

"If this is the way of the future, I will have none of it. I forbid you to continue."

"I don't have to listen to you anymore. I am a Shaolin master, too," sneered Chin. "This will be my future. Goodbye."

"If that is your future, so be it. I will live in the past," replied Master Wu with resolute conviction.

As Chin walked away, Master Wu turned to Garret and Tommy. "Do not join him."

Garret and Tommy avoided Master Wu's eyes as they followed Chin.

~

MASTER WU SPENT THE REST OF THE DAY IN HIS STUDIO, fasting, meditating, and praying.

He did that all the next day, too.

And the next day as well, until the bailiffs arrived and kicked him out. They left Master Wu with nothing other than the Shaolin martial arts uniform he wore: a plain, loose-fitting shirt with wide sleeves hanging almost to mid-thigh and baggy, pajama-like pants.

It was the lowest point of his life, and the master found himself staring at the sky, wondering if he shouldn't have listened to Sigong Zhang from Heaven and stayed at the mountain monastery. Shamefully, he even thought of taking his own life, which would accomplish nothing. It wouldn't bring back the lives of the three disciples entrusted to him.

But it would relieve his pain. And it would also ensure that he never made that mistake again.

His self-flagellation was interrupted by a tug on his jacket.

Master Wu looked down and saw a concerned seven-year-old boy.

"Hi, Mister. Are you okay?"

"I'm fine. Why do you ask?" Master Wu asked, curious about the young boy.

"Well, you keep on looking at the sky as if you're hoping

to see something, but there's nothing up there except clouds. All the stuff is happening down here."

The little boy nodded his head toward the vibrant, narrow street full of hawkers, lovers, haters, vendors selling crazy knickknacks.

The child extended his hand. "I'm Noah Reid."

"I am Master Wu."

"I know. I've seen you in action."

"You have?" Master Wu was surprised and cautious. Surprised because he had never seen Noah before, and cautious because he worried about what Noah might have seen.

"Yup. Sometimes I stand in your doorway and watch you. You are amazing. Can we go back inside your studio and you can show me some more?"

"Well, thank you, Noah Reid. But I don't live there anymore," Master Wu told him.

"Where do you live then?"

"Nowhere right now."

"Hm." The young boy thought hard for a moment and then his face lit up. "Let's go to my place. You can stay with us. I'm from Shanghai. I don't remember it because I was just two when we left. I'd like to go back and see it again someday, though."

The two began walking. A flicker of life emerged in Master Wu as the energy and ambience of the neighborhood soaked in. There was nothing he could do about the past, but being with this innocent boy ignited something that he had not felt for a long time—hope. Just like Noah said, *All the stuff is happening down here.*

"Maybe I'll go with you when you head back to Shanghai."

"Cool."

MASTER WU TREASURED THE TIME HE SPENT DURING HIS stroll with Noah, who chattered non-stop. When they arrived at the tenement building where Noah lived, it was up five flights of stairs—no elevator.

"We're almost there."

Master Wu squeezed Noah's hand as they walked to the end of the dark hall to the last apartment. It gave the sifu comfort that Noah squeezed back.

There was a sign on the door: "GOOD SHEPHERD SCHOOL."

"You wait here, please."

Noah entered to see his parents, George and Sarah, in their living room cum classroom. A few of their pupils were graduating, and they hoped to get scholarships for college. Without them, there was no way they could ever hope to go. Tomorrow was another application deadline, and George and Sarah were frantically going over last-minute details with the students.

"Hi, Mommy; hi, Daddy," greeted Noah.

"Hello, Noah," replied his mother, not bothering to look up. "Wash your hands and pour yourself a glass of milk."

"Mommy, Daddy, I made a new friend."

Without glancing up, George replied, "That's nice. Friends are good to have."

"Can he live with us?" asked the young boy.

Now Noah had their attention. It was one thing to adopt a stray dog or cat, but it was another to bring a human into the equation.

"Can we meet him?" asked Sarah in a calm voice.

"Sure."

Noah opened the door to the flat, and Master Wu entered.

This was not what George and Sarah expected to see. Instead of a boy Noah's own age, here was a Chinese man older than themselves.

And he appeared to be a Buddhist monk.

Quite the surprise for the Christian missionary teachers.

And then, another shock. From his standing position, the monk bowed his head so low that the top of his head touched the floor.

He straightened, stood tall, and announced simply, "I am Wu. I am a Shaolin master of Hung Gar."

Now, some people might complain if their kid came home and asked if someone could live with them, especially someone they didn't know anything about.

Not the Reids, though. Someone had always stayed in their living room or bunked in with Noah or, every now and then, stayed in their room, too. They'd never thought of doing a background security check or asking questions and weren't about to start now.

However, they did know that no one wanted to be considered a charity case, especially a middle-aged Chinese man, monk or not. Sarah noticed Master Wu's tired eyes and the stubble on his face. Her maternal instincts told her he needed something to eat, and she excused herself.

George smiled broadly and offered a gracious hand. "Very nice to meet you, Master Wu. Noah wants you to stay with us. If you are willing, we would be most honored if you would."

"I accept." Master Wu gave the Shaolin hand sign to George.

Noah nudged Master Wu. "You're supposed to shake his hand. Like this."

Noah took Master Wu's hand and shook it. "That's how you do it."

"I see."

Noah nodded approvingly as Master Wu shook George's hand.

Sarah re-entered, carrying a plate of cookies. She tripped on one of Noah's toys on the floor, sending the cookies flying. With lightning speed, Master Wu snatched the tiny delicacies out of the air before they struck the ground and placed them elegantly back onto the plate.

Noah dashed to the master and pulled on his jacket. "Can you teach me how to do that?"

"It will be my privilege, Noah."

12

THE ACCOUNTANT

HONG KONG - MONDAY 5:00 AM

G arret parked a borrowed silver Toyota Corolla in front of one of those ubiquitous characterless apartment buildings that Hong Kong—and in fact the whole world—had too many of. He didn't want to draw attention to his presence, which any of his personal cars certainly would. This building was in an expat complex, a place where overseas employees who worked in a foreign country could live, shop, and send their kids to school without having to mingle with the locals.

Garret hated these places that continued to nurture the colonial attitude that *coloreds* should be segregated from whites so as not to pollute Caucasian purity. For Garret, who had lived and breathed Asian culture since he was a teen, this attitude was an insult. He hid it, but just barely.

He stepped out of the car with his briefcase and strode briskly to the entrance where a uniformed guard saluted the senior lawyer before letting him in. Garret strode with the confidence of someone who knows his importance down the hall and knocked on the door of a particular unit.

Thirty-five-year-old prematurely balding Ron Armstrong, dressed in his pajamas, answered.

"What the...? I thought it was the maid. Garret, do you know what time it is?"

"It's time to get to work. I suggest you shower, shave, and grab a coffee."

Garret opened his briefcase and handed the accountant a thick file of documents and a USB flash drive. "I've gone over the Golden Asia financial statements and have flagged a few areas that need modification."

Ron winced as he gave the file a cursory glance. He restrained himself from hurling f-bomb invectives.

"We were up until midnight preparing these, and I dropped them off at 12:30."

"And I have been examining them carefully since then."

"You couldn't have found anything wrong. The team went through things with a fine-tooth comb."

"I didn't say there was anything wrong. I said I flagged some areas that need change. Get them done by lunchtime."

The implication of Garret's words needed no elaboration to Ron. "Cook the books."

Ron ran his hands through what was left of his greasy hair, perusing Garret's notes.

"This is a lot of number crunching. A lot."

Garret folded his hands, then spoke with an undercurrent of a threat in his baritone voice. "I pay you a lot of money. A lot. Goodbye, Ron."

Garret turned away and headed back down the hall without waiting for Ron's answer.

13

THE THUNDERBOLT

Somewhere else in the city, in a sparse modern flat temporarily provided by his new employer, Noah was dead to the world. After he finished at Master Wu's, he had to walk two miles before there was enough civilization to find another cab brave enough to pick him up. By the time he got to his apartment, it was past 4 a.m.

Noah sat at a table, snoring, his head propped on his right hand. A cup of cold coffee the size of a small bucket purchased at an all-night convenience store sat beside a thick open law textbook titled *Principles of Litigation*. He had a meeting scheduled with his new boss that morning and thought he should stay awake to brush up on his worst subject just in case he was challenged about complex legal disputes, but it was not to be.

The alarm clock on his cell phone rang and rang, but he paid no attention to it until his numb arm collapsed and his head hit the table. His foggy brain checked the time on his phone, then surged to alertness. The new lawyer moaned, "Reid, you are so dead."

He frantically pulled himself up and fumbled into the

shower. It was freezing, but Noah had no time to be picky. Besides, it helped wake him up. To save precious seconds, he brushed his teeth while showering, then used the shampoo from his hair as shaving cream and ran the razor over his face.

To add oil to the fire of his frazzled nerves, the water from the shower turned scalding hot.

"Damn, damn, damn." He hopped from foot to foot as the stinging water peppered his skin. He leapt out of the shower, barely patting himself with a towel before throwing a shirt and pair of pants on his still-damp body. Never mind that they were wrinkled. No time for ironing but, even if he wanted to press his clothing, that would have been impossible because he hadn't been settled in long enough to get an iron.

"Please, no, don't fire me...Mr. Southam, the plane was late. No, stupid, he knew my plane got in late. He was hassling me about where I was... Mr. Southam, the neighbor's dog died, and she wanted me to cremate it. No, numbnuts. This is a no-pets building."

Then a novel thought. "How about the truth, Reid? Duh. "I was late because I slept in because...because I wanted to see my sifu? My martial arts mentor?" That was another brilliant loser of an excuse.

With no time to look in the mirror to check for proper grooming, he shot out the door like Tokyo's bullet train with briefcase in one hand as he struggled to tie his tie with the other. There was just one problem. The back part of the tie still showed—a sure sign of a putz.

He didn't see it, but everyone else sure would.

～

UNDER A CLOUDLESS SKY WITH BLAZING SUN, A SWEATING
Noah jumped off the bus and peeled into a towering, eighty-
eight floored skyscraper. Weaving his way through crowds of
people and past three colorful fountains, he checked his
watch.

7:57 *I can still make it!.* Noah saw a tiny space in the lineup for the elevator. He jumped the queue and squeezed into
the elevator just as the door closed.

Noah counted at least another nineteen men crammed
like sardines along with him. All were cut from the same
cookie cutter, with dark suits announcing that they were
dressed for success, white shirts and gray ties. All glared at
him for jumping the line.

Noah wanted to shrink but then...*Holy babe-alicious
beauty, Batman.*

The babe was Olivia.

Noah shoved through the other guys, irritating them
even more, but no matter. He'd almost reached his goal.
There was only one person standing between him and his
goddess. He was only aware of her tantalizing perfume,
which was made even more attractive than her creamy skin
and long lashes. Noah melted, ignoring the other passengers as he fumbled for something, anything, to say. "Thanks
for holding the elevator," he blurted.

Olivia remained silent, but not the suit that stood
between them. "No one held the elevator. You butted in. I
hate butter-inners."

After this auspicious start, it was tension all the way to
the twelfth floor. The elevator stopped, and the disagreeable
man got off. As the door slid to close, Noah gave a little
wave. "Let's do lunch real soon," he called. "Friendly guy,"
he announced to no one in particular. "I like him. Maybe I'll
ask him for a drink next time."

With the obstacle out of his way, Noah edged closer to Olivia, who just as quickly eased away. He gave her his best Tom Cruise smile, a grin that would normally melt an iceberg.

No such luck. Olivia's eyes focused straight at the elevator door.

Her fragrance of roses, jasmine and Italian cinnamon was unavoidably alluring. Noah allowed himself to inhale her scent and daringly tried a different tactic. "I'm a lawyer with Pittman Saunders. And you?"

Before she could respond, the elevator halted again, this time at the sixteenth floor. The next suit's eyes threw daggers at Noah as he got off. "There are seven hundred seasoned attorneys in this building alone, half of us making three hundred Gs and more. Why would *any* secretary be interested in a rookie?" He darted out of the elevator.

Before the door shut and before anyone could respond, Olivia swung her purse at Suit Number Two. Shocked and more than slightly intimidated by her response, everyone on the elevator gave her a little space.

Everyone but Noah.

Noah snorted, "What does he know? The most important person in any office is the secretary."

Up, up, and away went the happy group, none daring to open their mouths for fear of having the wrath of the lioness inflicted upon themselves.

Except Noah. "I've got a black belt in *Hung Gar* Shaolin martial arts, second degree."

Olivia didn't say anything, but the short pudge beside her certainly did. In a fake effeminate voice, he mocked, "I'm so impressed. May I have your autograph? I'm just a lowly secretary and I love lawyers. Especially ones that know kung fu."

Still no word out of Olivia. At the eightieth floor, Olivia stomped off, then turned to face the cringing men. "I am not a secretary."

Every guy on the elevator froze and gawked perfectly immobile at this fearsome tantalizing woman who was not a secretary. With the echo of her footsteps thundering like cannon blasts leveled at them, none dared to move. As the doors closed, Olivia marched away, revealing an enormous *PITTMAN SAUNDERS* logo on the wall.

Completely freaked, Noah shouted, "That's my floor! That's my floor, and it's eight-o-one. I'm gonna get killed."

He frantically jabbed at the stop button, and the elevator lurched to a standstill. The doors refused to open, and the emergency bell shrieked. The remaining passengers glared at him.

"You are a complete toad, rookie," an ill-tempered suit leered. "You won't last two weeks."

The fast-wilting newbie lawyer glanced awkwardly around the enclosed box, but no savior was in sight.

14

UNPRECEDENTED

It's *8:09. God, I hope nobody missed me.* Noah raced from the elevator to the Pittman Saunders Conference Hall. The room was packed, and Garret was at the podium, pontificating.

Noah hoped to be close to Olivia and, as he scanned the room, he noticed that every one of the one-hundred-and-seventy lawyers, male and female, was wearing a tailored, conservative, navy-blue or gray suit. He felt like shrinking in his off-the-rack, outlet mall special.

Truth be told, for a guy who was a chick magnet, Noah was completely inexperienced in serious relationships with women.

Being raised by devout missionary parents and an ascetic bachelor monk had a lot to do with it. Sure, as with any red-blooded young man, good looks and a nice body were important, but that wasn't all. He needed, he wanted, someone with heart, with compassion, whose emotional IQ was more than watching the hottest reality bachelorette show.

His lack of self-confidence made sure he didn't trust any

girl who threw herself at him. *Why would anyone want me?*
He was more attracted to someone that was well, challeng-
ing, had an independent streak and most important, had
that undefinable quality, "zing."

Like the girl on the elevator who wasn't a secretary that
emboldened him.

He tried to stay incognito as he scanned the room
looking for her. The last thing he wanted was to have his
new boss, Garret Southam, see him slipping in late. The
second last thing he wanted was *the girl* to see him chewed
and singled out by Garret.

There she is. Noah quickly moved to the side of the room
and stood beside Olivia. He whispered, "Hi," but her eyes
remained fixed at the front of the room.

Settled in, Noah saw that the veterans pretended polite
attention while the twenty newbies hung on every word
Garret spoke. Garret's voice had a dominating authority that
matched his physical presence. With eyes like steel, every
aspect of his being announced, "This is a man who leads."

Like many good speakers, Garret's focus shifted
throughout the room while maintaining the impression he
was staring at you. Noah felt Garret's eyes boring into him.

"Unprecedented growth. Unlimited potential and
extremely difficult but immensely rewarding work. When I
started at Pittman Saunders, there were three lawyers and a
secretary. Now we have two thousand lawyers in twelve
worldwide offices. As senior partner and managing director
for the Asia Pacific region, I welcome you to realize the
unbelievable and to achieve the impossible. To enter new
cultures and experiences that will challenge every fiber of
your existence. At Pittman Saunders, we don't climb mountains; we conquer them."

This incited spontaneous applause which Noah over-enthusiastically joined. Nodding his head in acknowledgment, Garret gestured with broad sweeps of his arms for the clapping automatons to cease.

His regal baritone continued. "To the newest members of our family, I say be prepared for the ride of your lives. That you are here means that you are among the best of the brightest new minds in the world. Welcome. I look forward to meeting each one of you personally. At Pittman Saunders, we exemplify hard work and, above all, integrity. That's the Pittman Saunders way. That is my way."

Noah and the lawyers applauded again, this time even more enthusiastically. He chimed in with them, shouting "GAR-RET, GAR-RET," as the senior lawyer left the stage.

Not stopping his applause, Noah leaned over to Olivia. "He's got to be the biggest stuffed shirt in an office full of stuffed shirts."

Olivia kept her eyes straight ahead, but there was a hint of a smile on her face. Noah noted it, glanced confidently, and continued. "Gotcha. You like that, do you? He's a colossal blowhard, matched only by his pomposity and ego. Right? Right? I'll bet you even agree with me. Come on. I know you do."

Olivia's lips didn't budge, but it seemed to Noah that her slight smile was broadening more than a few millimeters across her perfect face.

"And now I have to go meet Mr. Senior Partner, the managing director for the Asia Pacific region," groaned Noah. "Just gag me with a spoon."

Noah saw Garret waving in his direction. Noah waved back enthusiastically and turned to Olivia. "Did you see that? He waved at me. I think I made a good impression."

Olivia's voice dripped honey. "You must have. Maybe even better than the one you made in the elevator."

15

NO FEAR BUT...

In the moody light, Chin stood at one end of a fifteen-hundred-square-foot clearing of red clay floors. Clothed only in a loincloth, his remarkable physique showed off rippling abs, biceps like granite and forearms like steel rods. While riddled with scars, his body revealed not a gram of excess fat anywhere.

Chin had spent much time in jungles and wildernesses around the world and the clearing was part of a tropical rainforest he had created in a cavernous warehouse-like space. With thirty-five-foot-high ceilings, Chin had personally chosen the towering green bamboo stalks with two-inch trunks; colorful moss and lichen hanging down in strings of orange, red and purple from mangrove trees with low thick-leaved grasses for ground cover. Torches sporadically placed on the walls created shadows that poked through the cavities in the flora.

With sounds of tropical birds tittering, animals bellowing and a devilish-sounding chanting in an unknown language pervading the air, there was the feel of impending darkness about to descend upon the earth.

Six henchmen carried a caged tiger to the opposite side of the clearing from where Chin stood. Snarling, snapping, pacing and trying to bite through the bars to get at its handlers, the feline was even bigger and more ferocious than the one Chin conquered at the airport. The animal thundered at the resolute, dour-faced Chin.

With feet staggered, toes forward, knees slightly bent and lightly bouncing on the balls of his feet, Chin threw his arms with balled fists into fight ready position in front of him and barked out, "Open the door! Now!"

Duke, Chin's son, a chunky, muscular twenty-five-year-old Asian hulk with a Mohawk, opened the door and quickly got out of the way. Father and son couldn't be more different. Duke had the appearance, approach and demeanor of a junkyard dog, whereas Chin, the ferocious psychopath, still maintained heritage elements of Shaolin mastery.

The tiger, seeing freedom and a feast, bounded out the open door and galloped directly at Chin, jaws wide open, incisors ready to shred the gangster. Its pent-up anger manifested with an ear-splitting, full-throated cry of defiance, and its quivering paws stretched out, prepared to sink its sharp claws in anything in its path.

Chin bolted fearlessly toward the tiger, yelling with Bruce Lee's signature animalistic scream. Both leapt at the same time. In midair, Chin's arms were faster than the feline's in attack. He jackhammered the feline's eyes, face and mouth, breaking the tiger's nose and causing a contusion in its right eye. Nose and eye spurted blood as man and beast crashed to the floor, landing on their feet.

The infuriated bleeding beast circled Chin, repeatedly thrusting a dangerous paw in its rival's direction. Each time, though, the steel-faced Chin deftly knocked the tiger's foot from harm's way. The foes locked eyes, neither willing to give up or exhibit even the smallest hint of weakness. Chin rotated as the tiger circled him, bellowing as it flashed its fangs.

Suddenly, the tiger exploded into the air. Voice thundering and teeth gnashing, Chin stepped aside just before the tiger's claws gouged his body to bits and the jaws severed his head.

The cagey Chin knew he needed more than muscle to stay alive. If it were simply a matter of muscle versus muscle, the tiger would be victorious in moments. But Chin had an advantage over the tiger. The tiger's thinking was linear and entirely concentrated on using its direct brute force to achieve its goal. Chin's secret weapon was to think unconventionally, to use an element of surprise.

The tiger lunged again at Chin, but now, instead of resisting—the normal response—Chin allowed the momentum of the tiger to swell onto him and push him to the floor. It was totally unexpected. The tiger momentarily lost focus, allowing Chin to deliver a series of bone-crunching blows to its head and body. The feline tried desperately to retaliate but, with broken ribs and a fractured skull, it was in too much pain.

Chin triumphantly lifted the beast over his head, whirling it around in a dizzying fashion like a figure skater executing spins. He spun faster and faster until finally, after releasing a scream that could be heard in Hell, he threw the tiger right across the clearing and into the cage it was delivered in. Catching a second wind, the tiger roared and with redoubled effort charged back at Chin.

Again, the unexpected. Chin held his ground, and a fraction of a second before the tiger arrived, he quickly leapt up and did a mid-air somersault. Descending headfirst, Chin locked his left arm around the tiger's neck. The tiger tangled its legs with Chin's, and the two locked in mortal combat as the tiger ferociously snapped at his opponent, trying to free itself from Chin's lock and trying to plant its teeth into any available part of his body.

Chin, like a ruthless robot, hammered the tiger on its already broken and bleeding nose with his twisted fist. The tiger spread its mouth wide, but Chin used his left hand to grab the debilitated tiger's mandible and his right to grab the tiger's upper jaw, preventing the tiger from clamping its canines into his flesh. There was a sickening CRACK! as Chin pulled the animal's mouth apart. Chin's arms blasted at the tiger's temples like jackhammers with Herculean force, knocking the beast out.

Chin lingered over the unconscious, heavily breathing predator and slowly wrenched its neck to the point of breaking. He stopped and gave the feline's fallen form a kiss. Chin was bruised and bleeding, but he was alive, and he was a conqueror.

This was not a show, nor was the fix in for the feline. The danger was real. Chin, long ago, decided that he could only keep his edge if his life was on the line for any circumstance.

As one of his henchman came over and toweled Chin down, Duke carried in a large crate with the inscription *JASMINE TEA—GOLDEN ASIA TRADING COMPANY*. Chin motioned with precise hand signals for his son to open the lid off the box.

Duke lifted a ham fist over his head and slammed it down hard on the wooden lid, sending splinters flying. He ripped off the remaining broken boards. Underneath was a layer of fragrant, luscious green tea.

Chin rifled through the tea and reached through it and

yanked out a false bottom, revealing an enormous cache of carefully packed cash of all nationalities. A smirk curled Chin's mouth. This man was on a first-name basis with death—and wealth on the level of the largest cartels.

This was the life that Chin, the epitome of Charles Darwin's concept of "survival of the fittest," had known since he was born.

Fifty-five Years Ago

Three-year-old Chin begged his father for a stuffed Panda bear. His father's response? "I'm not going to waste my money on you."

The next day, when his father was not there, his mother bought him the bear and took it to his bedroom.

"Thank you, Mommy!" Young Chin kissed her over and over again. "I love you!"

"Oh, I don't think you do. You're just saying that because I gave you a toy," replied his mother, pushing her son away.

"I mean it. I would do anything for you. Anything." He hugged her as tight as he could, repeating his streams of kisses.

This time, his mother responded. Chin felt her tongue licking his cheek. It felt kind of strange..."I don't like this, Mommy."

"I knew you didn't love me," pouted his mother, turning her back against him.

Chin leapt up onto her. "I do, Mommy. I do."

A cheap stuffed bear. That's all it took a warped, sick mother to turn her son into her sexual plaything. She taught him how to please her, how to drive her to ecstasy. He just did it...because he loved her.

Chin was too ashamed and afraid to let anyone know but, when he was seven, his father caught the two of them in bed together. The father was so angry he got a kitchen knife and repeatedly stabbed the mother until long after her death.

"Stop it, Daddy!" cried Chin but, of course, his little hands were no match for his father's strength.

In frustration, Chin jumped on his father's back when he was kneeling over his wife's body. Chin's downward force drove the knife from the backside into his father's heart. It was over in moments.

Chin was a jumble of emotions as he raced out the door. Hate. Love. Guilt. Joy. Despair. Relief...He wanted to wail, to unleash his dark confused shadows of torment, but knew he couldn't. Someone might find out and blame the deaths on him. He wasn't going to tell anyone. He didn't want to go to jail.

Guess how a seven-year-old kid on the streets supported himself? By putting to use the one thing he learned from his perverted mother...it was easier to please strangers for food than to please his mom. And it didn't hurt as much either.

When Chin was nine, he experienced a miracle. An expatriate American businessman and his wife decided to take him in. It was a crazy decision on their part, but they wanted to have children. Chin couldn't believe something good could ever happen to him but it was true—they wanted him as their son.

The happy life lasted four years. Of course, Chin had to perform certain chores. Five times a week, he spent the night alone in bed with either or both of his "parents," but that was nothing compared to what he had been doing previously. After all, they loved him so much, he would do anything for them.

And then the businessman's parent company went bankrupt. There was no more job, and the expat and his wife had to return to America. They tearfully told Chin they loved him but couldn't afford him and, even if they could, they had no formal adoption papers to bring him back to San Francisco with them. Giving Chin fifty dollars and dropping him off at a bustling market a few miles away, they told him he would always be in their hearts.

Grief-stricken, the thirteen-year-old somehow found his way

back to the apartment that had been his loving home. He wistfully sat across the street in one of the family's favorite noodle shops. Then, the wide-eyed Chin saw the couple get out of a cab with a boy who couldn't have been older than seven. He heard the man saying to the child, "We are going to love you forever." The wife kissed the boy and pulled him into her arms as they made their way through the apartment doors.

Chin was completely and utterly lost. Rejected, deceit and pain were all he had known his young life. It was a life he hated and would do anything to get away from.

That moment, he made a decision.

He would never allow himself to be taken advantage of again. He would be the master; he would be the one to be obeyed; he would be the one to be feared. The word "love" was stricken from his vocabulary.

And that's when he met Master Wu.

Present Day

"Hey, boss, you got a visitor."

Chin dropped the bundle of cash in his hand and stood up. "No one comes here uninvited. Who is it?"

"Some old guy. He won't tell me his name and he said you would definitely meet with him."

Chin sneered. "Tell him to get lost."

Suddenly, there were several loud punching bangs as the one-hundred-fifty-pound door to the room was shattered open.

Chin eyeballed the entrance.

Standing there was Master Wu.

16

CASH AND PANCAKES

HONG KONG - MONDAY MORNING

I n his gigantic master bedroom overlooking the pool, Tommy sat on his oversized bed with the gaudy yellow silk sheets in a rare moment of reminiscing. He saw Abby's artistry everywhere. When he told her he wanted a Chinese motif, she went to town and made him promise not to interfere. Her taste was exquisite, and the room could easily be a showpiece for a reality television show on luxury bedrooms of the uber-rich. Among the special items were the Chinese words meaning "double happiness" written in calligraphy onto a rice-paper canvas, an original Chinese ink painting of a horse in full gallop by legendary artist *Xu Beihong,* and a mammoth-sized, hand-knotted Chinese rug with a stunning array of colors in a floral design.

What touched him most, more than the exquisite and expensive items surrounding him, was an old photo on the mahogany night table beside his bed. It was a picture of him, his late wife and Abby, the last picture ever taken of Jocelyn, taken just before she went on that ill-fated aid mission to Thailand. Not a day passed since she died that he didn't spend time looking at this picture...and wonder what might have been and when he could have his revenge.

Now that Noah had come, that time was now. *Soon, very soon.*

Letting a final long gasp of air out, he tapped the picture —it was time to get back to work. Tommy turned from the photo to the large open suitcase sitting beside him on the bed. It was chock-full of bundles of currency from all nations, packed in the same manner as the money in the wooden crate that Duke destroyed. While primarily from China, there was Canadian, British, Australian, and American currency, too. He picked up one of the bundles and estimated that it must contain at least twenty thousand bucks in that one sheaf. *How many generations of pain were here?*

Abby popped in unannounced and gaped when she saw so much cash. "Where did that money come from, Papa?"

Trying to brush it off, Tommy shrugged nonchalantly. "Oh, that. It's from one of the casinos. I picked it up last night for a deposit this morning. That's the problem with being the boss. Sometimes, you got to do the grunt work."

"But..."

"No buts," interrupted Tommy. He swiftly closed the suitcase and asked jovially, "How about some of your famous pancakes for breakfast today?"

Abby scrunched her face. "Pancakes? I haven't made them since high school."

"But the memory has stayed with me forever."

Abby, biting her tongue, fixed a wondering gaze for a moment at her father, but Tommy didn't take the bait. This was not the time to get into a battle. She would ask him when he had had a few drinks and was less guarded. "You want maple syrup or blueberry sauce?"

"Let's go wild today. Maple syrup with extra, extra butter. And bacon."

"That's not good for your heart, but sure, why not?" She turned around and left, her face asking a hundred unspoken questions.

There is a whole lot of stuff that is not good for my heart. Tommy pulled on his hair as he put his head in his hands.

17

SUCKHOLES

MONDAY MORNING

Olivia strode briskly down the long corridor of the Pittman Saunders office with Noah tagging along behind.

"Hey, hey. Wait up," called Noah. "How about a little bit of meaningful conversation?"

Olivia kept truckin' as she snapped, "So what do you know about the Orient, Mr. Hung Gar, black belt?"

"Wow, you remembered. I made an impression. Am I ever glad to hear you speak. I was beginning to think you didn't like me."

Olivia froze in her steps, and Noah, not breaking stride, bumped into her and knocked her down. "Oops."

He offered his hand to help her up but she spurned the offer.

"I'm madly in love with you; isn't that obvious?" retorted the brainy beauty with a dismissive toss of her head.

Rather than being cowed by her disdain, Noah became more intrigued...and determined. "I was born and raised in Shanghai for the first part of my life and then moved to

Hong Kong. The school my parents set up gave scholarships to anyone who couldn't afford tuition."

Olivia tried to hide that she was somewhat intrigued. Maybe, just maybe, Noah might not be the idiot jock she thought he was. "Do-gooders are stupid."

"No worries there. Not a chance I would ever be mistaken for a gazillionaire philanthropist. I am very evil. My EQ, 'evilness quotient,' is off the charts." He fluttered his eyelashes at her.

She rolled her eyes as the two continued down the hall.

"I'm Noah Reid. And you are?"

"Olivia."

"That's a nice name." Noah waved his hands in a circular motion. "Olivia who?"

"Olivia Novak."

"You're Czech?"

"You studied geography. Give yourself a gold star," she answered with dripping sarcasm.

They arrived at the door to Garret's office. Olivia turned, reached over Noah's shoulder and started pulling the tie from the back of his collar.

"Hey, what are you doing? I spent all morning trying to be presentable," protested Noah.

She took a compact mirror out of her purse and showed him the exposed portion of the tie. Putting the compact away, she tucked the offending bit of tie under the shirt collar.

With a sardonic expression, her voice softened. "Well, Noah Reid, if you want to impress the biggest stuffed shirt in an office full of stuffed shirts, you can start by looking like a real lawyer."

~

In a big firm, there were offices, and there were offices. The bigger a fish you were, the more trappings you had. And when you were the biggest fish in the sea, like Garret Southam was, you had everything from an original Jackson Pollock painting on the wall to a custom-built, NASA-inspired Italian coffee-making machine sitting in the corner, waiting to satisfy your every caffeine craving.

Garret's private secretary, Jill Graham, greeted them in the well-appointed reception area of Garret's private office. She greeted Olivia warmly. "Olivia, I have so looked forward to this day. Mr. Southam is expecting you."

Olivia responded with a half-hearted smile. "Thanks, Jill."

As Jill led them into Garret's office, Noah speculated on how the hell Jill knew Olivia. *And what am I? Chopped liver?*

"Here you are," Jill said.

Noah and Olivia entered. While the view from the eightieth floor made no impact on Olivia, Noah was awed. With windows that went from floor to ceiling, he could see all of Hong Kong, from the green and cream-colored Star Ferries in Victoria Harbor to the skyline of some of the world's most spectacular skyscrapers: the Two International Finance Center, the I.M. Pei designed Bank of China Tower and, towering above them all, the one hundred- eighteen-story International Commerce Centre.

Garret beamed as he extended his hand to Noah. "Welcome, Noah. Good to have you aboard. Please take a seat."

The three took their seats in a triangle formation in front of Garret's desk.

"Thank you." *Wow, he didn't say anything to Olivia.*

Noah sat down slowly, cowed by the grandeur, but Olivia was nonchalant as she sat on the three thousand-dollar leather-covered ergonomic office chair.

Noah cleared his throat and began a well-rehearsed speech. "I want to thank you, Mr. Southam, for giving me this outstanding opportunity..."

The senior lawyer put a firm hand on Noah's knee. "Just call me Garret."

"Uh, yeah, sure." The neophyte began anew. "Thank you for the privilege of working with you. I was truly inspired by what you were saying just now..."

Garret interrupted again, "Reid, let me tell you a secret." He leaned toward Noah and whispered, "I hate suckholes. Unequivocally, completely, absolutely without reservation. Got that?"

Humiliated, Noah stifled a swallow as Garret leaned back on his nine-thousand–dollar, contoured office chair and relaxed. Throughout all this, Olivia had been trying to muzzle her pleasure at Noah's feeble attempts to cotton up to Garret but could no longer control herself. She burst out with a hearty laugh and folded her arms across her chest.

A bemused Garret continued. "Mr. Reid, have you met my daughter Olivia yet?"

Noah tried to keep from screaming as Olivia gave the same silly little wave to him that he gave to the obnoxious suit on the elevator.

"We've met," said Olivia with a hint of a smile. "Mr. Reid told me of his family's school."

Garret gave a knowing nod. "Ah, yes, the Good Shepherd. After the incident with your parents, I was requested to help continue their good work. I suggested changing the name to 'Kowloon Christian Academy' and I'm on the board of trustees. Never hurts having God on your side, especially when you live in a land where everybody thinks you're a white devil. Don't you agree?"

Noah was not only cowed, but floored. First, Olivia was Garret's daughter. Second, Garret knew about the school his parents founded. And this was the first he had ever heard about the continuance of their work under a new name. "Um. Yes, of course."

Garret waved his finger sternly. "No suckholing. Remember?"

"I mean that. Like I've spent my whole life trying to un-devilize myself," stammered Noah, pushing his foot not only into his mouth but now jamming it down his own throat. "Like, most people think I'm more Chinese than white."

"Yes, that's obvious," giggled Olivia. "The resemblance between you and Mao Tse Tung is remarkable.

Garret sobered and clapped his hands. Time to get on with business. "Noah and Olivia, you are both my new assigns. That means I dictate your lives."

Olivia's demeanor changed as rapidly as her father's. "As if you don't already," she muttered.

Garret ignored the jibe. He pointed to two sets of six-inch files on his desk and handed each one of them a USB flash drive. "These paper files are just executive summaries of Golden Asia's network of investments and companies. On the USB drives are the complete descriptions, company structures and their inter-relationships as well as the summaries. I expect you to get up to speed on them as quickly as possible. You're going to work with me on the Golden Asia file.

"Oh, come on, Dad," objected an exasperated Olivia.

"In the office, I am your boss, not your father," repri-manded Garret sternly to an unamused Olivia. "Golden Asia Land, Golden Asia Holdings, Golden Asia Imports, Golden

Asia Exports, Golden Asia Foods, Golden Asia Land Corporation and that's just a start."

"I know who Golden Asia is," said Olivia, gritting her teeth.

"This is the most important file we have, the most important file I have, the most important file Pittman Saunders has."

"This is complete and utter horse manure, Da..., Mr. Southam. I want to do something else."

"Olivia, you speak Mandarin, Cantonese and English. You read and write Traditional as well as Simplified Chinese script. You went to the right schools here, in Europe and in North America, but these are not the overriding factors."

Noah detected the change in Garret's tone, a little softer but maintaining its iron firmness. "You are my daughter but, most important, you are Abby's best friend, the daughter of Mr. Golden Asia, Tommy Sung, my lifelong best friend. You will concentrate primarily on the real estate holdings for now. Brush up on your commercial conveyancing. We are working the kinks out of a major development."

"You mean you want me to get a sewer permit or maybe evict some penny-ante squatters? What the hell did I slave for sixteen hours a day for four years at Harvard for?" huffed the exasperated new attorney. "I was hoping I could do something a little more exciting."

"Excitement thrills, but real estate bills. And I couldn't give a rat's ass about thrills. We will have dinner with Tommy and Abby tonight. I believe that will meet with your approval?"

Before Olivia responded, Noah cut in. "Um, sorry, but I can't make it. Previous engagement. I lined it up before I got on the plane weeks ago."

Olivia and Garret scrutinized Noah in amazement with the same thought. *You gotta be kidding.*

"Cancel it. Tommy is our rep at Golden Asia," said Garret in a voice that would brook no contradiction.

"No, sir, that's not possible." Noah was uncomfortable but firm.

"Well, in that case, you can pack up and leave for your engagement now. Don't bother coming back."

Noah swallowed, building up his nerve. "Uh, Garret?"

"Call me Mr. Southam."

Right. "Mr. Southam, didn't you just say you hated suck-holes? Well, isn't going to meet my friend, Chad, who I'm setting up a charity with, the most anti-suckhole thing in the world to do? And didn't you also say that integrity was important?"

"I lied." Garret's eyes seared Noah.

A tension-filled silence chilled the air as Noah handed the USB stick back to Garret. "Sorry you had to kill a bunch of trees for me," said Noah, motioning his head to the pile of paper on Garret's desk.

"What is so urgent that it can't wait until after our business dinner?" a vexed and exasperated Garret asked.

"Kids, Mr. Southam. The paperwork could easily wait, but the kids Chad's working with want to meet me. I can't let them down, and I won't."

"Is that really worth giving up your career for?"

"Mr. Southam, I was born to missionary parents and mentored by a Shaolin master. Jesus asked what is the point of gaining the world but losing your soul. From the Buddhist heritage of the Shaolin, I learned we must harbor compassion and help others sail to joy... Olivia isn't the only lawyer in town who reads and writes Traditional and Simplified Chinese. And not only do I speak Cantonese and

Mandarin, I speak Shanghainese as well. I'll get a job somewhere."

Noah began making his way toward the door.

"Reid," called Garret.

Noah froze into the moment and turned around, unsure what would happen next.

Garret growled, "This time only. But remember this. Pittman Saunders owns you, and I own Pittman Saunders. Forget this, and there will not be a next time. Understood?"

"Yes, sir."

Olivia twisted in her chair and her gaze fixed curiously on the straight-faced Noah. *What just happened? Dad would never put up with this normally. What's with this guy?*

18

REPENTANCE?

With Duke beside him, Chin marched up to the door, his steely eyes battling Master Wu's. His voice dripped full of disrespectful sarcasm as he addressed his former teacher. "It has been a lifetime since we last met, Master Wu. To what do I owe this pleasure?"

"It is the same now as it was before. I am concerned for your soul."

Chin threw a baleful sneer. "Did the white man's god finally get to you? Are you on your knees every day praying for salvation to Jehovah Jireh for the hopeless sinners of the world?"

Master Wu exhaled a long slow breath of air as he gazed around the gargantuan artificial rainforest. However, unlike others, he saw not prosperity, but hopelessness.

He intoned softly, but firmly. "It is not too late, Chin. There is still a chance... You were a monk. You were my monk, my disciple, my heir. You could have had it all."

Chin snorted. "Ten thousand percent of nothing is nothing. What you offered was worthless. Meaningless."

Wu looked at Duke. "Tell your father to repent. To change. He cannot win."

Duke struck out, locking his body with Master Wu's into a viselike hold. "Old man, you got nuttin' to say to me because you are a total loser."

Glancing at his father, the young man squeezed as hard as he could. A bit more and he would break the sifu's back.

Yet Master Wu did nothing to try and escape the death grip. Instead, he turned his sweating body to Chin's sharp gaze and asked softly, "Do you really want to kill me, Chin? Would that make you happy?"

"The world has surpassed you, and yet you cling to old-fashioned ways. Your existence means nothing."

The aged master unexpectedly let his body go limp. Caught offguard, Duke momentarily released his hold. That fraction of a second was enough for Master Wu to elbow him hard in the chest.

Duke buckled and Master Wu escaped. He leapt up and grabbed the top of the doorframe. He swung back and forth, gaining altitude with each subsequent move. Finally with his legs above his head, he let go of the doorframe and hurtled himself at Duke, still crumpled over.

He launched a quick barrage of left and right fists to his chest, temple and forehead and Duke collapsed backward in agony.

Master Wu turned to Chin and held his fists in fight-ready position. "As long as I am alive, I am your master. Principles, ethics, and morality are never out of date. They never die."

Chin scoffed. "Only power is honor."

Master Wu saw the futility of remaining. He turned and, with a leaden heart, walked away.

War is inevitable.

19

IMPRESSIONS

MONDAY MORNING

T he thing about being a new lawyer in a big firm
was that, even if you were the boss's daughter,
chances were you wouldn't get a corner office.
There was also a good chance you wouldn't have a private
office, either. And, if two lawyers happened to be assigned to
the same file, there was a reasonable chance that you would
have to share a space with your partner, especially when the
firm was experiencing what your dad, the senior partner,
called "unprecedented growth."

So when Noah and Olivia were required to share a small
office designed for one person, it wasn't entirely unexpected.
Too bad close quarters did not necessarily make for a close
relationship.

"You certainly know how to make a good impression,"
remarked Olivia, avoiding Noah's gaze as she began tackling
the mound of paper that was the Golden Asia file.

Noah took a deep breath as he turned to study the first
sheets of the thick file. "Well, you never informed me that
Garret Southam was your father. I thought you said your
last name was Novak."

"It is."

"Your mother remarried Garret, so he's your stepfather, then?"

"Why are you so nosy? How about some privacy?"

"I told you everything about me," Noah said.

"Oh, right." Olivia gently put the legal document down and glowered at Noah. "You want me to put you on a pedestal because you think you're so great. Well, guess what? I don't buy that. The world is a crappy place. I was eleven and I saw the plane carrying my mom blown up right in front of me. You bragged about being a lawyer trying to impress the *little secretary*. You tried to show off by telling me you were a chop-socky kung fu man. Then you tried to impress my father by saying how ethical and moral you are."

Scrunching his face, Noah inhaled as he lifted his arms in surrender. "Guilty as charged. I'm so sorry to hear about your mom. I admit that I overdid things and made a complete ass of myself...but that doesn't change the fact that I still don't know much about you."

Olivia stifled the urge to throw her laptop at this guy who wouldn't give up harassing her and settled for locking her eyes on him with a glare that could wither most plants. Then a light bulb began glowing in her brain. It was a glimmer, but glowing nonetheless. *He owned up and apologized. What guy ever did that?*

Patting an anger-suppressing index finger on her cheek, she said in a subdued tone, "After Mom died, I was shuffled off to a Swiss boarding school, and I hardly ever saw my father. I worked my ass off to get into Brown University. Then I did an MBA at the Wharton School of Business and graduated cum laude from Harvard Law School. Is that enough for you?"

Noah gulped, then regained his composure. "I was

thinking of something more...personal. You're not applying for a job with me, so I really couldn't care less about your resumé. Like who are you really, and why do you do what you do? And why did you lie to me about your last name? And are you really just a spoiled rich bitch?"

Olivia couldn't believe this guy just didn't give up. "I'm Olivia Novak Southam, age twenty-six. I was born in Hong Kong, and I have an IQ of 140, which means I'm probably ten times as smart as you. What I love to do more than anything else is to play jazz piano. I finished law school early and spent the last year in New York City playing the jazz circuit. I would have continued to do so except that I'm addicted to eating regularly, a habit most jazzers are unable to indulge in."

Olivia balled her fists tightly. She wasn't much of one to let out personal feelings. "Enough of that. I won't bore either of us anymore. I'm working with you because, for some reason known only to him, Dad put us together. I will make it as short as possible so that you will not have to put up with this spoiled rich bitch because I, for one, am not going to get stuck doing real estate conveyances that any storefront lawyer could do."

Olivia's eyes dared Noah to snap back. He didn't take the bait and threw her a curve instead. "I'm sorry to hear that..."

"I don't need any more sympathy."

"I didn't finish. I want to say I'm sorry to hear you have father issues..."

Olivia shrieked. "I don't have father issues!"

She was loud enough that coworkers across the hall turned to their computers and pretended nothing happened. She turned her attention back to the document in the Golden Asia stack, pretending she was concentrating on it.

Noah's voice was a shadow. "Just because you are angry with your father, don't take it out on the world...or on me."

Fury roiling her body, Olivia didn't say a word, and her expression indicated she didn't hear a thing. She got up and huffed out of the room.

Noah wasn't sure, but he thought he saw a tear rolling down her face. He folded his hands thoughtfully for a moment. If he was right, that meant she had a heart, as well as being knock-your-socks-off gorgeous.

20

SQUEEZE

MONDAY AFTERNOON

Ron Armstrong and half a dozen other accountants dressed in the obligatory conservative dark suits sat nervously around a table at Armstrong and Company's boardroom, pastries and coffee untouched. Eyes twitched, fingers tapped, legs jiggled as Garret perused Ron's revised documents, quickly scanning a page then moving to the following one.

The lawyer slammed the binder down. "This is bullshit."

"We haven't finished yet, Garret, because it's not just unethical; it's illegal on a mammoth scale," stated Ron.

"Since when has that bothered you?" asked Garret.

"Since we started to get investigated for accounting irregularities by some random government auditor two weeks ago. It's impossible to keep track of every single change because you make an alteration on one file, and it affects another, then another. It's a snowball effect."

"Is that worth losing $5,000,000 in annual billings?" asked Garret simply. "It's more than just Christmas bonus money we're talking about. Last time I checked, five million was one hell of a lot of change."

"But we could lose our designations," argued Ron. "The authorities already have us under watch, too."

"So what, Ron? Are you fearful of a few bureaucrats, because I'm certainly not," snorted Garret.

"The problem, Garret, is if we lose our designations, they are going to want to review all of Golden Asia's back records and statements. Then forget me. Pittman Saunders will be up a creek. We are talking about billions here, Garret."

"Epstein and Gallagher did it and they didn't get caught."

"They didn't have government auditors looking over their shoulders and breathing down their necks."

Garret walked over to one of Ron's minions and, with one hand, picked him up by the throat.

"Then don't get caught," growled Garret.

They all looked on in horror as Garret began to squeeze. The accountant struggled, waving his arms in the air, but he couldn't free himself from the lawyer's grip. His face laced with fear, he started gagging, and his arms started waving more frantically. Just before he lost consciousness, Garret released him, dropping him to the floor.

"Don't worry. You'll live," Garret told him. He glanced back at Ron. "But I can't guarantee the same result for you if my request is not honored. Do I make myself clear?"

"Of course, Garret," stammered Ron, resisting the urge to upchuck. "We all know what needs to be done."

"Good, because this meeting has just wasted eighteen and a half minutes. You've only got another two hours to make the appropriate adjustments." Garret's frosty eyes lasered upon Ron. "I went early to your home to give you more time. By throwing it away, you're just screwing yourself in the derrière."

The lawyer exited the room, and the accountants started buzzing with activity. Had they known what Garret knew, instead of spending time on accounting details, they would have been making travel arrangements to anywhere else in the world under names that were any but their own.

Garret himself was the anonymous whistleblower for the government auditor. He, more than anyone else, understood what the potential outcomes could be.

21

TIME WASTER

MONDAY AFTERNOON

The almost-a-Luddite Noah sat alone in the office at his computer. Using the two-finger hunt-and-peck method, he read aloud as he typed in the letters.

"Dear Olivia: I want you to know that I behaved improperly today during our encounter, and I am genuinely sorry for any consternation I have caused you. Sincerely, Noah Reid." He hit the send button.

Less than ten seconds passed before Olivia stormed back into the room. She held her iPhone up and waved it in the air.

"What's this patronizing piece of crap?"

"I was being pretensionless," said Noah, trying to defend himself.

"Pretensionless? Is that even a word. No. You were pretentious. And prevaricating, prickly, predatory…"

Noah interrupted, "How about precious? Or profound? I was trying to 'pologize.' Well, if that's how you feel, I take that back. I rescind my apology. Happy?"

Olivia glowered. "If you were really interested in me, you would put up with whatever I said or did."

"Who said I was interested in you?"

"Well, if you're not, why are you wasting my time?" She tramped out.

Noah leaned back in his chair and raised his eyebrows victoriously up and down like the mouse who just ate the cat. "I think she likes me."

Olivia popped her head back in. "Dream on, Reid."

Noah called out, "Enjoy your meal! If they do take-out, get me a Big Mac with fries."

Right.

22

PRYING FATHER

MONDAY EVENING

G arret could easily afford a chauffeur, but one of his life's pleasures was driving his Bentley Continental Flying Spur. The power, the smoothness, the sheer hand-crafted luxury was an escape from the constant tensions and crises inherent in running a mega law firm. Unless, that is, Olivia was riding with him and he wanted to have a meaningful conversation.

"What is your opinion of Mr. Reid?"

Olivia shrugged and looked the other direction. "Noah? He's okay."

Garret bit his lip. "How many times do I have to tell you that *okay* is not an acceptable response? It's a..."

"...shortcut for people who want easy answers without thinking."

"At least your memory is intact."

"Father..." Olivia only used the word "father" when she was angry at Garret. "Father, stop trying to set me up."

"I am not trying to set you up. I hired Noah because he was at the top of his class, he knows the Chinese language and culture and he has a black belt in Hung Gar."

"Which makes him a clone of you. That's even worse. He is definitely not my type. Definitely."

"He will be an asset to the firm and, believe it or not, setting him up with you was not even a remote consideration."

"Do not lie to me anymore. I am perfectly capable of finding men without you."

Garret snorted. "Right, I forgot about your stellar track record with persons of the opposite sex. Perhaps you prefer the artist I invested twenty thousand in that dumped you the moment the check cleared? Or how about the waiter who left you for a woman older than his grandmother because she was "more of a woman than you could ever be?" And let's not forget the fiancé you found in bed with another man? All of them fine upstanding candidates as Mr. Olivia Southam."

The problem with the truth was that the truth didn't lie...

"I wasn't serious about any of them."

"Your mother..."

"Don't bring Mom into this," she hissed in a voice tight with anger.

Garret ignored her. "Your mother entrusted me to take care of you. Whether you accept that or not, that is the primary responsibility of my life. If nothing else, I owe that to her. Cash is king and, if something happens to me, I have ensured that you will have a great deal of that."

Olivia spat out, "I'd rather be content in my own skin. At least I can sleep easy in it."

There's no point. Garret wasn't angry at Olivia, only exasperated, but at himself, not her. There was so much he wanted to say, but knew that he never could.

They continued in silence in their fifty-five kilometer drive to Macau. It was a drive Garret made several times a week and the forty-five minute journey on the three cable-stayed bridges, undersea tunnel, and four artificial islands gave him the opportunity to think and strategize without distractions

Garret had helped put Macau on the international gambling map with the enormous seven-million-square-foot Tiger Palace. When the word "Tiger" was mentioned in this former Portuguese colony, it was automatically understood that one was not talking simply about one building but an entire hotel, restaurant, residential, shopping, and entertainment complex.

In a land where extravagance was the norm, Tiger still impressed. No expense was spared to make the shining jewel in Macau's gambling tiara the most impressive and ostentatious display of human opulence ever exhibited.

Not to mention one of the most profitable casino complexes on planet Earth.

Arriving, Garret drove past the thousand-vehicle parking lot to the front of the building and parked under the casino's towering archway entrance, flanked by statues of eight imposing Chinese imperial tigers and eight ferocious dragons.

Miles, one of the valets, whisked to the car. "Good to see you, Mr. Southam."

"Likewise, Miles."

"Shall I detail it while you're here? No charge."

No charge. That was laughable because Garret's tip would be more than a week's salary. The same little ritual was played every time Garret came and with every valet that parked Garret's car.

"Naturally."

23

MOVE OVER VEGAS

MACAU - MONDAY EVENING

O livia's jaw dropped when she stepped through the twelve-foot bronze revolving doors and was met by eight saluting terra-cotta warrior statues. Mammoth. Monumental. Humungous. Ostentatious. Over the top. These adjectives barely scraped the surface of the Tiger Palace.

"Stop gawking and let's go. You can sightsee as we walk," stated Garret as he began to stride confidently down the lobby. Garret had put together many of the deals to get the Tiger Palace made so, to him, the complex was no big deal. He knew where the skeletons were buried, who got the bribes, kickbacks, and women...and who got killed when they put up barriers to successful completion.

While taken aback at her father's petty censure, Olivia bit her tongue as she accompanied him through the hotel. While it was old hat to Garret, Olivia was fascinated by the dazzling collection of Chinese artifacts including giant, laughing Buddhas made of bronze and porcelain, ornate vases ten feet tall and huge stone carvings of Ming Dynasty emperors.

Her eyes sparkled when she saw a sprawling enclosed living ecosystem where animals native to China resided, including monkeys, salamanders, badgers and a flock of cranes.

The *pièce de resistance,* however, was not of Chinese origin at all. The centerpiece was a caged habitat where eight Bengal tigers roamed freely. Gawkers of all nationalities and ages oohed and ahed at the fierce energy of the majestic beasts.

"Isn't that dangerous?" said Olivia, her voice tinged with tension and awe.

Garret whispered in her ear. "They're not as life-threatening as they look. The animals are injected daily with amphetamines and fed Chinese herbs to boost their energy levels, making them growl and pace ferociously almost constantly."

"Really?" She bit her tongue to prevent the animal activist in her from lashing out.

Garret shrugged. "Things aren't always as they seem. A little hocus pocus to make the customers satisfied. It's the name of the game."

"I see." Olivia knew there was no battle to be won here today.

She followed her father through the lobby to the three-thousand-seat restaurant, the Royal Tiger. Nine hundred and forty-seven attendants, chefs, waiters and other service personnel pampered the thousands of daily patrons with the freshest seafood that Hong Kong had to offer. Storage tanks by the kitchen displayed live carp, crab, turtle, frogs and shrimp swimming, blissfully unaware that they would soon be featured on a casino patron's plate.

But what caught Olivia's attention was the exceptional performances of so many skilled entertainers. Tonight's entertainment spectacle was the Artistry of China, the best of fifty centuries of Chinese culture boiled down into a ninety-minute extravaganza. With performers recruited from throughout China, the lavish production rivaled the *Cirque du Soleil.*

Her eyes went to the stage, where twenty performers leapt with breathtaking vitality. They performed cartwheels in tandem with other performers, not on the floor but on the hands and feet of acrobats, some who stood on the floor and others who lay on the ground with their feet in the air.

A different set of athletes flew through the air with rhythmic handsprings perfectly coordinated and synchronized in opposing directions.

A daring tightrope artist walked on the thinnest of ropes hanging directly over the audience. The restaurant patrons gasped in awe, anticipation, and fear that she would fall on them.

Pole climbers scurried like squirrels up thin pieces of bamboo and vaulted themselves to other poles, performing somersaults in the air during their brief flights.

Actor acrobats, dressed in classical costumes, performed acts of astounding agility that combined athletics, magic, dance and grace.

Others juggled glass bowls like meteors in the sky. One special woman rode a unicycle. With one leg on a pedal, she used the other leg to lob a dozen dishes onto the top of her head.

A multicolored lion train a hundred feet long snaked its way through the tables, weaving in and out through the other performers.

One group performed double and triple somersaults through space, landing precariously on partners' shoulders.

It was a symphony of strength, artistry, elegance and beauty.

"Do you approve? inquired Garret, amused at Olivia's wide-eyed wonder.

While she loved what she saw, Olivia wrung her hands in frustration as she watched the thousands of patrons ignoring the visual extravaganza, preferring to stuff their faces and gambling as if tomorrow didn't exist. "Doesn't everybody see what they are missing? This is amazing. You can't get this anywhere else."

Garret shrugged. "It's part of the furniture, part of the cost of doing business. Tommy went all around China recruiting these performers. If someone takes ten seconds to look at them before going back to the bar or slots or card game, it's worth it. That ten seconds separates us from anywhere else a customer may want to spend his money. It makes him or her feel special and makes the Tiger Palace bushels of money."

A tuxedoed maître d' named Wing arrived. "Hello, Mr. Southam and..." Wing waited for Garret to make an introduction.

"This is my daughter Olivia, Wing."

A smile crested on Wing's face. "Good evening, Ms. Olivia. Your private room awaits your arrival."

"Is Tommy here yet?"

"Mr. Sung is here somewhere. Always is. I'll let him know you've arrived."

24

CLIENT ENTERTAINMENT

MACAU - MONDAY EVENING

I n an empty, darkened stairwell, Duke and one of his father's men, Pau, dressed in tight-fitting black clothing, black gloves and black balaclavas that covered their faces, carried black custom-made cases two feet long, sixteen inches high and five inches deep. Their ebony, rubber-soled martial arts shoes guaranteed maximum traction on any surface, as well as ensuring minimal noise would be created.

They ascended stealthily, ominously, until they reached the top of the stairs to arrive at a locked door. Pau moved to open the door, but Duke grabbed his hand and shook his head emphatically, "Not yet! We get ready first."

Pau nodded, and the two opened their specially designed cases. Each one contained an unassembled crossbow. Handcrafted with contemporary precision, elements of their timeworn Chinese roots were visible—each end of the bow was finished with a carved dragon's head. These were not the bulkier repeating crossbows, but a smaller, lighter version. These slighter weapons were just as deadly as their larger cousins but were easier to transport. The drawback was they required expert marksmanship because one attempt was all you got.

They crouched and began assembling the weapons of destruction.

GARRET, ABBY AND OLIVIA WERE INTO THEIR THIRD ROUND OF drinks—Garret with his preferred neat Glenlivet twenty-one-year-old single malt scotch, and Abby and Olivia with their mojitos made with Trinidad's Angostura Old Oak white rum and mint leaves fresh from the Royal Tiger Restaurant's private garden.

"So, Abby, when are you planning to get married? Olivia refuses to allow me into her private life, so I have to ask you instead," chuckled Garret.

"Actually, I am thinking of going gay. Why do you think Olivia and I hang out so much together?" teased Abby.

Olivia leaned over and kissed her. "You mean you've been holding out on me, girlfriend?"

As the girls erupted into a fit of laughter that Garret didn't find particularly amusing, Tommy entered. All rose to greet him.

"Who am I, the Chinese premier?" joked the corpulent gambler. "I'm just a big mouth with a bigger stomach. Sit. Sit. Sit."

As they took their places, Olivia said in a formal tone, "Mr. Sung..."

"Wait. Who is Mr. Sung? What happened to Uncle Tommy?"

Olivia began again. "According to my father, this is a business dinner, which means you are now Mr. Sung."

Tommy rolled his eyes.

"Mr. Sung, I'm privileged to be working on your file…"

Abby couldn't take it anymore. "Dad knows you too well for that BS."

"And what happened to Irish-American-Asian fusion?" asked Tommy. He belted out, "*Oh Danny boy, the pipes, the pipes are calling…*" He then pretended to tickle the ivories as he beamed at Olivia. "You're too talented to be a lawyer."

"Stop it, Tommy." Garret knocked his knuckles on the table to get attention. "Don't give her any ideas. I've spent a lifetime trying to persuade her to follow me."

"No wonder you have a rebellious child, Garret. I can't stand looking at those wretched documents myself." He snorted. "Anyway, that's why I have you, Garret. Speaking of which, where is the young man you mentioned? Noah Reid, wasn't it?"

Garret's voice had a sting to it. "Mr. Reid took ill."

Tommy made pistols with his hands and pointed the "guns" at Garret. "Bang! Bang! He copped out on you," Tommy hooted. "Don't blame him. About the only thing more boring than Golden Asia is you. Unfortunately, I have no choice but to put up with you both." He turned to Olivia with mock lechery. "East Coast USA has turned you into a lady."

Garret grunted, not at all amused. "Watch it, Tommy. She's not into older men."

Tommy guffawed boisterously. "You mean, Garret, you're not into her with older men."

Wing entered with a bottle of Dom Perignon. He poured the champagne into tulip-shaped glasses and handed them to each person around the table.

"Your father may have convinced you to study law, Olivia, but the truth is, law is boring. Why don't I offer you a job being Abby's accompanist? I can get you gigs in every lounge in Asia. Then you can be with your *lover* all the time."

"Tommy!" muttered the increasingly irritated Garret.

Olivia loved Tommy. He was always fun, never took anything too seriously—the complete opposite of her father. "No, Mr. Sung. I think Golden Asia is fascinating. I've been studying it all day. The corporate structure is convoluted, unconventional and it would take the average forensic auditor half a lifetime to figure out who owns what and what goes where."

"But you're not the average forensic lawyer, are you, Ms. Einstein?" giggled the tipsy Abby.

Tommy pretended to fall asleep, snoring loudly. Then he perked back up. "It's amazing that you're still awake then. I'm falling asleep just thinking about it."

He got up, and there was a pixie glint in his eyes. "You should stick to playing piano."

Abby piped in. "I agree." She put her arms around Olivia and teased Garret. "We could make beautiful music together."

"I think we better change topics before Garret blows up," laughed Tommy, rocking his head playfully from side to side. "Tell me more about the missing Noah."

"There's nothing to say or, if I do talk about him, I will have a myocardial infarction," growled Garret.

"I like him already," teased Tommy.

25

GAME ON!

If you had no money in America, you played basketball. If you had money in America, you played basketball. Same deal in Asia. No matter how rich, poor, athletic or unathletic you were, everyone loved this game invented by Canadian James Naismith for the YMCA in 1891.

When his lifelong best bud, Internet cafe operator-cum-street kid worker Chad heard that his bro Noah was coming back to town, he reached out to him and asked him to help.

Noah gave him a one word answer. "Duh?" It was a no-brainer.

Arriving at the schoolyard for the night's game, the first thing Noah did was give Chad a brand-new leather basket-ball with the autograph of Chad's idol, Magic Johnson, on it. Although Chad was too young to have seen Magic play, the basketball player was a legend, not only for his skill on the court, but for his ability to face HIV with his trademark smile and love of life.

"GAME ON!"

After the tip off, Noah grabbed the ball out of the hands of the opposing center. He streaked down the court past the teenage drug dealers, car thieves, pampered rich kids, and garden-variety street punks. Noah deked around Chad and went in for an easy lay-up.

"Yes!" shouted Noah, pumping his fist high into the air.

"Ball hog! No worries; we'll get it back big time," called out the man-bunned Chad.

Chad fired the ball to fourteen-year-old Sam Xi. Sam charged up court, bowling over Lexus, one of the kids on Noah's team. Lexus knocked the ball out of Sam's hand but was the last to touch it. Chad motioned the ball to other players but finally inbounded it to Sam, who dribbled down the court.

Noah jumped in front of Sam. Sam changed direction but paid no attention and knocked Lexus down again.

Noah screamed, "Foul!" but Chad yelled out, "Shut up, Wuss!" and "Atta boy, Sam!"

Sam threw up a floater, banked it in for two, then turned to taunt Lexus. "Life's a bitch, eh? Take that and shove it up your ass."

Chad groaned because he knew what was going to happen next. The jab incited Lexus and the rest of Noah's team into a jumbo of a rumble. And it was no playground pussy fight, either.

Noah saw Lexus whip out a switchblade and charge at Sam. He took two steps to the side, kicked out his leg to Lexus' hand, sending the teen's knife into the air. Noah snatched it before Lexus could and pushed the punk to the ground. "No!" he yelled.

Sam yanked a chain out of his jeans, swinging it like a

medieval sword fighter and came at Noah. "Try me, white boy."

"Not here you don't," ordered Chad.

"Out of my way, Chad," shouted Sam.

"I got it, Chad." Noah chucked the basketball hard at Sam's abdomen. It didn't get through because the chain got in the way. Noah jerked Sam backward by his hair. His ego injured more than his body, Sam started yelling, "Child abuse! Child abuse!"

"Shut up, or I'll show you what real abuse is," Noah said calmly.

But even without weapons, the kids wanted to go at it, and it turned into a dog pile of kicking, thumping and slugging.

"Oh, shit," said Noah. He didn't really want to, but he had no choice. The reluctant combatant grabbed one kid from the pile by the neck, screaming, legs dangling. Noah threw the kid six feet skyward. Six inches before he crashed to the ground, Noah scooped him up and chucked him to the side.

Another kid ran at Noah with a knife, slashing viciously. Now totally on his game, Noah swiveled with a masterful aerial leg strike that knocked the boy several feet back before he smashed hard into the ground. His knife flew out of his hand, spinning directly to Chad, who quickly ducked out of the blade's way just before it would have landed in his throat.

Another group of kids swarmed to attack. Noah shrieked like a bulldog bat from hell as he charged at them. A triple spin kick put one punk out of commission; a flying sidekick leveled another; and one swift chop to the chest put another down.

A series of straight blast blows knocked three kids in a

row down, and Bruce Lee's trademark mighty backfists—bang, bang, bang—brought down those trying to attack him from behind.

Noah jumped back into the martial arts stance and barked at the group. "Anyone else want to rock?"

The boys jumped up and crowded around him. "You're so cool," "Teach me," "C'mon, Noah," "You're the man," "I wanna learn..."

Noah suddenly swung both his arms out, knocking everyone away. He shouted with a voice of authority. "You want to learn?"

"Yes!" they all cried out.

"Then you do it my way. No ifs, ands or buts. Got it?"

"Yes!" agreed all.

Noah kicked out and adopted a martial arts stance. "Then let's do it."

All the kids and Chad jumped into position. Noah led them in an exercise sequence. "Left, right, kick...Right, left, kick..."

Soon, it wasn't just the basketball kids but everyone in the neighborhood who saw how Noah dispatched the gang who wanted to learn. Young and old, grandfathers, grandmothers, fitness freaks, slobs, suits, singles, marrieds...

They all shouted with Noah, "Left, right, kick, punch...Right, left, kick, punch...punch, punch, right, left..."

26

LEAPING MONKS

MACAU - MONDAY EVENING

B ecause Olivia had not spent that much time in Hong Kong since the death of her mother, she wasn't completely familiar with Chinese customs and living styles, despite being born in Asia. This accounted for her surprise when Wing brought a large solid-gold container with the Chinese character for Tiger emblazoned on it.

Her eyes gleamed when Wing lifted the lid, revealing a mélange of shark's fin, sea cucumber, abalone, dried scallops and twenty other ingredients in a clear soup. "That looks and smells fantastic. What is it?"

Tommy's lips smacked in delight. "Monk Jumping over the Wall. My favorite."

With one hand behind his back, Wing ladled the soup into solid gold bowls. He stepped back and stood at attention. "Enjoy."

Olivia's eyes lit up as she took a sip. "Unbelievable. I'd forgotten how food is supposed to taste. This sure beats burgers, pasta, pastrami sandwiches, or anything else I ate on the East Coast."

"What did you expect? This is Asia. You think we're going to send anything good over to America? We keep the best for ourselves!" bellowed Tommy. "And we bring the best of North America over here. We get better Maine lobster here than they do in Maine, and better Alaskan king crab than you get in Alaska."

"That's just the start," Wing explained as he refilled everyone's bowls. "Not only do we have the best ingredients, we have the best chefs in the world. Your chef tonight was recruited from a seven-star Michelin restaurant, and yours is the only meal he is preparing. He had a small army working all afternoon." He placed the bowls in front of each diner.

"Why is it called Monk Jumping over the Wall?" queried Olivia, curiosity covering her face.

Tommy gave a knowing wink at Garret's daughter. "Legend has it that the amazing aroma of this soup wafted over a temple wall into the courtyard where Buddhist monks were meditating. The smell bewitched the monks, rousing them from meditation."

Tommy sniffed the air, then made a face of delight. "Try as they might, they could not put the thought of tasting it out of their minds. They prayed and chanted for hours, hoping to cleanse themselves from the evils of eating the flesh of a creature. However, the smell grew ever more appetizing as the soup simmered. Finally, the monks could take it no more."

Tommy arose and whipped off his jacket. "Ripping off their robes, they renounced their vows of vegetarianism and jumped over the ten-foot wall just to wet their tongues with a taste of the liquid ambrosia. It was food of the gods come to earth, corrupting the purest of the pure."

Garret laughed heartily. "The story gets better every time, Tommy. Last time it was a single monk. This time, you've got the whole damned monastery doing the jumping."

"Come on, Garret. I got most of it right," chuckled Tommy.

"And the damned French don't know how to count higher than five. There's no such thing as a seven-star Michelin restaurant."

Before Tommy could respond, Chin calmly entered the room. "If there were such an honor as a seven-star Michelin restaurant, my chef would certainly be its chef."

27

I AM GOLDEN ASIA

MACAU - MONDAY EVENING

D uke and Pau methodically assembled their crossbows. They screwed the prods together, then attached heavy-duty string to their bows' opposing ends. Each weapon was tested for tautness and resilience, by gently tugging on the string and then snapping it. Confirming that the bows met their satisfaction, they moved on. With precision, they attached the arbalest side plates, blocks, wedges and stirrups. They re-tested the crossbows, ensuring that they had correctly assembled two sinister killing machines.

They gave each other the thumbs-up. Duke unlocked the door.

The dark silence changed to the cacophony and garish illumination from the bright lights of a busy restaurant. A Chinese floor screen hid the two men but also blocked their view so they could not see the sources of the noise. Neither could anyone see them.

Duke took a quick peek around the screen to see the source of the mayhem—the Tiger entertainment show was in full swing. Patrons, some a little drunker, most a whole lot

poorer, were paying more attention to the sensational spectacle and noisily showing their enthusiasm.

The marksmen looked further down and saw Chin in a
private room about two hundred feet away.

"Get ready," ordered Duke.

"Sit down, Tommy. There is no need for ceremony,"
stated Chin, not even a hint of emotion in his voice.

Tommy sat as Wing whisked over a new chair for Chin.

Olivia and Abby weren't quite sure what hold Chin had
on their fathers, but there was definitely something not
right, despite Chin's calm demeanor.

"Tommy, Garret, Abby..." Chin glanced at Olivia. "And
you are..."

"Chin Chee Fok, meet my daughter, Olivia," introduced
Garret.

"Ah, my new lawyer. Pleased to meet you, Ms. Southam."

Olivia nodded, the feminist in her totally irritated that
this pompous bastard considered her his property. "Hello,
Mr. Chin."

"Just Chin is fine," declared the Tiger Master as he took
Olivia's hand and kissed it. "You're always hiding something
from me, Garret," he said in a condescending, reprimanding
voice. Eyeing Olivia as he would a piece of meat, he continued, "And it's perfectly understandable."

Olivia was puzzled. *Why wasn't Dad picking up this arrogant SOB and throwing him against the wall?* "Are you
connected with Golden Asia, too?"

"You didn't tell her, Garret?" Chin's steely eyes matched
his voice as he proudly confirmed, "I am Golden Asia."

Olivia looked at her father, perplexed.

"Mr. Chin is a silent partner who rarely makes an appearance. Mr. Sung is our everyday contact," explained Garret.

"I am not a partner. As I stated earlier, I *am* Golden Asia," corrected Chin definitively.

The room turned icy as Garret quietly addressed Chin with a sinister hush. "You have audited statements, including the ones the accountants prepared today. Any problems that exist are a result of you failing to deliver from your end."

Tommy shook his head helplessly as Wing ladled out a bowl of soup for the Tiger Master. "Chin, there are problems everywhere, driving us crazy. The unions are bandits. The cost of materials from Italy, China and India is skyrocketing. There's a lack of workers that know how to push a wheelbarrow, let alone build a fortress, bureaucrats wanting more ladies, bigger cars and more cash..."

Chin interrupted. "Cost overruns are normal. I expect that."

He put his hands under the table and, with a quick jerk upwards, upset it, spilling the luxurious soup, sumptuous Asian delicacies, and drinks onto the carpet. He exploded, "What I don't expect is to be cheated by my own people!"

He snapped his fingers, and Wing escorted in Ron, the accountant. Ron's hands were tied together, his face was bruised, his nose was broken, and he had two black eyes.

While Tommy and Garret remained calm at seeing the parasitic weasel, Abby and Olivia were aghast. *Omigod! Why doesn't Dad do something?"* Olivia wondered.

With his jaw broken, Ron slurred apologetically. "I'm sorry, Garret, but Mr. Chin came by in person to ask some questions about the file."

Chin snapped his fingers and, just as quickly, Wing

dragged Ron out. Chin leapt up, grabbed Tommy by the shirt collar and yanked him up to his eye level. He started tightening Tommy's shirt, making it difficult for him to breathe. "I made you who you are today, and this is my reward?"

Slamming Tommy back into his chair, Chin addressed both Tommy and Garret. "I am talking about the real money you've lost for me. The money that goes into your personal pockets. The money that goes into whores you've lost the ability to perform with. The gambling that is not done in my establishments. I'm talking about the absolute incompetence of management that I have trusted you with."

Tommy whimpered, forcing out labored words. "You have it wrong, Chin. We simply cannot convert those sums of cash easily."

Garret stood and asserted angrily. "The only reason you own anything is that I pull every string and bribe every two-bit official looking for mortgage payments for his mistresses. Not to mention putting together a corporate structure that makes you cleaner than the pope."

Chin hissed, "Paid with my cash into your pocket. Several billion, which is now missing."

Billion? Olivia and Abby gasped at the number. Tommy and Garret were not at all flummoxed.

A surly Garret studied Chin. "How does money that doesn't exist go missing? I'm doing my job, Chin, and doing it very well." He knew that Chin had no real idea of how much was gone.

Chin's face lifted in expectation and advanced to the door. "Remember who is feeding you." He whipped around, rocketing a razor-sharp martial arts throwing star directly at Garret's heart.

With reflexes faster than a cobra's, Garret snatched it out

of the air and hurled the deadly projectile back at Chin in the same fluid motion. The blur moved at a speed no normal person could see. Chin nonchalantly swiped the air and closed his fist. He opened his hand, revealing the star in his palm.

"Do not play games with me. Otherwise..." Chin waved his hands indicating a magic motion, "poof."

He strode out, erect, proud and arrogant.

A CROSSBOW ARROW CHANGES EVERYTHING

MACAU - MONDAY EVENING

Olivia and Abby were freaked, not only at Chin but at their fathers. While they had suspected there might be some unsavory parts to the work they did, this was the first time they had seen active proof.

"I'm not hungry anymore. I want to go home," whimpered Olivia.

"Me, too," Abby agreed.

"No. No. You hardly ate at all," said Tommy.

"Please, Uncle Tommy," protested Olivia.

"Uncle Tommy? You mean I'm not your client any longer? Come on, come on. Wing, get us another room. Now! Now!"

"Of course, Mr. Sung."

"Daddy, I want to go home!" blurted Abby.

With precision understanding, Garret glanced at Tommy and nodded. It was time to get the girls out of there.

THE MARKSMEN SAW CHIN STROLL OUT OF THE PRIVATE DINING

room. He gave an almost imperceptible but knowing nod in their direction before disappearing into the noisy crowd.

That was their cue to move into position. Pau and Duke quickly moved the folding screen a few feet so they remained hidden from the restaurant and casino patrons. That they could do so was another example of the power of money. Normally, tables and machines were packed right to the wall in order to optimize revenue. However, Chin had ordered that there be at least a twelve-foot gap between the door and the closest table. At the Tiger Complex, whatever Chin wanted, Chin got.

Duke and Pau planted their feet firmly. They took aim, getting their arrows positioned exactly right. Not an extra muscle moved, not an extra breath was spent. They saw Wing leading Garret, Tommy, Abby and Olivia out of the private room.

"Now!" Duke shot first, a few milliseconds before Pau. They watched in what seemed like eternal slow motion, even though the arrows raced forward with incredible velocity. The arrows rotated in the air like a space station hovering miles above the Earth. The shiny arrowheads reflected ancient and contemporary images of China as they flew past the Chinese acrobats, singers and dancers.

Finally reaching its destination, Duke's arrow pierced its target, slicing through flesh directly into the heart of a human body. Pau's arrow bypassed all and embedded itself in the wall of the private dining room.

Job done, the marksmen left just as unobtrusively as they entered. No one saw anything, and no one heard anything.

≈

WITH THE SHAFT OF THE ARROW PROTRUDING FROM HIS chest, Tommy was bleeding out, spirit rapidly ebbing away. There was no time for explanations, no chance for redemption, but there was one thing Tommy willed himself to do before he passed to the next world.

"Abby, Abby," he gurgled through the foam filling his mouth. "Goodbye, darling. I love you. Forgive me."

Abby and Olivia shrieked. Abby wanted to kneel next to her father, but Garret pulled her away and held her. "No, Abby. You must go. Immediately." Garret gently but firmly drew the girls away.

Pandemonium broke out as the other patrons, drawn to the girls' screams, saw Tommy's bloody, spasming body. Pain wracked his frame, his vision began to cloud and voices from another cosmos seemed to beckon. Through the fog, Tommy heard somebody shout, "Call an ambulance!"

Another blurted, "Medicine isn't going to help him anymore. Just get a priest. He'll be more use."

As Tommy convulsed in death throes, Garret took out a huge wad of bills, gave it to Wing, and spoke quietly, but firmly. "Distribute as necessary. Take the girls away."

He turned to Olivia and Abby. "You were never here with me. Do not argue. Do not say anything to anyone."

He addressed Wing. "The ladies were just entering the restaurant to join us, right?"

"Absolutely, Mr. Southam. We had not even made it to the Grand Room when the incident occurred."

"But, Dad..."

"For once in your life, Olivia, do not argue with me. Let me handle all the questions. And, whatever you do, if anyone asks you anything, don't contradict a word I say. You were never here. Now go."

Olivia had never heard her dad speak that way, and it

frightened her. What scared her even more was that he was absolutely in control of the situation, as if he had done this a hundred times before—as if he knew what was going to happen and was fully prepared.

Wing led the two girls away. Abby turned back and saw her father observing her wistfully. He gave a wave goodbye.

"No!" screamed Abby, trying to free herself from Wing's grip.

Wing tightened his hold, restraining her. "No, Ms. Sung. You can't go to him." He forced her to accompany him.

Garret knelt down beside Tommy for a final time. Tommy knew he had only seconds left. "Step one accomplished, Garret. Now it's up to you and Noah. I hope he's up to it."

"If he isn't, we'll all join you soon. We might anyway, even if he is."

With a last strength coming from an unknown place, Tommy's hand faltered as he tried to touch Garret's face. "We must not die in vain, Garret." With that, his eyes bugged out, his expression stiffened and his body went limp.

Garret held the lapels of his friend's jacket tightly and voiced hoarsely, "We won't fail, Tommy. Mary and Jocelyn will be avenged."

29

EXCUSES ARE FOR LOSERS

D uke and Pau raced through the door, then pounded down the stairs.

"I don't know what happened! I never miss," faltered Pau. He was freaked, knowing Chin's reward for failure.

Duke was silent as they exited into the interior loading area of the complex. In the garage were a dozen trucks coming in and out and one E-Class black Mercedes six-door stretch limo waiting for them.

Pau tried to bolt in the opposite direction, but Duke snatched him back. "You're going the wrong way, Pau." Pau struggled, but a ham fist to his head sent him reeling. The stronger Duke yanked him to the Mercedes, where inside Chin sat beside Ron, the human punching bag.

Duke pushed Pau into the limo, and the two sat in the seats facing Ron and Chin. Duke sneered at Pau, cowering with a fearful look of submission and snarled, "You can die fast, or you can die slow. It's your choice."

"No! It wasn't my fault! I don't know how it happened."

Pau shoved back against the seat, arms crossed protectively across his chest.

"Shaddap." Duke walloped Pau in the solar plexus, and Pau buckled over.

"Drive," commanded Chin, and the chauffeur began a smooth navigation out of the building's bowels.

As Pau made gurgling, belching noises, Ron looked as if his heart was hammering out of his chest, hoping against hope that he could avoid the inevitable. A bead of sweat formed at the base of his receding hairline.

Chin slapped the accountant on the knee. "Thank you for coming to the meeting."

"No problem, Mr. Chin," swallowed Ron meekly, whispering through jagged breaths.

"I want to show my appreciation for what you have done for us for so many years."

"That's not necessary."

"But it is."

Chin grabbed Ron by the throat and began to strangle the fraudulent accountant. He struggled, but the powerful Tiger Master delivered a crushing blow to his windpipe. As he tried to yell, Ron's tongue popped out. Chin reached into his throat, breaking his jaw, and jerked the gooey, fleshy organ.

Chin, blood streaming through his fingers, firmly yanked on Ron's tongue several times, finally tearing it out with a powerful jerk. The driver pushed the window button, opening the window. Chin tossed the tongue into a passing dumpster, then released his hold on the accountant as the electric window closed. With his crimson blood now covering the seating area of the car, Ron slumped back, savage pain distorting his features. He would never speak again, but he would live.

At least, temporarily.

"Next?"

Chin's sense of humor did not amuse Pau or diminish his fear. "I never miss," he blubbered. "You know I never miss. Something must have happened. Please, Chin, please. I have been with you since I was thirteen."

"Which is why you should know better." Chin's face darkened. "I know why you missed. You were not synchronized with Duke. You hesitated a fraction of a second after Duke gave the order, and that means Duke shot first, allowing the slightest gust of air—the kick from his crossbow—to blow on your shot. That diverted your arrow a millimeter at most. However, over the course of the two hundred feet the arrow traveled, that millimeter became several millimeters. Tiny, tiny, yes, but it made all the difference."

He spouted out a Chinese proverb ingrained into his being by Master Wu. "*Cha zhi hao li, shi zhi qian li!*" (A millimeter discrepancy leads to a thousand mile loss.

"I won't do it again. I promise I won't," begged Pau.

"No, you won't." Chin nodded at Duke to finish the man off.

"Why, Chin, why? I have been faithful and...and you gave the accountant a second chance. Why not me? Please, give me a second chance."

"Ron got a second chance because one thing Garret said was right. My corporate and financial structure is a maze that cannot be untangled. Not only are there traceable assets, but there are also undocumented funds. It would take several thousand hours to train someone else, and I don't feel like spending the time bringing another person up to speed. You? There are ten thousand like you in every city.

Every block has a tough guy that can easily be replaced by another tough guy."

Chin glanced to Duke. "What are your thoughts, son?"

"Excuses are for losers. The problem with losers is that they never know when to stop."

"Which means?" prompted Chin, as if he were teaching ethics to a student.

"Which means a loser will never change his habits. So, if he doesn't change, we have to change the situation for him."

With that, Duke swiftly delivered a hammer punch to Pau's midsection. Pau buckled over.

"I'll change! I'll change!" croaked Pau.

Duke grabbed Pau's neck and put it on his lap. Despite Pau's fight for existence, Duke easily held the failure down. He raised his right arm, bending it so his fist was beside his ear, then brought his elbow down on top of Pau's head. The stomach-churning sound of his skull being smashed permeated the car. There was no blood, but there was a small cave indented into Pau's head.

"Please," gurgled Pau, now on the journey to his next life.

Chin ignored Pau's pleas and looked at Duke. "This is a lesson. This is not a random killing or execution for the sake of pleasure. You have to ask, 'Why did he hesitate?' and the most likely answer is: doubt. Even though Pau carried through with the shot, doubt caused him to miss the target. Doubt will cause him to miss again if we allow him to."

"You couldn't have seen that. You were too far away!" whimpered Pau feebly.

"I see everything," said Chin. "Even though you were wearing a mask, I saw your eyes. They flickered and rose a bit as the group left the room."

"That doesn't mean anything!"

"No, Pau. It meant a brief moment of indecision. I can't have anyone working with me who does not follow orders completely." He turned to his son. "Understand, Duke?"

"Yup." Duke pulled his arm back and threw two hundred and fifty pounds of force into Pau's breadbasket.

"You're so friggin' useless." Duke raised his arm again and plowed his fist into Pau's head. As the fist made contact, he applied a corkscrew twist, crushing Pau's nose into his cranium. Pau lost consciousness, and his body froze. With the massive bleeding, the young gangster would soon be of another world.

Chin looked at the freaked-out Ron. "You heard what Duke said about doubt. I taught him that. You're a goner, too."

The tongueless Ron scribbled on his tablet computer. *You told me you needed me!*

Chin shrugged indifferently. "I just wanted to enjoy myself for a few moments watching your pain."

The now-mute Ron feebly waved his arms in protest.

"Slime. At least Pau was loyal to me." With that, Chin applied the same nose-to-cranium corkscrew twist blow that Duke used on Pau, and Ron joined Pau on the highway to Hell.

Chin nodded approvingly at Duke. "You've got promise. You're learning well."

Duke warmed. Praise from his father was rare.

30

NICE RIDE!

Noah watched a chauffeur open the door to a new Lexus LS that featured a sticker price of a cool quarter million. Lexus slid into the back seat and waved goodbye to Sam, Noah and Chad as they walked toward Noah and Chad's vintage MG sports car. "See you next time."

Noah gave him the thumbs up and shouted, "You got it!" as the luxury vehicle took off.

Noah whistled. "So that's how the kid got his name. That's one expensive ride."

"A car's a car. No big deal," said Sam emotionlessly.

Noah turned to look Sam in the face.

"It's a big deal to me," retorted Noah. I walked everywhere because we couldn't even afford bus fare when I was a kid."

"Yeah, well, you got it made now, Noah," snapped Sam, thrusting his hands into his overly dirty jeans.

Noah saw that the rips in Sam's pants were real, not the artificial ones that manufacturers put in to look cool. "I wish. Where you off to now, Sam?"

"Nowhere."

"Now that's not a real answer. You going home? Or maybe you want to hang with Chad and me? See a movie?"

Sam pulled out a little plastic bag of crack cocaine. "You want some? A hundred bucks."

"You're crazy, man." Chad tried to snatch the bag from Sam, but Sam yanked it back.

"You're gonna get locked up if you get caught," Chad snapped angrily.

"What you want me to do?" Sam snapped back defiantly. "Somebody's got to put groceries on the table."

"Well, you ain't gonna put shit on the table if you're in jail," retorted Chad.

"Whoa, whoa, man," interrupted Noah, the voice of calm. "What's the deal, Sam? You gotta know this is going to get you into a heap of trouble."

Pent-up rage from a kid who had been forced to grow up faster than he ever should have burst out. "My sister's three. My mom's got MS, and my dad just got busted for a B & E. He can't make an honest dollar, so he's gotta make a dishonest one. Stupid loser. Can't even do that right so guess who's left to put groceries on the table."

Noah had heard this story a thousand times if he heard it once. But there was a difference with Sam. His thinking might be warped but the kid had an unexpected sense of responsibility.

"Tell you what. I'll buy that hit and everything else you got on one condition."

"What's that?"

"That this is the last time ever that you do anything like this. Deal?"

Sam reluctantly took nine other small bags containing

the illegal substance from his pocket. "Deal. But I got a condition, too."

"You in the negotiating business now, Sam?" snickered Noah, starting to like this spunky kid. "What do I have to do?"

"You got to find me another way to make some money."

Not blinking an eye, Noah whipped out Master Wu's envelope. As he counted out a thousand bucks, he griped, "You drive a hard bargain."

"I got no choice, Noah."

Ain't it the truth. Noah forked over the dough. "Sounds about right. I'll see what I can do."

Sam jetted away, waving the cash in the air.

Chad blistered his buddy with a WTF look. "That could have kept me going for two months. And why did you lie to him? You can't get him a job anywhere. You know he's gonna be at it again."

"Yeah, but if he stays away from dealing for ten days, that's ten days more of freedom he's got. And ten days for us to try to figure out how to stop him from sliding down the slippery slope."

"How much more cash you got?" Chad asked bluntly.

"Not much. Why?"

"Because if you want us to solve Sam's problems fast, we gotta win a lottery, and we gotta buy a helluva lot of tickets if we want a shot of winning."

Arriving at the ancient MG, Noah and Chad hopped in to what they had affectionately nicknamed "the cockpit." Noah cranked the ignition. The engine coughed but then sputtered and died.

"No big deal." Chad got a wrench out, popped the hood, banged on the alternator and yelled, "Do it again!"

Noah tried again, and after a few nervous seconds of gear-crunching and growling, the engine rumbled to life.

Noah gently pulled the temperamental metal beast out of the parking lot. The leather seats were cut up, the windows had a few chips, and neither the odometer nor the speedometer worked, but hey, he and Chad were two guys in their twenties, riding in one of the most coveted sports cars ever built.

"You got to stop being an easy touch, Noah."

"As my parents used to say, 'It's not the healthy who need a doctor.'"

"Yeah," Chad said, "but, if the doctor gets killed, who's gonna take care of the patients?"

Noah sneaked a peak at Chad. "Certainly not a corporate lawyer, especially one that works at Pittman Saunders."

"That bad, huh?"

Noah yawned to emphasize the point. "I got assigned to the most boring job in the world. Got to check out the real estate contracts for Golden Asia. It's the ultimate cure for insomnia."

"Doesn't sound like you'll last long. You gonna hand in your notice tomorrow?"

"Well, uh, the place does have some fringe benefits."

Chad turned to see Noah grinning like a bird of prey feasting on a field mouse.

"You dirty dog, you. Damn, you work fast, Noah."

"As my illustrious and super-boring boss says, 'Real estate bills. Speed thrills.' So at least temporarily I'm doing both."

31

TAKING CHARGE

Garret's brain churned. He and Tommy knew that Chin would likely do something like this but didn't think that he would be so brazen as to have Tommy killed in such a public place with him being so close to the action. But then it hit him that it made perfect sense. Chin knew that none of Tiger's staff dare contradict him, and just the way, the Tiger Master had sent him and Tommy a message when he had the plane blown up that carried Mary and Jocelyn, he sent a message to him just now.

The difference was that this time, Garret would not bend —and that this was just the beginning of the plan.

While the situation was dire, it wasn't catastrophic. Killings in a casino were rare but putting out fires, even infernos, was routine.

First things first. Something had to be done about the crowd forming outside the perimeter of the cordoned-off area surrounding Tommy's body. They were all pointing, talking, crying and shaking their heads and, in a few minutes, pictures could potentially be all over social media unless Garret took immediate control in overdrive.

Garret made a call.

"Security," answered a bored young man.

"Listen up. This is Garret Southam. Shut down the internet and jam all forms of communication. Send a crew with high-powered magnets to the restaurant and discreetly take cell phones away briefly from customers to insert data-destroying programs."

The voice perked up. "Yes, sir!"

Seeing Wing approach, Garret sidled up and ordered quietly as he slipped him a thick wad of cash, "Keep the slots and tables open while security does their sweep. Give customers the cash to buy more chips. Keep them distracted. Also, get or make a bunch of coupons for the buffet that expire in fifteen minutes."

"Of course."

Busboys quickly reset the private dining room Garret was in with two used settings and two unused settings.

First responders were fast on the scene. A crime photographer snapped pictures of Tommy's body with the arrow sticking up while CSI techs dusted for prints and examined the arrow in the wall. There were two interrogators but, with most of the patrons bribed or incentivized away, those that were left were curiosity seekers, not real witnesses.

All, that is, except for Garret. Two policemen stood with him. One conducted the interview and the other recorded their conversation and took notes.

"Would you please summarize what happened, Mr. Southam?" one of the cops asked.

"Of course, Officer. I was having dinner with Mr. Sung in a private room that our firm reserved. Mr. Sung is involved in the management of this complex, and our firm, Pittman Saunders, is their corporate attorney. Mr. Sung was in a cele-bratory mood and had a few drinks, quite a bit more than he might normally have." Garret paused to consider, then continued. "Quite unstable, he knocked the soup over both of us."

Garret pointed to the stains on his shirt, jacket and pants. "We both had to clean up and left the room. As we left, two arrows came flying. One of them hit Mr. Sung, and the other planted itself into the wall."

"Can we assume the other arrow was meant for you?" the officer asked.

"No, I don't think that can be assumed at all." Garret frowned, as if the thought was foreign to him. "No one knew we were in the room. It was a spur-of-the-moment decision for two business associates who were also longtime friends to share a meal after we just ran into each other at the craps table. But, as you have requested that I speculate, I will do so. There are two possibilities. The first possibility is that we were the wrong people in the wrong place at the wrong time. In other words, a random act of violence."

"Do you think that likely?"

"What I think is immaterial. What is important are the facts. The Tiger Palace is an extremely successful entertainment complex. With its success comes enemies. What better way to destroy its reputation by having it linked to random murders of patrons or staff?"

"Right." The cop nodded as he continued writing. "You mentioned a second possibility."

"Yes. The second possibility is that both arrows were meant for Mr. Sung. One was insurance in case the first one missed."

"So you rule out the possibility that you were a possible target?"

"I'm a lawyer, Officer. And a damned good one. I never rule out any possibility, but let's go over the facts." Garret stood a little straighter. "I'm a senior partner specializing in corporate and commercial blue chip clients only. Do your due diligence on our firm, and you will discover an extraordinarily clean record. Pittman Saunders is extremely boring but extremely safe."

"Why were there four place settings if dinner was only for you and Mr. Sung?"

Garret continued with a hint of chastisement. "You don't know much about the entertainment industry, do you, son? The answer is public relations. Mr. Sung often spontaneously invited patrons, especially young ladies, to join him. Having structured his contract with the Tiger Complex, I can inform you that part of his job description is to spend $350,000 per month entertaining clients, patrons and any other potential for new business. What is called client development is an entirely normal legal expense. Had you come by, there is an excellent chance he would have invited you in the interests of maintaining an excellent relationship with our public defenders." Again, he paused and lowered his baritone voice so that it was barely audible. "I hope we can keep this low key, officers."

The two officers looked at each other. They nodded, indicating the questions were answered to their mutual satisfaction.

"Thank you, Mr. Southam. We will be in touch if there are any further questions."

The other police officer turned off the recorder and packed his notes. "I'm good to go."

The officers started to leave. Garret quickly joined them and discreetly placed an envelope into the bag of the policeman carrying the recording device and another envelope into the hand of the interviewing officer. "Thanks for your understanding," he intoned quietly.

"Always glad to be of service to the public, Mr. Southam."

Sɪᴛᴛɪɴɢ ᴀᴛ ᴛʜᴇ ᴇʟᴇɢᴀɴᴛ ʙᴀʀ ᴀ ʜᴜɴᴅʀᴇᴅ ᴀɴᴅ ꜰɪꜰᴛʏ ꜰᴇᴇᴛ away were Olivia and Abby. While Garret wanted them out of the way, they knew they were part of the unfolding story and had to know how it would play out.

When they were safely out of the immediate danger zone, they refused to accompany Wing any further. With chaos demanding his attention, Wing had no choice but to acquiesce to their demand.

Olivia and Abby had a complete view of the whole exchange. Their eyes filled with confusion and consternation. They knew their lives had just been forever changed.

Again.

32

COFFEE BREAKING

L ike always, Chad's Caffeine Emporium, a small internet café, was packed. It could barely squeeze in a dozen people at any time, but that was no big deal to the kids who hung out there killing cops, vampires and dragons in cyberspace, or dueled to the death with mercenaries and wizards, maybe half a world away, maybe on the computer next to them.

But, even though it was busy, money was in short supply, mainly because Chad wasn't really interested in being a coffee mogul. It was the kids who were important.

The gregarious Chad chatted them up, found out what made them tick and, if they needed a hand, he was there for them. Sometimes, it was helping with homework; some-times it was parental issues. Sometimes, there were kids like Sam who needed a hand to pull them out of shit before the cesspool dragged them in.

Chad loved them because, once upon a time, he was one of them. The hands that pulled him out of the abyss were Noah's parents, teachers who were more concerned about their students' personal lives than their academics. When

Chad and Noah met at the Reids' school, they got along like oil and water. That was pretty normal—you couldn't expect everyone to like everybody. However, one day Chad pulled a knife and stabbed Noah because Noah wouldn't give Chad the T-shirt he was wearing, and that's when the Reid parents stepped it up.

They found out Chad was an orphan and had been living on his own for months. Some people collected stray animals. The Reids collected stray people, and Chad became part of the Reid household. After that initial rough start, it took a while, but Noah and Chad became soul brothers.

It was that kind of brotherly heart to heart they were having at the Caffeine Emporium.

The love-struck Noah sat across from barista Chad, who was preparing cappuccinos for the two of them.

"So? Who is she? Who is this *fringe benefit*?"

Noah sighed. "A girl who has everything."

"Oh, one of those. Can't afford, can't touch, can't get to first base. I know too many of those."

"Olivia's different."

"You mean she's not a spoiled rich kid who thinks the world should cater to her every whim?"

Chad made perfect sense, but who said love was logical?

"Well...she's not that bad." replied Noah.

Chad tapped his forehead. *Think, bro!* "Not that bad means not that good. Let me guess. She makes Miss America look like yesterday's breakfast."

"Well...like I said...she's not that bad."

"You shallow bastard," Chad sneered disdainfully. "Falling in love with someone just because she's a hot babe? Do you remember Dad warning us about Cleopatra or

Helen of Troy or Mata Hari? Do you really want to step out on that menacing thin edge of the wedge? Duh."

Seeing Noah's lack of response made Chad realize that, for the first time in his life, Noah might actually be interested in someone of the female persuasion. He'd better just roll with the facts. "So, is she part of the secretarial pool or someone who hands out the muffins? Or maybe she operates the elevator?"

Noah sighed. "None of the above. She's a lawyer. And the boss's daughter."

Chad was flabbergasted. Intelligent women of means had always intimidated Noah. "She's gorgeous and smart. What's she doing with a slime ball like you? Hey, does she have a sister?"

"Damned if I know." Noah sighed again. "What can I do to make her see what a wonderful guy I am? That her life is incomplete without me? What kind of present can I get her?"

Chad rolled his eyes. "Gag me. Remember, we had the same problem every Mother's Day. What can I get you, Mom? And her answer was always the same." He put on a feminine voice. 'Oh, nothing, son. Just give me your love'."

Reverting to his natural voice, Chad offered, "The answer is you don't get her anything because you can't ever match up to anything she already has. So if she's everything you say she is, you gotta be different, think different, act different because you won't make an impact in a normal way."

"I'll get her a dozen roses," Noah announced as if it was the most original idea in the world. "No, two dozen roses."

"Duh," Chad scoffed. "Someone like that gets flowers from every guy who has ever hit on her."

"Mom loved flowers."

"Mom was the wife of a missionary who could barely afford the rent, let alone flowers."

Chad put the cappuccino in front of Noah. Like a true barista artist, he made a design using a combination of foam and coffee. This time, it was a rose. "Sweep her off her feet. Be different. Get her something she would never think of herself."

"Maybe daisies instead of roses?"

Chad made motions of tearing his hair out. "Hey, you got a picture of this ravishing creature?"

"Yeah, there's one on the Pittman Saunders website." Noah moved to one of the computers and started typing, narrowing his brows with unsettled intensity. "Something's wrong. I can't get in. Maybe they got some kind of firewall or something? My password is Reid, but I can't get in."

Chad walked over to Noah's computer and typed *r-e-i-d*. As the computer displayed Noah's opening screen, he said, "Bingo."

"How'd you do that?" asked Noah. "I mean, I'm not a computer geek like you, but I think I know how to spell my name."

Chad shook his head in disbelief over his friend's ignorance. "The light on the CAPS LOCK key is broken. It needs to be replaced."

"Then why don't you fix it?" Noah inquired.

"Funds are in serious shortage for this cowboy. Want to lend me some?"

"Gave everything I had to Sam. Wait until I get a paycheck."

"Hello, Noah," said an unrecognized somber voice from behind him.

Noah turned to see Chin staring at him. He recognized the man, and the hairs on the back of his neck began to twitch. "You, you're the one at the airport. The guy chasing down the tiger."

"You are most observant. Do you like tigers?"

Although there was nothing sinister about the appearance of the Tiger Master, there was something about Chin's matter-of-fact tone that made Noah shudder. "How do you know who I am? And who are you?"

"My business is to know everything about anybody associated with any of my enterprises. We have mutual acquaintances that I wanted to warn you about. They may not be good for your health. Goodbye, Noah."

Chin turned and strode to the door.

"You didn't tell me your name."

Chin turned back, sending two martial arts stars rocketing through the air, missing Noah and Chad by millimeters. The stars were sharp enough to slice through two cups. They embedded in the wall and then exploded like fireworks, sending a stream of sparkles throughout the air.

When they'd burned out, and after the smoke subsided, there were two twelve-inch holes in the wall.

"My name is Chin. Chin Chee Fok." Chin left without further comment.

"What was that about?" asked a freaked-out Chad.

"I have no idea, but he knows who I am, and he knows how to find me, so I think we should just carry on like normal." Noah took a long slow intake of air. "Nothing we can do anyway."

Chad's eyebrows rose as he glared at his best friend in confused amazement. "After that wacko, you're still thinking about her? Now?"

"You really think roses are a bad idea?"

"Trust me."

33

HOSTILE

HONG KONG - MONDAY EVENING

Garret had been driving for ten minutes. He checked the Bentley's rearview mirror to see Abby and Olivia, sitting numbly in the back seat. They had been so quiet he could hear the purr of the car. There were times when words could be a comfort but Garret knew this was not one of them. The girls had seen too much and anything he might say would only upset them or make them more suspicious of him. An inanity like, "Don't worry. Everything will be okay," would likely result in an explosion.

So he kept mum.

Garret needed the quiet time, too. His best friend had just been killed and he had been part of it.

And then the dam broke. Abby wailed, "It's not fair. Why?"

Olivia held her friend tightly. Staying silent, she knew Abby had to get the hurt out.

Tears streamed from Abby's eyes as she whimpered, "I should have suspected something. This morning, I found Daddy with a suitcase full of money. When I asked him about it, he told me it was from a casino."

Garret's ears picked up. He listened more intently but remained silent.

"Your dad is part owner of more than a dozen casinos. That's entirely possible," Olivia consoled her friend.

"Except, Olivia, the armored car service comes by to scoop up the cash every two hours, twenty-four hours a day. And the bills were in foreign currency. He said it was for a deposit."

Olivia turned from Abby and lashed out at her father. "You're Tommy's lawyer. You must know what's going on."

Garret focused on the road, trying to control his own inner turmoil. "I knew your father better than anyone else alive. If he said he was going to make a deposit, there is no doubt in my mind he made a deposit." *Just not at a bank.*

"You don't need to lie," Olivia stated calmly. "I saw what happened at Tiger. I saw you bribe the cops. Why didn't you want them to know Abby and I were there?"

"Your protection," replied Garret with a self-assured calm that masked his churning emotions.

"What the hell does that mean?" Despite their difficult relationship, this was the first time Olivia swore at her father.

"See no evil, hear no evil, speak no evil."

"Dammit, Dad. I'm not eleven," Olivia blurted. "Stop treating me like a child."

"Knowledge is dangerous. The less you know—or more important, the less anyone thinks you know—the safer you will be."

Olivia spat out in frustration, "That's the problem with you. Knowledge is not dangerous; it is power. You think you're protecting me by hiding things."

"No employee speaks to me that way," growled Garret.

"Is that what you really think of me? Well, I have news for you. I am not your employee; I am your daughter."

"As far as Pittman Saunders is concerned, you are an employee, an employee I am responsible for, including deciding what you're privy to on a need-to-know basis. As your father, who cares infinitely more for you than I care for my own personal well-being, there are things I don't want you to know about."

"You have a strange way of demonstrating that. After Mom was killed in the plane accident, you sent me away so you almost never had to speak to me." Olivia's voice steeled. "You told me to use Mom's maiden name of Novak for whatever reason. I never, ever had a cell phone, credit card or Internet account in my own name. It's like you were ashamed of anyone knowing I was your daughter. You never explained anything to me, but I deserve to know."

"Do you honestly believe that I would do nothing if I thought there was something I could do? The reason I haven't told you anything is that there is nothing to tell."

Before Olivia continued her tirade against her father, Abby interrupted with the whisper of truth and resignation. "Mr. Southam, I want to go back to New York as soon as possible. Obviously, I won't be helping in my father's business and there's nothing else for me in Hong Kong anymore. Can you help me arrange my father's funeral as quickly as possible?"

"Of course, Abby. Can we set it for tomorrow afternoon?"

"Can you do it sooner?" sobbed Abby.

Garret nodded. He had expected this response. "It's one in the morning. I can arrange for the service in two to three hours."

Abby's gentle voice intoned, "I would like that."

34

GOODBYE

Garret was non-stop all business on the phone as he drove to the morgue. It was a task that he performed every year or two for Chin, so he knew that a hundred thousand in cash would cover costs. No need to fret about the early morning hour. He kept several times that amount stored in secret places in the Bentley.

When Garret and the girls arrived, they were taken to the room where Tommy's body was stored. It had arrived shortly before they did. After Abby confirmed the body was indeed her father's, Garret ordered the attendant to remove the arrow. After carefully using a knife to enlarge the wound, he pulled the arrowhead from Tommy's heart, placed it into a plastic bag and gave it to Garret.

This process took less than half an hour.

The door to the room opened and three white-robed Taoist monks, along with two morgue attendants, entered the storage room. The monks handed white funeral robes to Garret, Olivia, and Abby.

They went to the washrooms to change while the attendants placed Tommy's body on a gurney.

When the trio, now dressed in funeral garb, exited the washrooms, Garret nodded at the monks, who lit incense sticks and began to chant. Carrying a framed photo of Tommy, Garret led the procession of monks as the attendants rolled the wheeled stretcher out of the morgue.

Garret was never one to leave things to chance. By evading an autopsy and careful examination of the body, he would avoid unnecessary questions about the legality of any of the pharmaceuticals that might be found in Tommy's corpse. This also ensured that the arrowhead in his heart would never be found, never be traced.

TWO HEARSES WAITED OUTSIDE THE MORGUE. ONE CARRIED Tommy's remains, Garret, Olivia and Abby. The other was for the monks.

It was a short ride to the crematorium. Master Wu was waiting outside when they arrived.

"Who's he?" whispered Abby to Garret.

"Master Wu was the father that Tommy and I never had. He's always out of the limelight, but he is always there for us," replied Garret.

Under normal circumstances, Olivia and Abby would have grilled Garret more but, in their present state, Garret's short, enigmatic answer was good enough.

They walked with the monks who chanted, sang, waved incense sticks, rang bells and beat drums as they rolled Tommy's body to the altar where it was lifted off and placed on the funeral pyre.

By 4 a.m., the altar had been prepared, complete with

ten oranges assembled to form a pyramid, incense sticks, a cooked fish and sweet candies. A lamp in the center was flanked by two lit candles symbolizing sunlight, moonlight and a human's eyes.

Abby and Master Wu approached the altar. Arriving, each picked up seven incense sticks and lit them. Holding the sticks in a single bunch with both hands, they held them worshipfully and prayerfully. They took three steps in tandem and stood before Tommy's body. Holding the incense straight-armed in front of them, they bowed three times. The smoke from the incense created little wisps that floated upward. Master Wu took the sticks from Abby and stuck them into a small sand-filled copper vessel.

The intensity of the monks' chanting and praying grew as Garret took out a roll of bills and placed it into a small earthen vessel. He took out a match and set the money on fire. Normal practice was to use fake money, but Garret refused to compromise for Tommy. As the fire died down, so did the performance by the monks. A single small bell tolled the end.

The monks placed Tommy's body into the brick cremation chamber and fired it up.

Garret turned to Master Wu. "Make sure he gets to where he's going safely."

"I will," nodded Master Wu.

"I'm staying, too," announced Abby.

"Are you sure? You may be here for twelve hours or more," said Garret. That was an exaggeration but Garret didn't want Abby hanging around.

"I have nowhere else I want to be," sobbed Abby.

"Understood." Garret whispered into Master Wu's ear. "Make sure she is safe and there's nothing but ash before you leave."

"I'm staying, too," added Olivia in a tone that brooked no argument. She hugged Abby tight.

Garret's chin jutted out as he answered, "I need all hands onboard to help with Tommy's documents. If Noah's all I have, it'll delay Abby's return to New York."

Abby turned to Olivia and the two locked eyes. "Go, Olivia. Please."

Olivia hesitated as a foreboding chill swept through her soul. She forced herself to ignore it, then nodded. "Of course."

PART III

BLEAK NIGHT OF
THE SOUL

RUNNING ON FUMES

N oah's fellow office mates shot him weird glances as he got off the elevator, carrying a large covered potted plant to the cubbyhole he shared with Olivia.

Stepping through the door, he grinned broadly and plopped it on her desk. "Happy birthday!" He whipped off the wrapping to reveal a Big Jaws X Venus flytrap plant slowly devouring the carcass of some poor fly.

Olivia's face contorted in disbelief. *Is he from Mars?*

Noah asked hopefully, "Peace?"

Not the right question at exactly the wrong time. She went ballistic. "Moron! Loser! You insensitive, unfeeling dimwit! I hate you! I hate you!"

She stood up, picked up the plant and crashed it on top of Noah's head. He just stood there, stunned, as she pelted him with her fists. He tried to restrict her as her arms pounded away.

"Hey, I'm sorry. The plant was my friend Chad's idea. I wanted to get you roses, but he said that was a bad idea."

She stopped flailing and screamed, "I love roses! What's

wrong with roses? My mother loved roses, and so do I! And who the hell is Chad?"

Memo to self: Kill Chad. Noah wiped some of the dirt off his head and picked up the poor Venus flytrap.

"Um...Chad is my best friend, or was my best friend until about thirteen seconds ago," he responded. He tilted his head and saw Olivia's eyes—there were tears.

"Hey," he said gently. He made a bold move and gently touched her. When she didn't object, he went a step further and held her hand. "I'm a good listener, and you need someone to talk to."

"I have nothing to say to you," she sniffled at him.

"Yeah, bad idea. Our conversations have been kinda underwhelming."

No response from Olivia, so Noah tried again. "Um...Uh...do you like falafels?"

"At 8:15 a.m.? Are you really that crazy?"

"I like them any time of day or night. Besides, I got here at 5:30 and need a break."

It was true. Although official office hours began at 8 a.m., all the lawyers, especially the juniors, got to the office by 6 a.m. at the latest. Noah had only popped out to get the carnivorous plant.

"Falafels give you the farts, and I don't think anyone in the office wants to smell your farts," mumbled Olivia.

"You've never had one before, have you?"

"What makes you say that?" she retorted.

"Because you wouldn't care about polluting the air with your personal gas if you had eaten one. You drown those little deep-fried chickpea balls lathered with hummus, hot sauce, and baba ghanoush...mmm, good."

Olivia continued to glare at Noah, and then her emotions poured out. "Last night, I saw the firm's biggest client get murdered with an arrow from a crossbow. I was with his daughter, Abby, my best friend. I was an inch away from being victim number two."

She demonstrated with her fingers just how close it was. "I was just at the crematorium before I came here, saying goodbye to Tommy. I should be with Abby now but am only here because we've got to wrap things up so she can get back to New York." Olivia's voice dropped. "And, somehow, and I don't know how, my father is tied up in this mess. And you have the audacity to ask me out for a falafel? What kind of proposition is that?"

Noah swallowed. "You're right." He hung his head. "Bad idea. Would you like to go for a Caesar salad instead?"

Noah's efforts at lightheartedness were starting to have the desired effect on Olivia. Closely observing her as her eyes wandered the room, Noah was positive there was the tiniest hint of a smile for a fraction of a millisecond. She stuffed her hands into her jacket pockets.

"Falafels are full of garlic."

"I'm not planning to kiss you." *Yet.* He gave his infectious smile. "Hey, I know life's a bitch, but you need to release all that garbage out of your system. Take up boxing or quilting...or you can take it out on me."

Olivia shuffled her feet and murmured, "I guess I just did."

Noah offered his arm; Olivia shook her head, but she followed him as he left the room. They entered the elevator and were the only two passengers. As it began its descent, without looking at him, Olivia warily took his hand and squeezed. If the ride never ended, Noah would think he had died and was en route to Heaven. Olivia's eyes concentrated on the elevator door. "I'm not doing this because I like you."

"No one likes me," Noah lamented. "Why should I expect anything different from you?"

"I'm just totally freaked out and need someone to talk to. You just happen to be convenient."

"I'm willing to be convenient for a long time. Forever, if necessary." Noah squeezed her hand a little harder.

"I don't like jocks," she countered.

"I'll take Mozart over the Green Bay Packers any day," Noah replied with a straight face.

She tried again. "I'm a high-maintenance person."

"I own an old British sports car. Try having one of those in Hong Kong. That's what you call high maintenance," Noah said.

36

THE OFFER

The atmosphere was much more contentious outside the elevator of Pittman Saunders parking garage. As Garret stepped out of the Bentley, Chin slid out unobtrusively from behind a concrete pillar and blocked his way.

"That was a touching service, Garret. Although 4 a.m. is an ungodly hour."

"It was the right thing to do. Tommy wanted to be cremated within eight hours of his death. Not an easy thing to arrange when he was the object of a murder investigation." Tommy had no such request but Garret knew that Chin had no way of knowing that.

"Which is why I pay you the big bucks. If it were easy, I could save myself a lot of money."

"You didn't need to kill Tommy," Garret fumed. "I explicitly relayed to you I would handle the situation."

Chin grunted with arrogance. "Yes, you told me that, but I didn't tell you the reason why I wanted him gone." He paused to let the gravity of the moment sink in. "I want you to be the head of Golden Asia."

Garret didn't hesitate. "With you pulling my strings on every move? I don't operate that way. No."

"Your salary will be bumped up to twenty million a year, Garret. Twenty million. Except for elite Hollywood entertainers, sports superstars and Fortune 500 CEOs, few in the universe make that kind of money."

"I can't be bought, Chin," Garret said. "You of all people should know that."

Chin replied nonchalantly, "It's worked so far. Think about it, Garret."

"And if I say no?"

"No one ever says no to me. But, in case you would like to be a hero and be the first, remember this. Everyone is expendable."

Chin's black Mercedes zoomed up. The door automatically opened, and Chin slid in. The car silently shot away.

Garret muttered with quiet vengeance. "Everyone includes you, Chin."

37

CONNECTIONS

HONG KONG - TUESDAY MORNING

Noah's choice of falafels had nothing to do with wanting to eat deep-fried chickpea balls wrapped in a pita or any connection with Hong Kong's small Middle Eastern population.

It was convenience and cost. Noah had still been pondering what to get Olivia before finally deciding on a dozen red roses. It just so happened that the 888 Florist close to the Pittman Saunders building offered the unsellable Venus flytrap at a 'humongous' discount. Noah instantly changed his mind, deciding the carnivorous plant was exactly the outside-of-the-box thinking Chad had talked about.

As Noah carried his special gift outside the florist, Hafez, the owner of the neighboring Falafel Palace, spotted him and gave him a handful of two-for-one opening special coupons.

So when Hafez saw Noah and Olivia entering, he gave a great big welcome to the couple. "Noah, so good to see you again."

"You really know this place," said Olivia, her respect for her workmate climbing a notch.

"Why else do you think I suggested it?"

Hafez seated them at a window table. "You want to use one of the two-for-one coupons I gave you? Save big money?"

"Sure," replied the sheepish lawyer as he gave one of his discount vouchers to the owner.

Olivia couldn't care less about Noah's financial situation. She just needed a caring ear. She looked across the table to see that Noah was really attentively listening.

"Pittman Saunders is Dad's only love. It has been ever since Mom died. I don't think he really wanted me after that. I'm not even sure he wanted me in the first place. He just went along with anything Mom wanted. Since then, he has maneuvered and manipulated me, all in the name of protecting me."

"Don't hold that against him. Most men find it difficult to express emotion."

Olivia turned away to hide her tears. "Can you imagine what it's like to watch a plane with your mother onboard blow up right in front of you?"

Now that was unexpected. Noah shifted uneasily. "Can't possibly imagine...Is that what happened?"

Olivia nodded. "I wasn't even twelve. Dad and I were waiting at the airport for Mom to come home and saw her plane land. And then, BOOM...Instead of my mom, there was a fiery inferno and then there were zillions of metal fragments where a plane used to be just moments before."

Tears welled in her eyes and rivulets of salt water ran down her cheeks. Her voice cracked as she whispered slowly, "You think somehow it's your fault, that you could have stopped it, or maybe it's God trying to punish you for some terrible thing you've done or for being the terrible person you are. The only one who understands is Abby. Her mom was on the plane with mine, and she saw everything, too..."

"You two go back a long way."

"Yes. My father and her father, Tommy, were best friends —just like Abby and me. We were inseparable."

"Right." A creepy feeling started to sneak up on Noah. He didn't recognize Abby's name but, in his examination of the Golden Asia file, Tommy's name was everywhere.

"Tommy Sung as in Golden Asia's Tommy Sung?" Noah was growing increasingly uneasy at the prospects.

"That's the one. Abby's now fabulously rich, owner of the biggest house on Victoria Peak..."

The falafels arrived. Seeing their somber faces, Hafez quickly left, letting Olivia and Noah eat privately.

Noah chomped slowly and thoughtfully, trying to make sense of Olivia's revelations. "This seems too coincidental. Do you ever think there's some possible connection between your mother's death, Abby's mom's death and now her father's death?"

"All the time. Why do you think I hate my father? I'm sure he's got something to do with Tommy's death. Last night opened my eyes to something that I...I..." Olivia struggled to continue. "Even as I hated him, I always respected him, but he knew that man. That scary, awful man."

"What man?"

"He said his name was Chin Chee Fok. I could tell Dad was scared. Noah, my father is never scared, but there was something about Chin...He also said he was behind Golden Asia, which means you and I are working for him, but I, for the life of me, haven't found anything the least bit suspicious."

Noah hid his sudden chill from Olivia. *Chin. That's who was at Chad's last night.* He shook his head. "I haven't seen anything with his name and my eyes are going buggy staring at the Golden Asia documents."

"My father didn't contradict him last night. If he's somehow part of what happened, I don't know who I could turn to."

"You can count on me," Noah said, taking her hand gently.

Olivia let out a sad, small laugh. "Noah, you're a very funny and sweet guy, but you are an ant playing with elephants. I don't need a peashooter. Dealing with Chin requires an elephant gun...."

She withdrew her hand from Noah's. "By the way, thanks for the falafel."

Olivia moved to stand up, but Noah boldly commanded, "Sit down, Olivia."

Stunned by his assertiveness, Olivia slumped back into her chair.

"You don't trust men. You don't trust anyone. I get that," stated Noah. "I don't blame you. What was taken from you was irreplaceable, and you're afraid of getting close to anyone because you're afraid that might happen again."

"I've already spent a small fortune logging frequent flyer miles on analysts' couches," said Olivia, her defense mechanisms shooting up like protective shields around her. "I don't need another shrink."

"No, you don't. But you do need to trust the world again."

"And that begins with you?" Olivia spat out sarcastically.

"I don't expect you to give it to me. I will earn your trust." Noah's firm eyes locked with Olivia's. "Now it's time to get back to work. Otherwise, your friend Abby will be stuck in Hong Kong."

Exiting the Falafel Palace, Noah was about to enter the florist next door when Olivia slapped his arm and asked crossly, "What are you doing?"

"I'm going to get you some roses."

"What's wrong with the *dionaea muscipula?*"

"Huh?"

"Dionaea muscipula... The Venus flytrap. I had one in Boston. Feeding it was my distraction from studying."

"Oh," uttered the flustered Noah.

"And flowers are so cliché. I must have had three hundred bouquets sent to me by doctors, lawyers, MBAs, gym instructors, plumbers, artists, engineers...anyone without an original thought in his head."

Memo to self: Give Chad a basketball autographed by Michael Jordan.

"And, Noah, thanks for the falafel. Next time, it will be my treat."

"Next time?" Noah gave himself an internal high-five.

Olivia moved a step closer to Noah. Close enough that a little gust of wind threw the scent of her lightly fragranced hair into Noah's face. Noah had to catch himself from stumbling.

"Next time. And can we not talk about touchy feely stuff? I prefer soccer and am a huge World Cup fan. And..."

"And?"

"Can we go for burgers and beer instead?"

"So we'll meet for meat?" Noah placed special stress on the words *meet* and *meat* to emphasize the pun.

Olivia rolled her eyes. "You are such a putz."

38

PLEASING THE MASTER

Noah and Olivia had been so wrapped up in their personal conversation that they didn't notice Duke discreetly watching them from a corner of the window outside the Falafel Palace. While he wasn't able to hear their conversation, their body language was more than sufficient communication.

As Noah and Olivia finished their meal and readied to leave, Duke ambled away out of sight and dialed a cell phone number.

"Dad, Olivia bit on Noah."

"Did they see you?"

"Not a chance. Too busy playing lovey dovey."

"Good work. Keep it up. Now we have options."

"You got it."

Duke walked away, grinning. A compliment from his dad was worth more than platinum.

Chin ended the call. He had taken Duke's call in the office of Eastern Commercial Bank's Stella Wei. Though she didn't have a finance degree or have more than a rudimentary investment knowledge, the financial institution found

Stella most useful for promoting the bank in special client relations.

"You look as if something is on your mind, Mr. Chin," said Stella in a soft, caring voice.

Chin's voice was ice. He had zero interest in Stella's expression of concern. "Something is always on my mind. It's a normal state of affairs. If it weren't, I'd be dead."

Stella quickly re-assessed and pulled back. *Stick to business.* "True, and here is something else for you to think about. I was assigned a small portion of your portfolio, two million dollars. In the month that I've had it, I have generated a ten percent return."

"Two hundred thousand?"

"It's 201,674.33 to be exact."

Chin's attitude warmed and he took another look at Stella. Rather than being businesslike and androgynous in appearance like most bankers, Stella's form-fitting mauve dress strategically emphasized the curves in her well-formed bosom and her twenty-one-inch waist.

"That's very good news. I'm excited about the prospects."

"I'm excited that you're excited," murmured Stella, not bothering to disguise the double entendre in her voice.

"Please stop calling me Mr. Chin."

"I will when I am of more use than handling your banking affairs."

Chin paused a moment to control his irritation. He never liked mixing his personal life with business affairs. His experiences with women rarely lasted more than a few days, but business relationships took time to develop. Women who thought they could be useful on an ongoing basis were particularly problematic. "I don't think that's a good idea, Stella. As long as you make me money, that will be more than satisfactory."

Ignoring Chin's seeming lack of interest, Stella pushed ahead. She had never lost a conquest and she wasn't about to begin now. In a low, smooth I'm-interested-in-you kind of tone, she cooed, "People bore me, but money fascinates me. Men with money fascinate me even more."

"I am not an easy man, Stella. My standards are very high. You remember Mr. Sung?"

"Of course. Your representative. Very capable."

"Unfortunately, Mr. Sung no longer works for me."

This was news. She had spent much of her time, in and out of office hours, nurturing the relationship with Tommy. "You fired him?" she asked guardedly.

Chin's eyes bored into Stella's. "No." He leaned over and whispered. "I killed him." As Chin leaned back, he saw the slightest glint of fear on Stella's face but, for people like Stella, ambition always trumped anything else.

"Chin, may I apply for his position? Perhaps we could have dinner tonight?"

"What's on the menu?"

Stella cooed, leaned over to Chin, took his hand and moved it to touch her bosom. "Me."

Chin withdrew his hand and stood. Stella was twice the age of his preferred conquests... but she still had usefulness. "I have some work to do tonight and will have further instructions later."

"Of course."

Chin made a cell phone call. "Duke, get half a dozen of our best ready. We're going to war." He turned back to Stella. "Give me your address. Someone will pick you up in several hours. Don't disappoint me."

Stella could feel the fire burning already. "I won't."

39

A LONG DAY'S JOURNEY

TUESDAY EVENING

I t was incredible. Noah had fully expected to be harassed and interrogated by Garret for taking the previous evening off and then deluged with whatever files were discussed that night but instead there was nothing.

No email. No telephone call. No communication with the end result being that he and Olivia were largely left alone.

Then at ten o'clock, he and Olivia received the same terse text message.

Swamped dealing with Golden Asia details. Get up to speed faster.

The deluge was coming and, even though Olivia was less than ten feet away from him, Noah used his full powers of concentration to focus on matters concerning Golden Asia.

He felt his brain about to burst but he was learning nothing new from the reams of paper, the digital files on the USB stick, and nothing from trolling the Internet.

The only conclusion that could be drawn from all material was that Golden Asia was a conservative, straight-as-an-arrow group of companies involved in real estate and the import and export businesses. Tommy was the only officer listed on all the companies, either as president, chief executive officer or board chairman. Garret had the power of attorney to act on Tommy's behalf. Taxes were always paid on time; accounting records were sterling. While some marginal Internet websites indicated that there may be some underhanded dealings from the company, nothing had been substantiated and fell more into the category of jealous rumors from competition rather than fact. The truth was, there was no way for anyone to find out the inner workings of Golden Asia because it was completely privately held. There was no fiduciary obligation to release hardly any information at all.

Noah found even less real info on Chin, but what little there was seemed to indicate that he was a ruthless gang leader. Again, nothing concrete and, furthermore, there was nothing linking Chin Chee Fok to Golden Asia. Noah had tried a variety of spellings, different order of words, but nothing that came close to Chin Chee Fok was remotely revealing.

There was something disturbing, though. When Noah tried to follow up with the authors who published material even slightly negative about Chin, none could be contacted. Emails bounced back, phone numbers were disconnected, and a number of the writers had vanished or died mysterious deaths.

There was, however, tons of stuff about Tommy. About his extravagance, from the thirty-million-dollar mansion to his extensive collection of rare whiskies to his legendary gambling habits of losing and winning several millions in a day to his womanizing of the most beautiful starlets in Asia. What was maddening, though, was that while there was considerable mention of his connection with Golden Asia, there was really nothing available that described what Golden Asia was involved in other than the mention of the import and export businesses and real estate ventures.

Which meant there was nothing to tie Tommy to Chin.

At 5 p.m., Olivia looked up from her desk. "Good night, Noah. I'm going to get Abby and spend the night at her place. I'll have to break the bad news that she can't leave tomorrow and needs to spend a bit more time in Hong Kong to tidy up affairs."

"Be safe. Don't do anything I wouldn't do," replied Noah automatically and he went right back to work.

It was completely frustrating. Taking a new tact, he decided to check the news. Maybe there was a clue somewhere about Tommy's grisly execution.

You've got to be kidding. There was absolutely nothing about Tommy's death, in mainstream media or social media. No pictures, no videos. It was as if it never happened.

Noah surmised that the tentacles of the public relations department at the Tiger Palace reached into every part of public and private media in Hong Kong. Either that, or Chin's staff was the most covert of covert operations, or Garret's talents were wasted with Pittman Saunders and he should be made head of the CIA, Interpol and Mossad combined.

AT 9:30 P.M., WITH HIS CONCENTRATION DEGRADING, NOAH decided he would do what he always used to do whenever he was losing focus—spend time having Sifu kick the crap out of him.

He got tsk-tsk looks from the other eager beavers as he

donned his jacket and left. He didn't care. He knew his biorhythms and, at that point, he was pretty well useless. Anyway, there was always tomorrow.

Tie loosened, hair disheveled, stubble on his face...it had been a long day.

Little did he know it was just beginning.

40

YOU'RE KIDDING

TUESDAY NIGHT

N oah got off the bus in the grotty, familiar area. The driving pellets of water hadn't let up much, and the sodden young man jogged through the narrow back alleys, passing seniors walking their pet birds in cages, vats of hot water in a temporary kitchen where a street vendor cooked noodles to order, a barber slathering shaving cream onto his customer in front of a smoke shop, and two ladies haggling over the price of a live chicken, until he reached the familiar unmarked building that was Master Wu's studio.

THE FOYER WAS EMPTY. NOAH PUT HIS BRIEFCASE DOWN AND removed his soaked clothes. He opened the briefcase and took out the bundle containing his martial arts uniform. He quickly changed, then sprinted into the main studio hall.

Omigod.

There, sparring with Master Wu, was about the last

person he expected to see—Pittman Saunders Senior Partner for the Asia Pacific Region, Garret Southam.

Garrett emulated movements from the sun. Fiery masses of strength, breathtaking powerful moves. Left, right, center. High, low, medium. Unpredictable hand and feet combinations, yet each handled expertly with razor-sharp reflexes. Crossing arms with double kick out.

Fire pelted by hammer fists and sweeping leg motions. Straight directed blows like solar rays characterized each element. Like the sun, the punches and strokes radiated energy and domination.

Each blow was masterfully parried with swift counterattacks, combinations of feet, hands and uppercuts. With a lightning series of palm thrusts to the head, hammer fists to the abdomen, and a sweeping sideways kick coming from left, then right, Wu's foot landed on the cheek of the unbalanced Garret, knocking him to the ground.

Wu had just defeated a man twenty years younger and thirty pounds of muscle heavier. Wu pulled Garret up, and they made the Shaolin salute to each other—body upright, right hand clenched in a tight tension-filled fist, left hand open and covering the right hand. The hands were placed in front of the chest and a bow from the waist followed.

Garret turned to Noah. "Your turn?" he asked pointedly.

"Didn't know you saw me here."

"I see everything, Noah Reid."

Trying the element of surprise, Noah leapt at his superior with a spinning move, his left foot directed squarely at Garret's head.

Garret's reflexes were fast and, with a quick forearm movement blow, he knocked aside Noah's foot, sending him hopping to the side.

Undeterred, Noah asked, "Do I get fired when I kick your ass?"

"I fire people for kissing ass, not kicking ass," snarled Garret.

Noah charged in full frontal attack like a bull. Left, right, feint, attack.

Garret fended off the combination as if swatting flies. He was angry. "You are so disappointing me, Reid. Let's begin your education now."

Garret advanced with a ferocious assault of the Ten Form Fist. Noah crouched into a deep, low Horse stance, raising his hands with the Tiger claw. The wary Garret attacked Noah with blazing speed with the traditional animals of the Shaolin Temple: the Dragon, Snake, Leopard, Tiger and Crane were all on display. Adding insult to injury, Garret quickly assumed the same Horse stance that Noah did. However, before Noah could react, Garret knocked him down with ease.

With passion searing his voice, Master Wu urged Noah, "Harder!"

"He hasn't got it in him," scoffed Garret.

Noah panted, "I...do...so..."

Garret launched an attack like a suicidal kamikaze pilot, throwing every micron of energy he had into every punch and kick. Noah was not intimidated and fought back. The rust disappeared, and Noah's technique was superb—he matched Garret's energy with his own focused attack.

It was a small act of war with Hung Gar Tiger and Crane style of Shaolin kung fu as the weapon. It was a war of wills, war of strength, war of ability. Pinpoint attack at vital organs, pinpoint accuracy of defense from both experienced warrior and young Turk. When Garret as Tiger leapt to strike, Noah as Crane used his gentle, quick steps to keep his balance. With an intricate combination, Noah skillfully maneuvered in and was on the verge of conquest but, with the tremendous flair of a raging feline, Garret grabbed Noah in midair and slammed him to the ground.

Changing tactics, Garret changed to an older style of Hung Gar, and jumped into a wider stance with lightning-fast footwork, momentarily confusing Noah. A quick side-kick sent his younger opponent to the floor. As Noah rose, an arcing leap kick to his chest sent him sprawling, and he landed defeated on the floor. Garret put his foot on Noah's neck, one strong thrust away from snapping it and ending Noah's life. "Like I said, you are so disappointing, Noah Reid."

Terror filled Noah's eyes until Garret took his foot off his neck. Noah crawled to his knees.

"Why do you care?" panted Garret's new charge.

Garret glanced over to Master Wu, then to the young lawyer. "Because, Noah, one day, you are going to be me. And the stakes that I play with are not just some shadow-boxing in some safe studio like this. I play for keeps. And, when we play for keeps...more than just your ego gets broken."

Master Wu glared at Garret, chastising him with his eyes. "You were young once, too, Garret. Have the same patience with Noah that I had for you."

"To be patient, you need time, *Sifu*. We don't have a lot of that," replied Garret.

"But a river goes at the speed it goes, no matter how hard you try to force it to flow faster."

"Stop!" shouted Noah, staring at Garret. "I've been wracking my brains since I saw you but now I remember who you are. You came to our apartment to see Master Wu when I was a kid. I had a huge shiner but saw you out of the corner of my eye."

Garret said nothing as Noah continued. Noah studied Garret. "One of them was you. Was the other Tommy?"

Master Wu nodded. "Yes." He turned to Garret. "You can tell him now."

Garret cleared his throat, then lasered his eyes on Noah's. "When I was young, there were three of us that wanted to take Hung Gar to the universe. Master Wu was our sifu. We failed miserably and we fell. Tommy, me and Chin Chee Fok." Garret took out an old photo and pointed to Chin, trademark attitude and arrogance already in evidence.

"That's Chin?" gasped Noah, pieces of the picture, starting to come together. "I saw him at the airport. He chased and caught a tiger with his bare hands."

"Tommy and I joined his gang but, when we wanted out, he killed our wives."

"So what's all this got to do with me?"

"You are going to help me kill him."

Noah gulped and looked at Master Wu. The old man nodded.

"No, no, no. I didn't sign up for this," protested Noah.

"No, you didn't," stated Noah's sifu. "I did."

Garret's voice took on a subdued tone. "Let's go for a ride. I'm going to show you something."

41

TIGER, TIGER, BURNING BRIGHT

HONG KONG - TUESDAY EVENING

I n the clearing of Chin's man-made jungle, Stella stood outside a large circus-sized cage. No longer in business attire, she was dressed in a flesh-toned string bikini that left little to the imagination. Her eyes fixed on a tiger pacing angrily. It circled around its hoped-for victim: Chin. He was stripped to the waist and, dressed in loose-fitting martial arts pants, he was as fine and fit a human specimen as she had ever seen—and she had seen many.

Chin paid no attention to Stella as tiger and Tiger Master's eyes bore into each other. Standing twenty feet away from the feline, Chin gradually tilted his head to the left, then right, staring hard at the tiger, almost as if trying to hypnotize it. Mesmerized, the tiger lost its impatience and sat down. It began to purr. Never for a moment letting his gaze leave the tiger, Chin gently made a few footfalls and then knelt on the floor, about a dozen feet away from the feline.

The tiger silently and calmly paced over to Chin. It licked his face over and over. With a hint of a smile, the man caressed the animal. This soothed the animal even more, and it allowed Chin to put one arm around its back, reaching toward its belly.

The tiger purred gently and looked away from Chin. Chin's face turned to sadness as he began stroking the beast's back with long, smooth, rhythmic strokes. The beast relaxed even more and dropped its entire body to the floor. The animal was still as Chin buried his face into its nape. The stroking continued as Chin lifted his face off the tiger's body. His face was full of tears as the tiger breathed its calm, long, heavy, smooth breaths.

With a sudden movement, Chin grabbed the animal by the nape with one hand and with the other gave a lightning jerk that broke the tiger's neck. Paralyzed, the tiger struggled to twitch but had lost its mobility. Stella entered the cage and handed the knife to Chin.

With one expert cut from the finely sharpened blade, Chin sliced the tiger's throat. As the animal started to bleed, Chin put his mouth to the cut, drinking in as much of the tiger's blood as he possibly could. As he was unable to catch it all, some of the red liquid spilled onto his face, arms and torso. Finally, the beast stopped moving, and a bloodied Chin stood up.

Stella sidled up to him. She took his hand and placed it on the top of her bikini. "I have something special for you. Take a look."

Chin balled a fist. *What makes her think that she's anything better than any other woman? I shouldn't have wasted my time with her.* "Of course," he stated without enthusiasm.

He pulled the front of the bikini and then glanced at her with intrigue. It wasn't her perfectly formed, translucent-skinned breasts. Chin had seen thousands of those. What was special about Stella's was that on the nipple of one of her voluptuous mounds was a Bengal tiger tattoo, and around the other, a red-crowned crane.

"Ready for dinner?"

THE VIEW FROM THE BALCONY OF CHIN'S PENTHOUSE WAS fabulous. The Sai Van Bridge could be seen from the steaming, oversized, sumptuous hot tub. Even more attractive than the view of the night panorama was the view of Stella's nude body wrapped around Chin's. Every cent she spent on the spa and personal trainers had sculpted her into one of the most inviting creatures ever to grace the earth, and all was on full display.

"No man should look as good as you," she said softly.

Chin didn't react. He knew who he was. "No man does."

Stella playfully stroked his abs of steel. She wanted to talk about something else but was smart enough to know that it would finish her chances with Chin. "I will leave in a few minutes."

"Aren't you waiting for me to say something?" Chin had her pegged to a T.

"I am at your service, at your pleasure, not mine."

"I am expanding operations here and in North America. Toronto, San Francisco, Vancouver, Los Angeles and New York will all share in the Tiger." The intensity of his glare melted Stella. "You are capable, Stella, but you are not capable enough. Tommy was my puppet, but Garret Southam pulled the strings... and you are hardly in his league."

Stella did her best to hide her hurt. "Mr. Southam is a brilliant lawyer. A master of strategic organization and negotiation, not to mention corporate structure and finance."

"Which is why I want you to completely but discreetly monitor all the banking activities of Pittman Saunders, Garret's family and Garret himself."

Stella fondled Chin. "I won't disappoint you."

Two people entered. One was a doctor of traditional Chinese medicine who wore a stylish Chinese jacket embroidered with twin dragons. The other was a manservant, complete with white jacket and bow tie. The doctor carried in a large grinding bowl and pestle made from volcanic rock while the manservant wheeled in a cart with three globe-like covered trays, one larger, one medium, one smaller. The two arrived at Chin and Stella's hot tub and bowed.

The doctor raised the lid off one of the globed serving dishes, and inside was the skinned fur of a tiger's tail. Beside it were the bones from the tail. He took several of the bones, put them into his grinding bowl and used the pestle to start grinding. "This was an especially fine tiger. Its bones will make you stronger, even invincible."

The manservant lifted the lid off another tray. Inside was a steaming whole tiger's head, fur still intact. The servant took a knife and carefully sawed off the top of the head, just above the eyes.

While he did so, Stella spooned out the two eyes. She put one into Chin's mouth and ate the other.

Finished cutting, the manservant lifted off the top of the tiger's head and handed Stella a golden spoon. She used the spoon to feed the cooked tiger's brain to Chin.

Meanwhile, the manservant went back to the cart and took the lid off the smaller tray. Contained underneath was the tiger's penis with the testicles still attached, an aphrodisiac of legendary powers. He expertly sliced them into bite-sized pieces, then placed them into a cast iron skillet and doused them generously with cognac. He took out a match and lit the cognac, causing it to flame up.

As the cognac burned, the servant gently tossed meat in the pan, ensuring the organs were evenly cooked. Once the fire was out, he placed them onto a silver plate. Stella skewered each of the sautéed testes with a chopstick, feeding one to Chin and eating the other herself.

She then used her hands and body to massage Chin until they finished eating. Lips touching, Stella fully embraced Chin. He lifted her off him and sat her on the hot tub's edge.

The doctor finished grinding. He placed the powder into two brandy snifters and poured cognac into them, then handed one to Chin and one to Stella.

The doctor and manservant bowed and left.

Chin and Stella downed the potent drink slowly. Stella noted that there was a change in Chin's mood as he sipped. In his eyes was both a look of obsession and resolve, mixed with the distant look of the ancient mystics. Perturbed, she quietly queried, "Am I doing something wrong?"

Almost to himself, without looking at the boy toy, Chin replied, "Strength without honor is weakness. I am not weak."

Chin stood up and climbed out of the hot tub. Stella stared with fearful awe. Somehow, and she knew not how, Chin's physique looked even more invincible than ever.

Chin stalked away, leaving a confused Stella alone.

42

WHAT GIVES?

One of the black Mercedes from Chin's fleet blended in with the night as it leisurely wound its way up Victoria's Peak. Although Duke was looking outside the car window, he didn't really pay attention to this prime residential area of multimillion dollar homes. Instead, he reflected on his family.

He had no idea who his mother was. His father had sexual relations with upward of five hundred different women a year, each one as disposable as a used Kleenex. Knowing his father, Duke figured that Chin likely had little use for his mother other than to bear him twenty-five years ago. Where she was or even if she was still alive was unknown. Nor did he have any idea why she might have been chosen to carry Chin's child.

Honestly, Duke didn't care. Chin had been father, mentor, teacher and protector to him. His greatest desire was to meet or exceed his father's expectations. Duke never had any issues of teenage rebellion. He worshipped Chin, so there was never any need to rebel against God.

Like his father, Duke had never had a meaningful, intimate relationship with another human. He'd tried both men and women, but neither of them exerted any kind of interest beyond a desire to relieve him of his occasional horniness. Duke thought he didn't have much of a libido because he was too busy trying to emulate his father, but that was not the truth. The reality was, Duke's system was pumped so full of steroids that his sex drive was less than thirty percent of an average young man his age. Even if he knew, he'd continue with the body-enhancing drugs because it was just a cost of doing business.

While not at all a model father, Chin was able to instill in Duke what he considered the most important traits necessary for success: obedience and excellence. Failing in either meant death. That included his right-hand man, Tommy. Chin hated any kind of personal exposure. Not that he was afraid of being famous, but notoriety just got in the way of empire building, especially if that empire was one of the world's largest criminal enterprises. The stakes for what Chin did were too high for any other punishment to suffice. When it was clear that Tommy was no longer completely reliable, his usefulness was over. Even their relationship of over thirty years was unable to save Tommy from his fate.

That was why, at that moment, Duke was finding it hard to understand why his father wanted to keep Garret, Olivia, Noah and Abby alive. As the lawyer and chief architect of the Golden Asia conglomerate, Garret had intimate knowledge of every part of its operations. Could his father have made a tactical error by trusting Garret too much? Olivia and Abby were totally insignificant. If it were up to Duke, he would make use of them for fifteen minutes then dispose of them in the open sea. And Noah? Noah was a pipsqueak. He'd fall over the moment someone blew on him, so what was the point of his existence?

However, his father said, "The goal is not death but terror," so there must be a reason. What that reason was, was totally unknown to Duke. To this glorified street thug, keeping useless vermin around was an excruciating command.

The car crawled to a stop in front of Tommy's house. The chauffeur turned the car lights off, and Duke sat, awaiting his next order.

43

THE KING IS DEAD

HONG KONG - TUESDAY EVENING

After Garret and Noah left, Master Wu assumed the lotus position in the middle of his studio. He began meditating, praying and reflecting. Now that Noah knew, the burden he carried for the young man grew heavier by the moment. *The time is nigh.*

Chin entered with his posse silently. Wu sensed his presence, but his eyes remained closed. The grandmaster intoned quietly. "The superior man, even for the space of a single meal, does not act contrary to virtue. In moments of haste, in seasons of danger, he cleaves to it."

"Do you think you haven't told me enough times that I wouldn't remember the Analects of Confucius? Stop talking philosophy. You know why I am here." Chin's voice held menace.

Master Wu opened his eyes and stood. "There will always be someone stronger. There will always be someone smarter. There will always be someone richer. This is a game you cannot win."

Chin shook his head. "I made mistakes but those are long forgotten. I learned my lesson then. But you have failed to progress. You live in yesterday. There is no glory of the Shaolin. There never was. There is only power."

"You think breaking someone's neck or arm is power. You believe that inflicting pain on someone weaker than you shows strength." Master Wu shook his head sadly. "That is why you can never be a true master. No one can apply strength to achieve virtue. Not you, not me."

"That was bullshit to me then; it's bullshit to me now," Chin said, his voice relaxed.

"You will not insult The Way," responded Master Wu with resolute conviction.

"I will say whatever I will say," smirked Chin, "and no one will stop me."

Both men sprang into the ready-for-battle martial arts stance. Chin snatched up a tufted spear and flung it at Master Wu's head. Wu moved his head slightly, and the spear missed by a quarter of an inch. With an agility beyond mortals, Wu made a flying handspring to an ax by the wall. He pulled it smoothly from its holder and launched it at Chin. Spinning like a maddened whirligig, it flew through the air.

Chin's men stood in awe, not only of their master, but of the old man who had taught him. They had never witnessed such a powerful demonstration and their blood ran hot.

With reflexes sharper than the ax blade, Chin pulled the ax out of the air by its handle and, in the same motion, propelled it with even greater force back at his former sifu. Wu dodged it and the ax gouged a deep cavity in the wall.

Chin remained on the attack. With the terrifying speed of a feline, he leapt at Wu. A Dragon palm strike from Chin targeted Master Wu's ribs. Wu brushed off Chin's blow, countering it by ramming a rapid-fire series of Leopard blows at Chin's abdominals. However, twenty million sit-ups performed over the decades made Chin's stomach muscles immune to blows that would have killed an ordinary man.

Wu raised his arms in Dragon claws and lunged to grab at Chin's groin, but Chin quickly positioned his hands and, with unexpected fingers, thrust his thumbs into Wu's eyes. The aged master howled in pain and backed off. Sensing blood, Chin sprung to attack the suddenly vulnerable master. He yanked three daggers from the fold of his jacket and launched one, two, three pointed projectiles at the weakened Master Wu's head, abdomen and legs.

The first two missed, but the third found its target and embedded itself into Master Wu's thigh. Blood gushed out. With a kamikaze-like scream, Master Wu jerked the dagger out of his leg and flung it back at Chin. However, severely debilitated, Wu's throw had only minimal power. Chin contemptuously flicked his index finger to deflect it out of harm's way.

Full of confidence, Chin bombarded Wu with a blitzkrieg of combinations...left arm, right arm, left kick to midsection, right kick to the head, double kick to the chest...and more. The bruised and bleeding master could not withstand Chin's relentless onslaught.

A final double fist to the back of Master Wu's neck sent him unconscious to the floor. Chin's pointed eyes glared at the immobile old man, full of contempt and loathing.

He heard clapping and turned to see his thugs applauding his victory.

Chin acknowledged the tribute with a swift twist of his head. "Let's go."

44

SMOKE AND MIRRORS

TUESDAY EVENING

R ain drenched Noah and Garret as they arrived at a huge development site. A large billboard announced:

Golden Asia Developments
The Concept For The Future

As they examined the framework of the massive structure, it was clear it was a combination residential, entertainment, retail and corporate complex under development. Covering several city blocks, it was larger than anything Noah had ever seen.

Gaping holes were strewn around the site, interspersed with partially built buildings and mud everywhere. Backhoes, tractors, hundred-foot-tall cranes and other building machines were lit up with Christmas lights even though it was far from the yuletide season. All of it contributed to an odd juxtaposition of East and West over this stupendous, monumental and commercialized Shangri-La.

Garret and Noah walked to the chain-link fence

surrounding the property. Garret nimbly scaled the fifteen-foot fence and then leapt to the ground on the other side. Noah followed suit.

Garret waved his arm over the enterprise. "This is the future of Golden Asia. When we are done, this will be paradise. You can shop, eat, do business, play tennis and never leave our complex. And, because we own everything, we make money on everything."

"Garret, China has tried complexes like this before. There are whole pockets of buildings—they call them ghost cities—where builders have built but no one has bought. Ordos, Dongguan, Hangzhou. There are hundreds of thousands, maybe millions, of empty units in block after block after block."

Garret's voice softened with melancholy. "But you forgot one thing. We do not build for today. We build for tomorrow. The Golden Asia complex is hardly a white elephant. There is a mass exodus from rural China to the urban centers. Most of the people are poor and can afford very little."

"That proves my point."

"But people do not stay poor forever. They scrimp, they save, they put a dozen people into a bedroom and, sooner or later, they start accumulating wealth, and they will want to buy their own personal piece of real estate. If we build now, we build in today's dollars. If it takes two, five, ten years to fill them up, inflation will guarantee a healthy profit."

"That's for the mainland. That's not going to apply to Macau."

Garret was exasperated. "Reid, you are absolutely wrong. Hong Kong and Macau are now the top tourist destinations for Chinese from the mainland. When we complete Golden Asia, this will be a breathtaking entertainment and residential complex that will be the envy of the world. Besides, we have a secret weapon."

"Which is?"

"Legalized gambling in all of the five complexes, rivaling the Tiger Palace. The best of Europe, America, Russia, Africa and China will be authentically and vibrantly represented. We will make Las Vegas look like a sleepy little hamlet. Every Chinese will want to visit here or own property here. They will have all the benefits of travel without ever having to leave our enclave."

Noah took a deep breath. What Garret was saying was not only visionary and awe-inspiring, but the chances of success seemed like one hundred percent—if he could finance it for the proper term.

"What's this going to cost?" he asked.

"Seventeen billion dollars by the time we are finished."

Noah's jaw dropped. "You'd have to be one of the richest hundred people in the world to afford that, and that's assuming you put every nickel you had into the investment. No one's going to put that much dough into a single investment. You've got to be kidding."

"Mr. Reid, I never joke, but perhaps you are now realizing why I need total commitment from everyone I work with. This is one of the largest non-governmental projects ever undertaken."

"But seventeen billion?"

Garret nodded. "And climbing. We have the best minds and the best materials in the world working on this. Land, construction, approvals, not to mention kickbacks, bribery and ladies for the bureaucrats are just the tip of the tip of the iceberg."

Garret waved over the vast project. "Our architects were the lead architects at the last world's fair. Our engineering firm is building the new state capital for Thailand and is responsible for the Vancouver-to-Vancouver Island Causeway. We own our own mine in Italy from where we quarry and stockpile marble. To ensure that we have an adequate supply of teak for building our furniture, we have purchased a forest industry company in Myanmar. And our entertainment advisers have been recruited from Cirque du Soleil and Lucasfilm, the creators of the *Star Wars* movie franchise."

Garret turned to face Noah. "Yes, it is an enormous amount of money but, when you study the talent we have assembled and are assembling, it will pay itself back many times over. My job for thirty-five years has been to guide the corporate and financial structure of Golden Asia, making sure that nothing, but nothing, goes off track."

Noah inspected the superstructure, letting Garret's words sink in. He began to see connections and how the various players fit in. Noah gave Garret an approving nod and spoke in a soft tone. "Your real job is to make Golden Asia legit."

"Very astute, Noah." Garret nodded. "Yes, but we're on hold now. Take a closer look at the construction. Flecks of dust on the girders, supplies are short, the equipment has not been turned on in several weeks, the labor unions are about to blacklist us. The project has run out of cash."

"How can that be if you were keeping as close an eye as you said you were?"

"Well phrased again. Golden Asia should not have any problems at all. But it does, and there is only one reason I'm alive right now. Tommy was Chin Chee Fok's choice. Years ago, I advised against it, but Chin insisted."

"Who exactly is Chin?" Noah asked. "He seems to be everywhere, but I can't find any connection between him and anything. Definitely not a seventeen-billion-dollar project."

"And no one will ever find that out. I'm damned good at my job, Noah. Chin is the most vicious Triad leader in the world. I have set up all Chin's companies, all his accounts. That's why, try as he might, Chin doesn't own me. He needs me because only I know where every cent is. The only funds I don't control are those that are not given to me. If Tommy didn't give me something, I can't be held responsible for it."

Noah's eyes widened with astonishment and fear. His new boss was not the "biggest stuffed shirt in a company of stuffed shirts." Not only was he a Shaolin Hung Gar master on par with Master Wu, perhaps the greatest living Hung Gar grandmaster, but he was the brains behind legitimizing a criminal operation with assets in excess of many small countries.

"But why do you need me to kill him?

"Lex talionis."

An eye for an eye, a tooth for a tooth.

Noah's eyes widened and he jawed, "You want to bankrupt Chin by taking the only thing that matters to him. His empire."

Garret suddenly noticed a slight movement in the wind and instinctively pushed Noah aside. An arrow whizzed by Noah's ear and twisted into a pole behind him.

"Follow me, Noah," shouted Garret.

Garret led Noah on the run of his life. Slogging through the muck and mud, Garret and Noah leapt onto the top of an iron beam on the first-floor frame of one of the buildings.

Dancing along the girder, they zigged, zagged and hid behind a concrete pillar as an armada of arrows streamed by.

"We'll never make it!" screamed Noah.

"Then stay here and die," called Garret as he leapt to the ground and charged away.

"Oh, shit." Noah reluctantly ran after Garret. The sharp, pointed missiles continued their barrage. To avoid them, Garret changed direction every two steps. "Do the opposite of what I do," he yelled. When Garret took one step right, Noah stepped left. When Garret made two steps left, Noah made one to the right, keeping the pattern inconsistent.

With arms raised straight up, senior and junior lawyer rushed toward a pile of lumber. They took a short hop and lunged to the top, hands first, kicking their feet upward, then pushed off the top of the lumber with their arms, executing handsprings to the roof of a storage shed. Without breaking step, they raced fifty feet, then performed hand-springs into a double somersault before landing on the ground. Garret took cover behind a concrete pillar while Noah ducked behind the huge wheels of the adjacent building crane.

"What now?" panted Noah.

"Keep following me," replied Garret.

"That hasn't been very reliable advice so far," shouted Noah, his breath coming in irregular gasps.

"You're still alive, aren't you?"

Their attackers came into view. Six elite, very fit killers, primed and ready for a direct attack. Walking directly toward the pillar and crane, they tossed their repeating crossbows aside. They'd run out of arrows, but that was no big deal. A construction site was a Fort Knox of potential weaponry.

"Go!" Garret and Noah blitzed from their hiding places.

Four gangsters grabbed anything in sight—lumber planks, hammers, rivets— and hurled them at Garret and Noah. The other two found a stash of nails that they launched, handful after handful, of the sharp rods. The lawyers jumped and dodged behind a barricade of concrete slabs, just in time to avoid being skewered.

Garret saw a huge excavation, deep enough for ten stories of partially built underground parking. Leaping into the air, Garret executed a twisting and twirling aerial, allowing him to evade the deadly, hurled objects as he landed just inside the crater.

Noah combined somersaults and handsprings to get out of danger's way, and he vaulted into the hole next to Garret. They tumbled down the embankment, veering from side to side to evade the battery of construction materials hurtling toward them—plastic tubes, concrete slabs, steel clamps, brackets and joint pins thrown with the arm strength of Major League baseball pitchers.

Their assailants started a giant bulldozer and jumped aboard. It crawled methodically down the side of the excavation, lights pinpointing the rolling, slipping lawyers.

Arriving at the base of the parking understructure, Noah hid behind a concrete wall. Constantly on the go for the last ten minutes, the two lawyers had been as nimble and agile as the acrobat performers at the Tiger Palace, defying death with their phenomenal flashy maneuvers from weapons and assailants, and they were far from done. They sucked in air like thirsty dogs lapping water, trying to catch their breath. They had maybe thirty seconds before the bulldozer caught up to them.

45

DISSONANCE

HONG KONG - TUESDAY EVENING

I nside the mansion on Victoria's Peak, Olivia and Abby sat on the living room couch, remembering Tommy as they listened intently to yesterday's recording of their performance on Abby's iPad of his favorite song.

> Oh Danny boy, the pipes, the pipes are
> calling
> From glen to glen, and down the
> mountainside.
> The summer's gone, and all the flowers are
> dying.
> 'Tis you, 'tis you must go, and I must bide.

During the recording, a cell phone rang, and they heard Tommy's hushed voice in his part of a conversation. "No, I haven't heard from Chin yet, but it's only a matter of time...Really, there's nothing else to do...Abby is in less danger if I'm not around. Chin never makes useless kills...I know...Yes, that's Abby singing. Voice of an angel, isn't it? It'll be the last time...Chin will never find the money, and neither will you. I guarantee that...I will hold you to that promise and chase you from Hell to Heaven if you do not keep it...Goodbye, my friend..."

It was eerie listening to a conversation that predicted and foreshadowed a person's death. It was even worse when that person was your father.

"Now do you believe me, Olivia?"

"I never doubted you. I just didn't realize the extent."

"Our fathers are tied to the hip, even more than we thought," Abby said quietly.

"Which means, Abby, so are we, even more so than I thought."

From the sofa, Abby and Olivia heard the doorbell ring.

"You expecting anybody, Abby?"

Abby shook her head. "Nobody even knows I'm back in town yet."

"Then don't answer it, Abby."

"I am so not planning to."

Whoever was at the door started pounding.

"Follow me," whispered Abby.

Olivia nodded as Abby led her quickly into the dining room. Abby pressed a hidden button by the china cabinet. The cabinet slid open, revealing a hiding space. Abby and Olivia entered, and Abby pressed another button to close the cabinet.

The sound of jackhammer blows continued. Suddenly, there was the sound of the door crashing down.

Olivia covered Abby's mouth, stifling a gasp. Whoever was at the door had just broken down a custom-made five-hundred-pound door with his bare fists.

For ten minutes, the girls heard someone upturning furniture and banging on walls. It was all they could do to stay still and silent.

Then the sound stopped. Olivia watched her cell phone and waited until five minutes passed. She nodded to Abby. Abby pressed a button, opening the door. They were freaked to see a huge man with a crowbar coming after them.

"Your dad has stolen my boss's money. A lot of it. Chin wants it back. Do it and you'll live."

Olivia followed Abby as she bolted up the stairs. The hulk began an unhurried walk behind them. They entered Tommy's bedroom and locked the door.

Olivia made a call. "Daddy, we need help. There's a giant threatening to kill us. He says Abby has his boss's money."

Garret's calm voice sounded, "Panicking will not help. I'll deal with it. Where are you, Olivia?"

"At Abby's house."

"Stay put. I'll send Noah to get you."

Noah? Abby ran to her father's dresser and pulled out a gun. Shaking, she leveled the deadly weapon at the bedroom door. She saw their hunter's arm punching through. Abby took aim and fired several rounds.

The girls heard a thud. Abby tiptoed to the hole in the door to see their assailant bleeding. He tried to stand up but the blood loss was too great. He collapsed, dead.

As the girls tiptoed around the body, Olivia praised, "Nice shot, Abby. I didn't know you spent so much time at the range."

"I don't. Never even fired a peashooter."

At the top of the staircase, they peered down to the foyer and shrieked—there were two tiger paws, a tiger's liver and a tiger's heart lying on the marble floor.

GARRET KNEW HE COULDN'T LET HIS CHURNING EMOTIONS

show. It required every bit of self-control to keep his cool when he spoke to Olivia. He couldn't let Noah see concern either. "Go to Olivia. She's at Abby's house. The address is..."

"I know where it is. I've been studying that damned Golden Asia file."

Noah was about to take off but Garret called, "Wait!"

Noah stopped and turned. "Yes?"

Garret's voice was strong and full of emotion. "If I don't make it, tell Olivia she was right to hate me. Now go!"

"Will do." As Noah took off, he heard the rattling, beeping sound of the bulldozer. He turned his head to see his hunters jumping off and preparing a fresh barrage of artillery. Noah surged off in a dead run to the other end of the uncompleted parking structure. As his aggressors approached, Noah leapt into the darkness.

GARRET JUMPED ONTO THE VACATED BULLDOZER AND PUSHED it full throttle. Noah's attackers turned to him but, before they could catch up, Garret reversed the vehicle, jumped off and scooted up the embankment, leaving the bulldozer to charge ahead at the attackers.

Arriving at ground level, Garret threw trashcans, a small cement mixer and cylinder blocks at the ascending goons.

With light-speed footsteps, Garret raced to the entrance of the complex, jumped into the Bentley and took off. He had made several mods to his car that allowed it to accelerate to one hundred thirty miles per hour in nothing flat. He needed every bit of it as he raced through the series of bridges and tunnels that connected Hong Kong and Macau.

Garret's pursuers matched him in speed with their own turbo-charged Mercedes. The driver accelerated into

Garret's car, and Garret gripped the wheel tightly to keep
the Bentley from spinning out of control.

The Mercedes punched the rear again, knocking the
Bentley off to the side ever so slightly. It was enough for the
Mercedes to inflict a hit on the driver's side of the car.

Garret slammed on the brakes. To stabilize the car, he
jerked the steering wheel as hard and fast as he could. Tires
screeching, the Bentley spun around and collided into the
oncoming Mercedes.

The unanticipated collision caught the Mercedes driver
off guard. He steered hard left to avoid the protective
concrete wall. Momentum carried the car for another two
hundred yards before the driver was able to bring it under
control and to a stop. The Mercedes turned, and the driver
revved the engine.

"Bring it on," said Garret as he floored the accelerator of
his parked Bentley. Throwing the car into drive, Garret
pushed the car faster than it had ever been driven.

More than half a million dollars in two cars were racing
at a hundred-plus miles an hour right at each other. Neither
driver was willing to give an inch.

A fraction of a second before impact, one of the passengers in the Mercedes yelled, "Stop!" But it was too late.
However, just at the point of impact, the roof of the Bentley
opened, and Garret was ejected thirty feet into the air.
Flailing his arms, he grabbed onto the bridge's suspension
cables.

The two vehicles collided. There was an ear-deafening
explosion, and the passengers in the black Mercedes were
incinerated instantly. A tattered Garret watched the fireball
flare up, then he climbed down the bridge's tower onto the
main deck. He hobbled away, slowly but alive.

But not all the henchmen were in the ball of flame. A

second Mercedes rolled up and four lethal foes stepped out and strode toward the lawyer.

There was no point in trying to fight. Garret was exhausted and outnumbered. *Better to try to save some energy for later than die a fool's death now.*

The biggest man bashed Garret in the stomach, causing him to keel over. A tremendous uppercut followed, and Garret lapsed into unconsciousness. Not the rest he needed or was hoping for.

46

THE SUPERIOR MAN

HONG KONG - WEDNESDAY - EARLY AM

I t was a typical busy night at the Coffee Emporium when Chad got a call from Noah. "Hey, man, you want to go shoot some hoops?"

"Not now, Chad. I need help. Get outside. Five minutes!"

"I got a room full of teens going nuts here. Can it wait?"

"Sorry, bro. Gonna wage war and I need soldiers for battle. We're going to pick up Master Wu, too. He's not answering."

Now that's an army. A new lawyer. An old martial artist. A barista. "Will do."

Chad called out, "Sam, can you take over for awhile? I'll pay you."

Sam gave two thumbs up. "You said the magic word. Pay."

"Bandit," called Chad as he heard a honking outside. He ran out to see Noah in a beater of a Toyota.

"Nice ride," grinned Chad as he hopped in. "Where'd you pick up this sardine can?"

Noah snorted as he stepped on the gas. "Thank God for

the MG. Teaches you how to hotwire a car. This was the only thing around."

Chad shook his head in pity. "You are working for one big-ass boring-as-shit company, Noah. I explored the Pittman Saunders website and it is so clean, it squeaks. And it's biggest client, Golden Asia, is just as bad. I don't think you'll last there five years."

"Ya think? I might not last until tomorrow. The real stuff is off book. Golden Asia is the front for the organization of a brutal Shaolin Triad leader—Chin Chee Fok."

"Never heard of him."

"Exactly. Garret's job is to make sure nobody knows too much about him or his holdings. There are holding companies of holding companies. Garret has sanitized the whole operation, which is what you found."

"So what's the plan?" Chad asked.

A fitful Noah shivered, silently brooding. This was not at all what he expected when he entered law school. "I'd like to quit but I can't. I'd like to go back to LA, join some buddies in their new intellectual property law firm. Or another one can get me into the mailroom of a big Hollywood talent agency...but I can't."

"Wow, Olivia's done that to you in one day."

Noah glanced to his best friend, his partner in arms in almost everything that was important to him in life. "No, dummy. It's because of you. You had to become a do-gooder and now I'm hooked on the kids, too. No way I can abandon them and if you're gonna spend your time making lattes, one of us has got to make some dough."

"Don't you watch TV? The only way you leave organizations like that is when they carry you out in a body bag." Chad crossed his arms across his chest, grinning at Noah. "If there's a hell below, we all gotta go."

"Yeah, be careful of what you wish for. Garret wants me to kill Chin."

"Now you're talkin'!"

WHILE NOAH DROVE, CHAD KEPT TRYING MASTER WU'S number but there was no answer. Noah had a sinking feeling in his stomach as he parked the "borrowed" vehicle in front of the master's studio.

Noah and Chad leapt out of the Toyota and rushed into the old building.

It was Noah's worst fear come true. Master Wu was unconscious, bruised, bleeding and seemed to be at the point of death.

"No, please, God!" yelled Noah with a quick prayer.

Noah pressed his fingers and thumb at strategic healing points on the top of Master Wu's head while Chad ran to the bathroom and got a wet cloth and some water. Noah knew that Wu would never consent to Western medicine, preferring the five-thousand-year-old Traditional Chinese Medicine techniques of his good friend, Dr. Tang. While hardly a practitioner, over the years Noah had observed the doctor as he treated Master Wu and his students, including himself.

"He's not moving or nothing. Shouldn't you push a little harder?" asked Chad as he wiped the blood from Wu's face.

"No. I just need to increase the circulation," said Noah, moving his fingers to healing points on the hands.

In the Chinese healing cosmos, all parts of the body interconnect through energy, or *qi*. That was why head trauma could be treated by massaging the back, or blood pressure might be changed by manipulating the spine.

Noah pulsed his digits, then exhaled a grateful sigh—the master groggily opened his eyes.

"Are you trying to scare me, Sifu?"

Master Wu blinked hard, trying to focus, then said quietly. "You've arrived, Noah. You're ready to take my torch."

"I...No, I'm not."

Wu gripped Noah's hand and spoke weakly. "Yes, you are. I'm eighty now and the only reason I kept teaching is so that you could carry on the legacy. Once I thought it might be Chin, but that was my mistake, a mistake that has taken me the rest of my life to try to correct."

Master Wu sighed, regret etched on his face. "And then, I thought it might be Garret, but his time with Chin tainted him. Once you break an egg, you can never really put it back together properly."

The elderly master struggled to sit up. His eyes fondly caressed Noah. "From the time you brought me to your parents, I saw that you were special."

Noah's face sobered. "Sifu, I was always the kid who got beaten up by the school bully. Nothing too special about that."

"But it was how you reacted after such moments. You didn't give up, but it was more than that. As I trained you, I saw something in the character of your parents and in you that I did not understand. I saw a humanity that transcended anything I ever experienced, that went far beyond the superficial world."

Master Wu balled his fists and lifted them to Noah. "Strength is not merely muscle. There will always be someone stronger than you." He pointed to his temple. "Nor is knowledge a matter of intelligence only. If brains and brawn were the only ingredients for honor, we would be ruled by robots." He took Noah's hands. "But I look at the great leaders of history: Genghis Khan, Jesus Christ, Winston Churchill. What did they all have? They had big bold hearts. When people experienced that, they would follow them to the ends of the earth."

"I'm no hero. I'm a chicken."

"And that is what will make you strong. Use your fear, and let it morph into courage. You have that heart, Noah. I have waited from before you were born for now. You didn't win a scholarship to university or to law school. I asked Garret to set it up without you knowing. Just as I asked Garret to hire you. Because I believe there is something else for you, Noah. Do you remember, Noah, about the superior man?"

Noah fidgeted a bit, then nodded. This was a truth he always suspected but had never been able to confirm. He spoke in a barely audible voice.

"The superior man has neither anxiety nor fear. There are three things of which the superior man stands in awe." Master and disciple recited together the age-old words of Confucius. "He stands in awe of the laws of Heaven. He stands in awe of great men. He stands in awe of the words of sages. The superior man in everything considers right-eousness to be essential."

Noah nodded. "You've waited a long time for me, Sifu."

"If there is one thing I learned from your parents, it is patience. If the Jews waited thousands of years for their Messiah, a few decades is not worth complaining about." Master Wu took Noah's head and turned it to the painting on the wall that Noah gave to him so many years ago—the tiger and crane entwined together.

"What do you see, Noah?"

Noah's breathing sped up. "I see that...it is time to release the Tiger."

TWO MINUTES LATER, CHAD AND NOAH DROPPED MASTER WU off with seventy-five-year-old Dr. Tang. "Sorry, I can't stay, Dr. Tang."

"Go, Noah. I will take care of him," croaked the kindly doctor. "But you should get some rest. You need to regain strength."

"Dr. Tang, sleep is highly overrated. Ask any law student."

47

THE INTRUDER

I n his lush rainforest space, Stella watched with horrified fascination as Chin pummeled an already battered and bruised Garret. Tightly bound to a chair, the defenseless Garret refused to wince, irritating Chin all the more after each devastating blow.

Two bruised purple eyes mocked the Tiger Master. "Hardly a fair fight, Chin. Didn't think that was your style."

"I'm not here as your battle opponent," Chin scorned. "We will wait for the right time for that. I'm here as your master. I want the information."

Garret coughed out blood, then snickered. "I told you I will not be your Joe Boy anymore."

Chin leaned down to Garret's eye level. "What do you possibly gain by turning me down? Even now, Garret, I will forgive you. You will be king of Golden Asia."

"I would be your puppet."

"You already are," smirked Chin.

Garret spat. "I want freedom. I wanted it fifteen years ago and I want it now."

Chin stood up and shook his head. "That's too bad."

Chin delivered another bone-crunching wallop to the face. "I want the access codes to all of my accounts."

Garret looked up at Chin, daring him to hit him again. "Not telling you is the only thing keeping me alive right now."

"Wrong answer." Chin straightened his right leg and twirled it with a solid blow into Garret's stomach.

"Works for me," burbled Garret.

A second smash kick sent Garret crashing unconscious to the floor.

"Keep an eye on him, Terry," snapped Chin as he left the room.

"You bet, Chin," said the burly thug, eager to impress his boss.

NOAH AND CHAD WERE IN THE TOYOTA, AND THE OLD VEHICLE valiantly clawed its way up Victoria Peak. "So where exactly are we going?" Chad asked.

"The biggest house on the hill."

"Oh, that one. Owned by Tommy Sung. Girls up the yin-yang, parties with swimming pools full of booze, one of the richest guys in Asia. The dream of every guy in the Orient."

"More like nightmare than dream. He got killed by a crossbow arrow last night," Noah said.

Chad swallowed. The car sputtered as the mountain's incline got steeper. In fifteen seconds, at a forty-five degree angle, the Japanese beater completely conked out.

"I didn't think we were going to have to walk up Mount Everest." Chad groaned when he saw there was another half-mile of increasingly steep terrain to go.

"Let's go." Noah hopped out of the car.

"Can you piggyback me?" asked Chad.

ABBY AND OLIVIA DASHED INTO TOMMY'S BEDROOM AND locked the door. Abby opened a dresser drawer and threw her dad's socks onto the floor. She felt the drawer's inside corner, then pushed her finger on a small round wood button, that was disguised to blend in with the wood panel.

The girls heard a clicking sound and the drawer's false bottom opened, revealing two loaded handguns. Abby handed one of them to Olivia. "Do you know how to use this thing?"

"No, but I've seen *Dirty Harry* ten times," quipped Olivia.

Abby groaned. "Be serious, Olivia. You like guns?"

"No, I like Clint Eastwood. And he's a piano player, too."

"Get him to teach you."

Before Abby could make a comeback, the women heard gasping sounds downstairs in the direction of where the front door used to be.

Suddenly, all the house lights went off.

"Another intruder," whispered Olivia.

The two girls tiptoed quietly outside the bedroom door. They couldn't see anything but weren't going to take any chances.

They fired blindly.

"I surrender!" shrieked Noah.

Just as suddenly as the lights went out, they came back on. A momentary power outage at the worst time possible.

"Noah?" responded a startled Olivia in stunned disbelief, looking down to the front entrance as she and Abby picked themselves up off the floor.

"No, I'm the damned ice cream man making a home

delivery. Of course, it's Noah, and this is my friend, Chad." Noah noticed the bleeding animal parts. "What's this?"

"It's a souvenir. What else? Where's my father?" Olivia demanded.

Words sped out of Noah's mouth as he and Chad raced up the stairs. "We were in WWIII with some guys who ambushed us at a building site. He kept them distracted and told me to give you a message…"

Before Noah could tell Olivia what Garret said, he spotted the dead thug in front of the bedroom door. "Holy shit! Did you guys do that?"

Olivia snarked, "Of course we did. It's a lesson for you in case you cross me."

Chad scrunched his face as he turned to Noah. "This is your new girlfriend?"

"I am not his girlfriend!"

Yet, said Noah to himself. "Your father said if he didn't make it to tell you that you were right to hate him."

"I don't hate him. I don't hate him." Olivia started crying, then whimpered to Abby, "Your dad is gone and mine will be next."

Noah took control. "Chin won't kill him. And he can't kill you, either. If he did, Garret would never break. He would never reveal where the money was." Noah pointed toward the body of the dead thug. "If he was trying to kill you, you would be dead. This guy needed to take you alive so Chin could have leverage. A ballbreaker like him isn't used to playing footsy."

Fear filled Abby's voice. "He said my father had money that belonged to his boss, Chin. He told me to get it back to him."

A sobering thought stopped Olivia's tears. "Noah, how can we save my dad?"

Noah inhaled, thoughts racing and digesting. He replied grimly, "The only way to get your father back is to give Chin his money back. My guess is that the only clues to its whereabouts are somewhere in this house or at the office."

"Why not Olivia's dad's home?" asked Chad.

"Pointless. There is nothing there," Olivia said. "No furniture, no desks, no beds, no hiding places. Dad leads two lives. His public persona is of an extraordinarily powerful lawyer. His private life is that of an ascetic Shaolin monk. At home, there's not a television or even a radio around."

"Okay, that's one less place to muck around looking for stuff that can't be found," breathed Noah. "Abby and Chad, you stay here and tear the place apart. Olivia and I will head to the office. Abby, we need a vehicle. Last thing we need is to get arrested for stealing a car."

Abby offered, "Cadillac, BMW, Rolls, Mini-Cooper, Range Rover, Mercedes, Ferrari..."

"Range Rover," affirmed Noah.

"Wait a sec. What are we trying to find?" asked Chad. "The trail of a money launderer can be buildings, artwork, yachts..."

"No," said Olivia firmly. "We are looking for something that can store a huge amount of cash. Secret bank accounts, probably offshore, is my best guess."

48

NEEDLES IN A HAYSTACK

WEDNESDAY - 4 AM

At this ungodly hour, even the eager beavers at Pittman Saunders were few in number. The deserted parking lot gave Noah the pick of any spot he wanted for the Range Rover. On the way up to Pittman Saunders, Olivia and Noah had the elevator to themselves.

"This is where we first met. Weird, huh?" said Noah.

"Be thankful I'm a cheap date."

"Can you put that in writing?"

"Do you ever stop joking?" Olivia scowled.

"It's a stress reliever. Try it sometime," suggested Noah.

"I like men to be serious."

"Then you should have gotten along with your father just fine." Noah gave her a *gotcha* look as they exited the elevator. "I'll go check out the computers in our office, and you check your dad's out. We're searching for needles in cyberspace. The slightest hint that something seems different."

"I don't need to be told over and over again. We're not married," Olivia said, eyes focused ahead as they walked.

"I can fix that too if you like."

CHAD HAD TAKEN OVER TOMMY'S HOME OFFICE, BRINGING IN every single computer he and Abby could find in the house. There were seven desktop computers, ten laptops and eight tablets sitting in front of him.

Chad frowned. "Every one of these is different. None of the information is the same and they're not even connected. What gives?"

Abby gave a little shrug. "Actually, he didn't really know how to use any of them. Every time he had a problem, he just bought a new one. He never bothered with any kind of technician."

"I wish I'd known him sooner. He could have outfitted my whole café with the ones he wasn't using," sighed Chad. "It could take hours to go through them all."

"We don't have hours." Abby slumped down on a sofa in the office.

All of the computers, laptops and tablets suddenly began smoking. Chad stared, knowing there was nothing he could do and that any information on them was now irretrievable.

"Now that's not the work of a technological illiterate. Pretty damn impressive," marveled Chad.

Abby gaped. "What happened?"

"Could be anything, but my guess is that your dad must have had timing sensors put in so that if one or some or all of them weren't turned on in a certain period or in a certain way, they would all self-destruct. You're sure your dad never had anybody working with him on the computers?"

"Well, I've been in New York so I don't know, but he never did before, and I doubt he did while I was away."

"In that case, I think your dad was a lot smarter than you gave him credit for."

Abby's cell phone dinged with a new text message. A frown appeared when she saw that the sender was her father. She quickly opened the message. *Thanks for the breakfast. I loved the extra butter, maple syrup and bacon. Can't wait until you make pancakes again.*

She showed it to Chad. "Somebody's idea of a cruel joke, impersonating my father."

Chad stared at the text. "You know, I think this genuinely came from your father. Unless I miss my guess, that message was programmed to be sent by one of the computers just before it went kaput."

Abby's eyes widened as a light bulb in her brain turned on. "He specifically asked me to make pancakes for him. He has never done that. He hates Western food. If he wants me to make them again…"

Abby quickly scurried out of the office and headed to the kitchen. She pulled out the jar of flour she used to make breakfast with. She reached into the finely ground white powder and pulled out a Ziploc bag with a USB flash drive inside.

She held it up for Chad to see. "I think I've found what we're looking for."

Chad took out his own trusty laptop and powered it up. "Let's plug it in and see what's on it."

SITTING AT HER FATHER'S COMPUTER IN HIS OFFICE, OLIVIA felt as if he was looking over her shoulder as she skimmed thousands of documents and files. Nothing appeared out of the ordinary. Digging down a few layers of folders, she found one oddly called *Heaven*.

She opened it and began to tear as she perused it. There were dozens of pictures of her parents and herself at all stages of their lives, including Mary and Garret's wedding, Olivia's kindergarten graduation and the happy family on a cruise around Aberdeen Harbor slurping down Lau Kee traditional seafood noodles on one of the small boat restaurants.

She picked up her cell phone and punched in a number for the thirty-seventh time in the last hour and a half and, for the thirty-seventh time, there was exactly the same response—the call went directly to voicemail. "This is Garret Southam, senior partner for Asia Pacific at Pittman Saunders. Please leave me a message."

At the sound of the beep, Olivia whispered, "Daddy, where are you?"

She examined the computer's photos again and saw a photo of herself with both her parents standing by an airport ticket counter. The picture showed a dashing, rugged Garret lifting scrawny eleven-year-old Olivia over his head, with Olivia holding a sign reading, *Don't Drown, Mom*, and Mary, a Heidi Klum lookalike wearing a Red Cross uniform.

Noah entered, frustrated. "I got nothing. How about you?" He saw Olivia's tears, then moved to the computer. Seeing the photo onscreen, he softened. "Is that your mom?"

Olivia nodded. "That was the last time I saw her."

"She's beautiful...just like you."

"She was even more beautiful inside than out..." However, there was a job to do, and Olivia snapped out of her reverie. "I couldn't find anything. It all seemed like the same stuff Dad gave us before, except more stuff and more boring. Nothing that looks like secret accounts squirreled away."

Olivia's cell rang—it was Abby. "What's up, girlfriend?"

The voice at the other end of the line replied, "It's Chad, Olivia, not Abby but feel free to call me girlfriend anytime...Hop onto a computer and keep this line open."

IN ANOTHER PART OF THE CITY, THE CONVERSATIONS BETWEEN Olivia, Noah, Abby and Chad were being monitored and watched with exceptional interest by Marco, Chin's computer geek. Chin and Stella sat in front of Marco in plush theater-style seats in a special conference room.

All eyes in the room were fixed on an eight-foot high-definition screen in front of them and two smaller four-foot screens on either side of it. The large screen broadcast the live conversations between Noah, Olivia, Chad and Abby from Garret's office. One smaller screen showed Chad and Abby inside Tommy's home office. The other screen showed Garret's computer monitor.

They watched and listened in on the conversation.

"Olivia, I'm not seeing what's on your dad's monitor. Can you check that everything is plugged in properly?" asked Chad.

Olivia checked the screen, running her hand over the keyboard and the back of the monitor.

Marco gritted his teeth. "Don't do that," he growled.

"What's wrong, Marco?" asked Chin.

"Everything seems okay, Chad."

"No, I'm still not getting a feed. Try pulling each cable out and then sticking it back in."

"Whatever you say."

Olivia checked cable one. *"How's that?"*

"Nope."

Olivia tried another cable. "This one?"

"Nope."

The smaller screen that mirrored Garret's computer screen went black. Marco screamed, "Plug it back in!"

"How about this last one?"

"Nope. Don't worry about it then. We'll have to do it the old-fashioned way. Just follow my instructions."

Garret's mirrored screen remained black. Marco was about to blow a gasket. He was helpless to do anything other than listen.

"Sure." Olivia sat at her father's computer. "What do you want me to do?"

"Go into a folder called Heaven.*"*

"I did that already. There's just a bunch of family pictures."

"No. Go to the control panel and find computer options."

Olivia typed a few strokes and then moved the mouse. "Got it."

"Now turn on the 'show hidden files' option."

Olivia made a few clicks. "Done."

"Okay. Go back to the Heaven *folder, and tell me what you see."*

Olivia started perusing the previously hidden files, and her jaw dropped. "I can't believe what I'm seeing."

"What are you seeing?" yelled Marco.

"Believe it."

"What are you looking at?" queried Noah.

Chad replied, "These are an elaborate maze of encrypted accounts. I can't tell specifically what they are, but the labeling system indicates they are all from the Eastern Commercial Bank."

"That's the Pittman Saunders corporate bank," said Olivia. "They are all over the files my father wanted me to study."

"I can't access these files from my end, but open them up, and tell me what you see."

Marco started pulling on his hair. "What the hell have you got there?" he muttered at the black screen.

Olivia typed some more and grimaced. "Forty strings of numbers. Seems like they are bank accounts. Can you get into them, Chad?"

"I've been trying but no luck. That's why I called you."

"Wrong person, Chad. You keep at it and let us know what you find."

Thirty tense seconds passed by. Chad let out a loud vexed grunt. "These guys could teach a lesson in bank security to the Swiss. No can do."

Olivia's eyes lit up. "Oh. Oh! I can go to the bank and get them to tell me what these accounts are. After all, I am one of the Golden Asia attorneys."

"You're not going without me, Olivia," said Abby over the phone. "I'll meet you there when the bank opens. Bye."

The screen went dark.

"The bank doesn't open for another few hours. We can try to find your dad until then," said Noah.

"If my father doesn't want to be found, there is no way to find him."

"In that case, we can grab a few ZZs."

"How can you think about sleep right now?" shrieked Olivia.

"There's nothing else we can do until the bank opens so we should grab a little rest."

"WHAT HAPPENED?" SHOUTED AN ANGRY CHIN. "WHY ARE ALL the screens black?"

"When that idiot Chad told Olivia to unplug and replug the cables, she disconnected our feed."

"Marco, can't you just hack into the bank's computers from here? Seems like the obvious thing to do," grumbled Chin.

"Not possible," said Stella. "How many organizations like yours do you think there are in Asia of at least your size? How many countries have presidents whose main job is siphoning funds from their citizens into their personal coffers, all of them demanding a level of protection that makes America's Homeland Security seem like child's play?" asked Stella rhetorically. "There are at least seventeen of them at our bank...I know because I service many of them."

"What do you suggest, Marco?" asked Chin.

Marco drummed his fingers onto the control desk while looking at Stella. "Sometimes, you have to do things the old-fashioned way."

Stella sidled up to Chin and rubbed her body on his. "First things first," she purred.

49

HEAD GAMES

WEDNESDAY - 6:25 AM

Office workers snickered as they passed Noah and Olivia's office and saw the two of them slumped over sleeping on their desks. One grinning lawyer took out her cell phone and snapped a picture.

"What are you so happy about?" asked her office mate.

"I've been trying to get on to the Golden Asia file as long I've been here. Never got a hint of a sniff. I can understand Garret putting his daughter on the file, but that other slacker doesn't deserve the gig." She texted the picture and smirked. "Okay, Garret Southam, now what do you think of your new hire?"

"He works people to death on Golden Asia."

"Garret's driving a Bentley. Not to mention the Lamborghini in his garage."

"Money isn't everything."

"Only paupers say that."

As their co-workers ambled away, the alarm on Noah's computer rang. He and Olivia groggily awakened. Wiping the sleep out of his eyes, Noah cleared his throat and joked to her, "I guess this means we are officially sleeping together."

"Let's go, Reid. Abby's meeting us at the bank."

Noah and Olivia rose out of their chairs and strolled nonchalantly past an office full of onlookers who gaped at the mussy, messy duo who looked like they had barely slept and spent the night partying.

At precisely 9 a.m., the doors of the Eastern Commercial Bank opened and a flood of customers rushed in, including Olivia, Noah and Abby.

Stella stood at one of the teller stations behind a *Closed* sign. Although she was seemingly occupied, she flipped the sign to *Open* when the trio got to the front of the line. She cheerfully announced, "I'd be pleased to serve you here."

Noah, Olivia, and Abby stepped to her service station. Noah and Olivia pulled out business cards and handed them to Stella.

"Pittman Saunders. We are Golden Asia's attorneys," asserted Noah in his best corporate voice. He handed her a slip of paper. "May I have the balances on these accounts please?"

"Of course." Stella typed in one of the numbers. She studied the notes then typed some more and looked at the notes on the new page. She repeated the process several more times, then frowned.

"Can you hurry up please?" asked Noah, irritated at the lack of progress. "We have a lot of work to do on the file.

Stella nodded. "Please bear with me. There is a considerable amount of follow-up and protocol that needs to be exercised."

Not the answer they wanted to hear, but they had no choice.

For the next forty-five minutes, Stella went through the process for the next thirty-nine numbers, with the same results each time. "I'm sorry, but every one of these accounts has restricted access," she said regretfully.

Noah glared. "These are Mr. Sung's personal accounts from Golden Asia Investments. There should be no issues."

"I'm sorry, but I don't have the authority to override this."

Abby started crying. It was not something she wanted to do, but Noah had told her to shed tears if there was any objection at all. *Do whatever it takes, Abby.* "He passed away, and I want to finalize the settlement of his affairs. Please."

"I understand that, but all of these accounts were frozen this morning."

"By whom?" demanded Noah.

"I can't tell you that. Client confidentiality." Stella looked genuinely sorry that she couldn't help them.

Noah inhaled deeply. "If you don't tell me, I will ask my boss, Garret Southam, who is the Pittman Saunders senior attorney for the Asia Pacific region and who personally leads the Golden Asia team, to move all of our firm's accounts."

Fear was in the teller's voice. "Then I don't know what to do because Garret Southam is the one who froze them."

"We were here right at the bank opening, and we did not see him here. When did he do that?" asked Noah.

"Mr. Southam has special banking privileges. He has concierge service on demand, twenty-four hours a day, seven days a week, including holidays. I wasn't around to take his call, but it could have been anytime between closing yesterday to opening today."

Noah thumped his fist on the counter. "This is not acceptable."

"I'm sorry, but when accounts are frozen, especially if there is a suspicious death, only the most senior management has the authority to lift the freeze. Given that it was Garret Southam who gave the order, I am doubtful your request would be granted. At the Eastern Commercial Bank, we are particularly concerned for the privacy of our clients. Shall I call someone for you?"

Noah shook his head. "No, we have wasted enough of our time here."

As Noah, Olivia and Abby left the bank, all three shared the same thought.

Where the hell was Garret?

STELLA WATCHED THE DISTRESSED OLIVIA, NOAH AND ABBY until they left the bank and were out of sight. She put the *Closed* sign back on, then walked to her office where Chin waited.

"Did you have to keep me waiting that long?" asked Chin sternly.

"There was a problem." She handed him the sheet of paper Olivia gave her. "Those are the numbers of the forty secret accounts. Some are personal; some are from private numbered companies. The reason I took so long is that none of them has any funds in them, and I wanted to verify that before coming to you."

Chin's fist hit the desk so hard that it shattered. "Nothing? There must be a mistake."

"No mistake. The money is somewhere else," cried Stella.

Chin threw her a dismissive sneer, stood up and walked out.

"Where are you going?" Stella called out.

"There is nothing for me here anymore," said Chin.

Stella quickly chased after him.

BACK INSIDE THE RANGE ROVER WITH OLIVIA AND ABBY, Noah called Chad for an update. Both girls had infrared transmitters in their purses that linked to Stella's computer when she searched the account for information. "We came up with zeros at the bank. How about you?"

"Nothing. When I checked into the bank's computer system, it showed there were no funds, but there was something more than that. What's crazy is that there were hundreds upon hundreds of no-money transactions. And I mean, like, from zero from one account to zero to another. How about you?"

Abby was genuinely puzzled. "Daddy went to the bank all the time. He was a regular there. Not only that, fooling around with bank accounts was about the only thing he knew how to do on a computer."

Olivia added, "And I recognized the names of those companies and accounts because that's what my father had me studying from the moment I got here. He billed a fortune to Golden Asia to make sure no one could ever figure out the chain of title, that no one knew who owned whom or what."

"That means both your fathers had banking privileges on the same secret accounts but never used them for any transactions of value?" asked Noah. "Things just aren't adding up. Why would Garret freeze accounts that had no money in them? Why did Tommy get him to set them up in the first place?"

"Here's more craziness to throw into the mix. They knew what they were doing," said Chad. "Although a lot of the transactions were done at the bank, records show there was never a teller involved."

Noah breathed deeply. He was going to take a stab in the dark. An intelligent guess, but still a guess. "It's got to be camouflage. Garret wanted to throw the scent off the real hiding place of the funds. So the question is, Olivia, who would your father have trusted with the info or the money?"

Olivia answered immediately, "He's a lawyer. Trust is not in his vocabulary."

As they slowed for a stop light, a bicycle courier rode up beside them. Without missing a beat, he reached into his knapsack and tossed a grisly package in through the driver's side window. Olivia and Abby shrieked—the severed bloody head of a red-crowned crane cut from the base of its neck landed on Noah's lap. This rare bird, a symbol of luck and prosperity, was ghastly in death.

"Hey, what's going on?" shouted Chad.

Noah gripped the steering wheel with one hand, and picked up the bird's head with his other hand and put it on the dashboard. "Someone's playing head games. Chad, we're on our way back. There's got to be a clue hidden somewhere at the house."

PART IV

FURY UNLEASHED

50

COOL CUCUMBER

HONG KONG - WEDNESDAY MORNING

A lesser man would have been dead long ago. Both of Garret's eyes were beaten black, his ribs were cracked and his cut ravaged lips were bleeding. Determined to prove his worth to Chin, Terry was relentless in his assault on Garret.

He leered, "Mr. Southam, Mr. Chin said not to kill you until you tell us where the rest of the money is. I know you got to be hurting, so why don't you just be a good boy and tell me who's got the dough and where it is?"

Garret whispered, "Listen, Terry, you don't really want to die, do you?"

The young tough plowed a right into Garret's stomach. "No, sir. That's why I've got to keep you alive until you talk."

Terry pummeled Garret again. And again. And again. Each blow was harder than the previous one. The force from a final blow toppled the chair, and Garret's head knocked against the floor. The lawyer was unconscious and worse, maybe dead.

Terry started blinking uncontrollably. This lifelong

involuntary habit gave away his fear—not at the thought that he'd killed a man but at what Chin would do to him if Garret didn't recover.

"Damn you, Garret. Wake up," said the worried gangster as he poured a cup of water over Garret's face. There was no response. "Oh, shit. No, no." The beast leaned over to check for a pulse when suddenly Garret propelled himself up and bit off Terry's ear.

As Terry reeled back, screaming in pain, Garret turned and head-butted him; Garret's forehead broke Terry's nose. With the area where his ear used to be and his nose both gushing blood, Terry tried to launch power fists at Garret's cranium. However, the thug was seriously weakened, and his feeble blows had no impact on the wounded but built-to-the-hilt lawyer.

His legs had the strength of a railway car. Garret, still tied to the chair, pushed off and launched himself into an aerial somersault.

Suspended for a moment, with deadly aim the chair came down hard. Two legs landed on Terry, penetrating his body, piercing his heart and lungs—instant death. Garret searched for any kind of sharp object to free himself from the tightly bound ropes.

The lawyer couldn't find anything but he did witness the eerie post-mortem twitch of Terry's body.

Garret pulled himself and the chair off Terry's body. Even though mobility was difficult, Garret used his right hand to reach into one of the holes created by the chair, right into the corpse. Forcing his way through the gangster's flesh, he grabbed a couple of ribs, snapped them and pulled them out. Using their sharp broken edges, he cut through the cords binding him and freed his hands, body and legs.

Glowing in victory, despite every part of his body screaming in pain, Garret took Terry's cell phone out of his pocket and coolly strode out of Chin's manmade jungle.

51

END OF BASKETBALL

Dead end after dead end. Whenever it seemed Chad was making progress, it turned out to be another smokescreen. *Think outside the box, Chad. You've been searching all the normal places, done all the normal things, so maybe that means the key is in an abnormal spot. Okay, Chad. What is the most unlikely spot on a computer to find banking information?*

Chad's eyes opened—maybe it was hidden in plain sight with something so disconnected no one would ever suspect it. Like the *iTunes Media* folder.

Chad opened it and saw all the normal songs, books and podcasts. Also, a curious file had a game-like name called *King of Kentucky*. It was the only file on the computer Chad couldn't crack. The King of Kentucky was an encrypted file with contents yet to be determined. Chad picked up the phone and called Noah.

The young lawyer picked up. "Got anything new?"

"Yeah, but I have no idea if it means anything or not. I found this last hidden file but, for the life of me, I can't get the sucker to open, no matter what I try."

"What's it called?" Noah asked.

"King of Kentucky."

"No way. When I was a kid, I asked Master Wu what he wanted to be if he wasn't a sifu. He said, 'King of Kentucky.' Open it. It's got to mean something."

"That's the problem, Noah. You didn't hear me. It won't let me and keeps on asking for a password. I have no idea what the hell it is, but the password question is, 'What is the tie that binds?'"

"'Blessed be the tie that binds' is the name of a hymn," said the missionary's kid. "Try Jesus or God. That's the tie that binds Christians together."

"Duh, been there, done that. I've tried everything: Jesus, God, Son, Holy Spirit, Jehovah, Trinity and then all kinds of combinations."

Noah groaned. "Check on who the composer is and try that."

"Okay, the guy is John Fawcett. Nope. John. No. Fawcett. No."

"How about trying something connected to Fawcett's life? That might be something that binds."

Chad's face contorted as he tried, then rejected, new possibilities. "Chapel? No. Wainsgate? No. Carter's Lane? No."

～

Inside the Range Rover, Noah sang thoughtfully, rummaging for other ideas as the car climbed the now familiar Victoria Peak.

"Blest be the tie that binds
Our hearts in Christian love;
The fellowship of kindred minds

Is like to that above."

"Nothing connects. Who is doing the tying, and who is doing the binding? Anything out of the ordinary?" asked Chad.

Olivia offered, "What if there's a different kind of connection other than the Christian one?"

"My father was a Taoist," said Abby. "He would never even dream of using a Christian reference."

"Chin, Tommy, Garret. What do they all have in common?" puzzled Noah. He tapped thoughtfully on his leg as he drove. "I got it. It's Master Wu. Try Master Wu, Chad."

Moments later, Chad replied. "Sorry. I tried every possible combination. What was his real name or full name?"

Noah sighed. "As long as I've known him, he was always Master Wu or Sifu."

Noah glimpsed at the dashboard as the Range Rover pulled into Tommy's driveway. The head of the dead crane seemed to stare at him, inviting him, questioning him...Noah's eyes lit up. "The tie that binds is not a people; it's a system, it's the philosophy, it's the school. What binds Garret, Tommy, Chin and Master Wu is the Tiger and Crane. Try *Hung Gar*."

The Range Rover pulled into the circular driveway of Tommy's home.

CHAD TYPED IN *HUNG GAR*. THE PASSWORD WORKED! HE shouted, "Bingo!" but there was no opportunity to celebrate.

With Abby, Olivia and Noah out of the house, Duke had quietly slipped into the mansion and had hidden in a closet in the adjacent room.

Before Chad could utter a word, Duke grabbed him. He covered his mouth with his giant pudgy hand, muffling all sounds Chad tried to make. "God, it took you long enough to figure that out." He entered a number into his cell. "The code is Hung Gar."

IN CHIN'S THEATER ROOM, MARCO TYPED *HUNG GAR* INTO THE computer. "It worked!"

Chin gritted his teeth. "Of course. See what's in the file."

"That's where we need some time." Marco shook his head. "I got in, but it's going to take a while to figure out what the hell is in here. There are over five thousand files with very little description."

Stella sidled up to Chin and purred. "Since we have some time, why don't I make it pass away a little more pleasantly?"

Chin emotionlessly lifted her up by the throat with one hand.

"You found nothing."

"Because there was nothing to be found," gurgled Stella as she floundered in the air.

"You wasted my time. If you had been monitoring my accounts properly, you would have known that."

"I just assumed..."

"You assumed wrong. You also assumed that because you threw yourself at me like a nymphomaniac cat in heat that I would be swayed by something I can get from anyone, anywhere, male, female, or animal."

"No, no. You are the best. You are the best sex I've ever had," spluttered Stella, trying desperately to say something to assuage Chin.

"Unfortunately, I cannot say the same about you. But, even if you were, I have no room for incompetent amateurs."

Chin began squeezing. Stella battled for her life, kicking and clawing, but her efforts were futile as Chin stared blankly, watching her life ebb away. He tossed her still body aside.

He punched in Terry's cell number and barked, "Bring me Garret!"

"Sorry, Chin, Terry ain't available," taunted Garret on the other end of the line. In his best Arnold Schwarzenegger voice, Garret growled, "Hasta la vista, baby."

The phone went to a dial tone. Chin raged, "Bring me Olivia!"

WHEN HE ARRIVED AT TOMMY'S HOME, NOAH HAD BARELY PUT the luxury SUV into park when a group of thugs who had come with Duke descended like raging Mongols upon them. While Chin's son had gone inside, they had hidden outside, waiting for this moment. One opened the passenger door and yanked a kicking, flailing, and screaming Olivia out.

Three others readied arrows in the barrels of crossbows. When Noah opened his door, he was greeted by speeding arrows destined for his heart. He slammed the door shut. Good thing Tommy had bulletproof glass put in. The arrows splintered when they hit the window but this gave the bowmen enough time to rush to the luxury SUV and jam arrows into the door locks, disabling the door locks and electronic window mechanisms, making it impossible for Noah and Abby to get out.

They helplessly watched Duke's henchmen shove Olivia

into the black Mercedes that had appeared from down the street.

Noah started pounding on the window when he saw Duke coming out the front door, carrying Chad by the throat. Standing in full view of Noah in front of the Range Rover, Duke lifted the struggling Chad with his left hand. He cocked his right arm and, with one super punch from the mass of two hundred and fifty pounds, he completely mashed Chad's face, breaking through his skull. Reaching in through the bloody skull, he grabbed the cerebral arteries and yanked them out.

"Chad! Chad!" screamed Noah.

Duke tossed Chad's bleeding corpse onto the front windshield of the Range Rover. Then the gangsters calmly poured gasoline over the vehicular prison. Duke lit a match and tossed it onto the car. The car ignited as the gangsters boarded the Mercedes and drove away.

"What are we going to do, Noah? It's bulletproof glass. We can't get out," whimpered Abby frantically.

"I've got an idea and we have five seconds to find out if my theory is right. Hang tight, Abby." Noah started the car and aimed it directly at the stone wall surrounding the property. He floored it, and the flaming vehicle crashed hard into the wall.

The impact of the crash scrunched the car, but what Noah hoped for happened. The doors sprung open. "Run!" yelled Noah.

He and Abby jumped out of the car and raced away. BOOM! The car exploded. The force threw the two to the ground. They crawled gingerly to Chad's remains.

Noah kneeled over his deceased friend. "No, Chad. You can't leave. It's not right."

Abby gently tapped his shoulder. "We've got to go, Noah."

"I just need a minute, Abby," lamented Noah.

"We don't have the time, Noah."

"But, even if we leave now," Noah said, "I have no idea where to go. Olivia could be anywhere."

"I think I can help with that answer," called a familiar voice.

TRANSFORMED

HONG KONG - WEDNESDAY MORNING

Noah and Abby looked up to see a disheveled, beaten, and bleeding Garret getting out of another of Chin's black Mercedes.

"You're one tough mother," said Noah in pained admiration.

Even though his body was wracked in agony, Garret felt cocky because of the compliment from a fellow martial arts master. "You should have seen the other guy." He took another two steps, but stumbled and collapsed.

Noah wrapped his body around the convulsing man. He called to Abby, "Are there any acupuncture needles here? I need to stem his pain. If we use morphine, it will dull his senses and we need Garret to stay sharp."

"Right." Abby dashed into her home as Garret stopped shivering and lay unconscious on the circular parking lot.

Knowing exactly where the thin steel rods were stored, Abby returned quickly to see Noah gently extricating himself from Garret.

She handed the acupuncture needles to Noah and five minutes later, Garret resembled an oversized voodoo doll with a hundred needles stuck in the top of his head, his cheeks, his wrists, his stomach, his ankles and his toes. Noah hovered over the senior lawyer, constantly tapping the needles, moving from body part to body part.

Abby looked askance at Noah. "Do you know what you're doing?"

Noah confidently replied, "Every Shaolin master needs to have a basic understanding of Traditional Chinese Medicine. When massaged, the needles create a kind of electric current in the body that allows it to heal faster. I've had Dr. Tang do this to me and Master Wu a thousand times."

"That's supposed to be reassuring?" gaped Abby. "I've watched a thousand hours of Lady Gaga, but I still can't sing like her."

Noah tapped the needles on Garret's body. For what seemed a lifetime, there was no response.

"I could have called emergency and they would have been here in fifteen minutes," complained Abby.

Suddenly, Garret's body started trembling and he bolted upright. "What the hell are you trying to do to me, Reid?" he croaked.

Noah gasped with relief. "You're alive!"

"Isn't that stating the blatantly obvious?" asked the irritated Garret as he started pulling the thin needles out of his body. "Let's get Olivia. And, Reid, you put most of these damned things in the wrong place."

"It was my first time," admitted Noah.

"You don't get points for losing your virginity. You could have killed me."

"But you're not in pain. Right?"

Garret glared at Noah. *Are you stupid or something?* "Next time, just give me a handful of Tylenol. Let's go."

"But where?" shot Noah. "They just grabbed Olivia and took off."

"You'd know if you joined us for dinner that first night," admonished Garret. "We're going to the Tiger Palace in Macau."

Garret jerked—he saw Chad's body. "It never ends," he said softly. Sensing Noah's loss, he added, "And it won't end unless we make it."

Garret stood tall. "We will make them pay, Reid. All of them," he said painfully but confidently.

Noah nodded and seethed, "I'm going to kill the bastard that did this to Chad. And if Chin so much as touches Olivia...I will make sure he pays, too."

Garret looked at Noah—there had been a change. A toughness, a determination that wasn't there just hours ago. *Maybe Master Wu was right.* "Let's go."

Abby led them to the ten-car garage. Noah's eyes widened—every vehicle had a sticker price of over $100,000, especially the $2,000,000 Bugatti Veyron.

Garret saw Noah ogling the Italian vehicle. "Sorry, Noah. The Bugatti won't fit the three of us." He pointed to a Porsche Panamera Turbo. "Zero to sixty in four seconds."

Noah tried to get into the driver's seat, but Garret pushed him aside.

"I drive a sports car. I think I can get us there," protested Noah.

Ever the lawyer, Garret presented a convincing argument. "Your bucket of bolts is hardly a performance vehicle. My other cars include a Lamborghini and a Ferrari. And I know how to get to the Tiger Palace Complex. And you are used to left-side driving in LA. We need someone who can drive a vehicle at two hundred miles an hour from the right side."

Garret got into the driver's seat, Noah rode shotgun and Abby climbed into the back.

Adrenaline energized everyone, and forgotten were deaths, beatings and attacks. As Garret started the car, he proclaimed, "Prepare yourselves, children. There's a wild ride ahead."

53

BINGO!

W ith her hands and arms duct-taped behind her back, Chin dragged Olivia into the theater room. She withheld the gasp in her throat when she spotted Stella's corpse at her feet.

The Tiger master shoved her into a chair. "The bold are free from fear. Are you afraid, Miss Southam?"

Olivia attempted a brave front. "No."

Chin smirked. He grabbed a fistful of Olivia's hair and forced her head down to get a close-up of Stella's brutalized body. "You recognize Miss Wei, do you not? She was momentarily useful, but then she disappointed me. Just as Tommy did. Now where is my money hidden?"

Chin slapped her so hard that Olivia almost toppled from her chair. Her cheek burning from the blow, Olivia forced out, "I don't know anything. I just got back from New York. I have no idea what is going on with you, my father or Golden Asia."

"Maybe that's true; maybe it's not. But your father will definitely know."

Chin released his viselike grip on Olivia's hair, then

twirled a lock of it around his finger. Reaching into his pocket, he pulled out a throwing star and used its razor edge to cut the tress off. Chin noted her trembling and slid the star across Olivia's neck, barely touching the skin. There was no blood, but there was now a thin scarlet line on her skin.

"You have no reason to fear...unless your father continues his refusal to cooperate. I did want to scare you, though, at the restaurant last night."

"Killing my father would have accomplished nothing," muttered Olivia.

"You're right. Garret was not the target." Chin stooped to face Olivia. Although her fear welled to a rapid boil, Olivia instinctively knew that control of her emotions was mandatory if she wanted to stay alive.

"You were. Not to kill you but to blind you in one eye. It would have been painful beyond comprehension as the arrow embedded itself close to your brain. But you would have lived. And Garret would do whatever I asked to make sure I didn't do the other eye or any other part of your body."

Olivia could no longer control herself. She shot out a kick with her leg, which affected Chin not a whit. She tried to leap up but Chin clamped her head down hard. "I like you. I enjoy a challenge."

"Having me tied up like this is hardly a challenge. But you'll get one when my father shows up," hissed Olivia.

Chin's arrogant eyes pitied her. "Your father has not been a challenge to me for a long time from even before I arranged for a certain plane accident, which I believe you also witnessed." Chin's voice turned to ice. "After that, Garret was mine. Just as you will be."

Chin slowly unbuttoned Olivia's blouse. He took a

martial arts star and ground one of the points dangerously close to her navel.

Olivia's expression went blank. She wanted to scream again but realized that would only feed into Chin's control of her. These kind of men fed off fear. She chanted inwardly. *You will not win. I will not lose. You will not win. I will not lose.*

CHAD WAS NOT THE ONLY ONE WHO HAD TROUBLE TRYING TO figure what the heck the King of Kentucky was all about.

Super-geek Marco was equally stymied, until..."Yes!"

Chin spun his attention away from Olivia. "You've got it?"

Marco nodded vigorously. "I've gone through file after file after file. Most are dead ends or put there as a smoke-screen to throw someone off track. The average hacker would never find those but I..."

Chin interrupted. "Just tell me."

"Okay, okay. I have found half a dozen Swiss bank accounts. I've been breaking into those ever since I was in grade six. This will take me no time at all. Fifteen minutes tops."

"Excellent." Chin made a call. "Duke, Garret and Noah's usefulness has ended. Eliminate them."

54

THE HEAT IS ON

MACAU - WEDNESDAY NOON

Garret's driving had two speeds—fast and faster. Noah and Abby gritted their teeth in horrified adrenaline-pounding fear.

"Mr. Southam?"

"Yes, Abby?"

"Who are you and my father, really?"

"We are two men who love their families, two men who made a mistake. We will do whatever is necessary to protect the living and avenge the dead. And, if we can't, we will die trying because you and Olivia cannot continue to live in the shadows of regret, wondering what might have been, the way your father and I did.

A monster of a pick-up truck, a Dodge Ram 3500, pulled alongside the Porsche on one side. Another of Chin's seemingly ubiquitous black Mercedes zoomed in and flanked the other side, sandwiching the Porsche in the middle.

Garret said with uncompromising strength. "Hold on. Things are going to get nasty."

That was an understatement. The Ram and Mercedes

took turns sideswiping the Panamera. It was one hell of a rocky ride. Garret gripped the wheel tightly, refusing to allow the car to swerve out of control—the direction kept shifting abruptly as the assault on the vehicles escalated as they accelerated.

Garret sped up to one hundred and forty miles per hour, but the opposition's vehicles had no difficulty keeping pace.

The Ram and Mercedes converged on the Porsche's sides, trying to squeeze it like an accordion. However, the Panamera was built like a tank; they had little to show for it other than burning rubber and flying sparks.

Suddenly, Garret slammed on the brakes, allowing the other cars to shoot ahead. He did a one-hundred-eighty degree turn. With a burst of speed and tires spinning furiously until smoke belched out, he put German engineering to the test by hitting one hundred sixty miles per hour in under six seconds.

The other vehicles screeched to a halt, spun around and hurtled forward, but Garret had too much of a head start for them to make much headway.

The windows of the Mercedes opened up, and a marksman leaned out with a crossbow and arrow. It wasn't the easiest target to hit at breakneck speed, and the marksman shot and hit the Porsche's window, shattering the glass.

The arrow grazed Noah's ear. "Ow!" His ear started bleeding.

Pissed, Noah saw an arrow coming for Garret. He grabbed the steering wheel to steady himself and head butted the speeding missile out of harm's way.

Even in the midst of war, Garret had to admire that move. "Did Master Wu teach you that?"

"I made it up two seconds ago," called Noah, releasing his hold on the steering wheel.

The fractions-of-a-second loss allowed the Ram and Mercedes to catch up. With deadly aim, the Ram accelerated into the rear left side of the Porsche, destroying its equilibrium. The passenger side wheels lifted into the air, and it took every bit of driving prowess Garret had to make sure the car didn't tip.

Noah dove out of the passenger side and hung onto the car door frame. The crazy move was enough to put enough weight on the passenger side so that the car righted.

"Did you just think of that, too?" yelled Garret.

"No, that came from watching Captain America movies," quipped the smartass.

Now the Mercedes took its turn, inching ahead of the Porsche and trying to muscle its way to the front.

"Not on my watch, soldier." Garret put the pedal to the metal and shoved the Mercedes out of the way. "Got you."

It was a precarious, bone-chilling, thrilling ride navigated by instinct and powered by sheer adrenaline. Now at one-hundred-seventy-five miles an hour, Garret knew it was only a matter of time before either the Ram or the Mercedes would inflict a lethal blow.

Noah jumped into the back seat and opened the rear window. "Slam on the brakes when I count to three," he ordered.

"You got to be kidding me," Garret couldn't believe what Noah would be thinking of next.

"Can you stop questioning me?" Noah asked. "Just do as I say. One. Two. Three."

Garret obediently slammed on the brakes. Noah took out a throwing star and leaned out the window as the Ram screeched alongside. He propelled the metal star with full force and accuracy. It shattered the Ram's window. Noah's next star sliced into the driver's jugular.

As the driver's blood sprayed the vehicle's interior, the Ram spun out of control and smashed into the concrete bridge ramp. It exploded into a flaming spectacle.

But the black Mercedes had crept up dangerously. Noah saw Duke's sights set on the Porsche. Duke fired but Garret quickly jerked the steering wheel—the arrow sliced the side mirror off the car.

Noah worried, "That gorilla's good."

"He should be. He's Duke, Chin's son," glowered Garret.

Noah shook his head. "We gotta go on the offensive. Sooner or later, Duke's going to connect."

"Try this," said Abby, taking some martial arts stars from her purse.

Seeing Noah and Garret's quizzical expressions, she explained, "They were in the same cabinet as the acupuncture needles."

Duke was loading another arrow into the crossbow when Noah launched three stars at him. He shot an arrow that destroyed one of them. He nabbed the other two mid-air with the same calm as his father and Garret.

Noah saw Duke disappear into the car, then re-emerge, this time shouldering an assault rocket launcher. Noah blew out a resigned gasp of air. "We're done for. He's breaking the honor code."

"What honor code?" Abby asked.

"The unwritten code of the Shaolin." Disappointment mixed with worry appeared on Noah's face. "He violated the Way. The only weapons we use are those we can control with our bodies. No guns, no artillery and no explosives."

"Then get out some more of those stars, Noah," yelled

Abby, checking out the back window to see their foe less than twenty feet away.

"I don't have any more but, even if I did, they'd be useless. And no one could miss from that distance."

Darkness of inevitable doom fell upon the Porsche.

55

WHY?

MACAU - WEDNESDAY AFTERNOON

M arco shook his head. "Dammit. All the accounts are here, but I got a problem. It's voice- and fingerprint-activated. I have enough stuff of Garret and Tommy so I can break through that, no sweat. Trouble is, they've put in an extra personal access code, and it seems only Garret knows what it is. It's not in any of the records of any of the account managers. Nothing is working, and I tried everything I could think of, boss."

Enraged, Chin lifted the chair Olivia was tied to and threw it at the big screen in front. He made a phone call and screamed, "Leave them alone! We need Garret! Alive!"

NOAH WATCHED HELPLESSLY AS DUKE FIRED THE PORTABLE rocket launcher. However, instead of heading directly at the Porsche, the warhead overshot the racing vehicle. Fifteen hundred feet later, it hit a low-flying traffic helicopter, which exploded like the fireworks finale on the Fourth of July in New York City.

Duke pulled himself back inside his car as the black Mercedes braked to a halt and then drove off in the opposite direction.

Noah was baffled. "He could have killed us but didn't. Why?"

"This was the outcome I was hoping for," Garret said in a low tone. "What that means is they finally discovered they still need me. It also means that Olivia is still alive. If they hurt Olivia, Chin knows I will never give him what he wants. If he kills me, then he'll never have the information he needs unless...The bottom line is that Chin wants me...and I want him."

"Um, do you mind if I drive?" asked Noah. "Garret, you need a break and I've never taken a car worth more than a bagful of Big Macs for a spin."

No wonder Olivia likes him. Noah's fun. "Be my guest." Garret pulled to the side of the road.

~

THE TIGER PALACE WAS THREE BLOCKS AWAY, AND NOAH gunned it one last time before slamming on the brakes in its driveway.

56

FALLEN WARRIOR

G arret led Noah and Abby as they flew out of the car and into the entertainment palace, hurtling past the terra-cotta warriors, caged Bengal tigers, patrons, acrobats, entertainers and staff. They waded through gambling tables, slot machines and a hundred-yard-long buffet to arrive at their goal of the huge picture of a tiger taking up the entire wall at the other end of the casino.

"This is it," said Garret. "We just need to figure out how to get in."

"You don't know?" asked Noah.

"Never had to get in by myself."

They started feeling the walls for hairline cracks or hidden switches, but the surface was smooth.

"Hello, Mr. Southam," sounded a voice familiar to Garret. He turned to see Wing with Duke standing in front of him. "Mr. Chin wishes to see you alone."

Scanning Duke's solid body, Noah didn't see anything other than muscle. *The harder they come, the harder they fall.* "No dice. I'm going, too," asserted Noah.

"Me, too," added Abby.

Duke stepped in front of Noah. Without the car masking part of his body, Chin's son was huge. "Alone means alone."

Hate was in each man's eyes as Noah retorted, "You are not only fat, but you are *real* ugly."

Infuriated by the insult, Duke launched a barrage of obscenities as he lunged for Noah. Noah quickly side-stepped the hulk, and Duke's fist plunged into one of the toes of the tiger painted on the wall.

"Did I also mention you're stupid and a lousy shot?" taunted Noah.

"At least I'm not dead, which is what you're going to be in three seconds," snarled Duke.

This would be no genteel martial arts competition. It would be down-and-dirty fighting. Each man was a master of the Five Traditional Animals of the Shaolin: the Dragon, Snake, Leopard, Tiger and Crane. The battle would be brutal in nature, but exquisite in its execution of the martial arts. Noah showed the power of the Dragon as he attacked Duke's vital organs.

Crouching like a Snake, Duke sprung out to repel Noah, who countered with the focused, ferocious movement of a tiger's paw. Noah's tiger-like quickness blocked Duke's hand and, with the velocity of the feline, jabbed his hand toward Duke's throat.

Duke parried the attack and used the Crane's quick foot movements to catch Noah ever so slightly off guard and power-kicked him in the thigh. Wincing in big-time pain, Noah lost his balance. Duke, as the Crane, stretched tall and kicked out, but Noah reached for inner strength. Forcing himself to ignore the physical torment, he found a new element of power—the element of Metal. Hard like iron, he resisted Duke's attack and, with the power of a steel bar, he hammered his arm on Duke's back, causing him to stumble.

Garret tried to intervene, but Noah snarled, "No! This is my time!"

"That was dumb," mocked Duke. In a singsong falsetto voice, he added, "Baby could use the help."

With both combatants exhausted, sweating and breathing heavily, the battle continued through sheer willpower. Gathering strength, Duke drew from another power source—Water. His arms and legs attacked Noah like the relentless pounding of waves upon the seashore.

Noah could not withstand the barrage and stepped back, but Duke relentlessly pounded on. However, Noah refused to break, angering Duke. The huge man reached into an inside fold of his jacket and pulled out his knife. With blazing speed, he stabbed Noah in the gut.

Noah's eyes filled with hate. "You broke the code." He repeated this louder. "You broke the code in the car and you broke the code of honor now."

"Who gives a shit about honor?" Duke smirked.

"I do." With the knife still in his stomach, Noah became an inspired dervish, kicking and hammering. Duke grabbed for the knife and pulled it out, causing more blood to flow. Instead of weakening Noah, the gushing blood infuriated and inspired him. He began a rapid series of combinations of left, right, upper, kick, kick, right, right...with a final pirouette ramrodding Duke into submission.

A desperate Duke tried in vain to knife Noah again, but Noah easily deflected the attack and, with a swift kick, directed the knife into Duke's heart. The hulking man's eyes bulged. As his mouth gurgled, then foamed, Noah staggered over and twisted the knife until Duke keeled over, dead.

Noah stood over his vanquished foe, panting as he bled.

He was in mental and physical shock—he had never killed a man before.

Garret walked up to him. "Now you know what blood tastes like."

Suddenly there was the sound of thunderous applause. Noah turned to see the restaurant guests, casino patrons, and even the Chinese acrobats, giving him a standing ovation, thinking the battle between Noah and Duke was staged. Shouts of "Bravo! Fantastic! Best show in town!" rang through the celebratory atmosphere.

One giggling girl came up to Noah, "Can I have your autograph? I watched the whole thing from the time you entered. This was just so perfect."

She handed him a pen, and Noah signed. "Thank you and..." She whispered in his ear and nuzzled her boobs against Noah's chest as she handed him a card. "That's my room number. Come up anytime." She made a little roar like a tiger. "*Raar!*"

As she left, Noah collapsed in an agonized heap to the ground. The combination of the strenuous battle and loss of blood was too much. Abby grabbed a tablecloth and, using a table knife to cut off a strip, she tied it tightly around Noah's middle to stem the bleeding.

Garret picked Wing up by the scruff of his neck. "Now get us up there, Wing."

Suspended a foot off the ground, the swinging Wing whined, "I don't know how. Mr. Chin always does it himself."

Noah, lying on the ground, looked up at the huge picture of the tiger. He struggled to stand up and stumbled to the wall. From the restaurant's impressive collection of martial arts weapons, Noah picked out an ancient gold-headed spear with a jet-black shaft.

Noah eyed the tiger, aimed the spear and hurled it. Bull's eye. The spear slammed directly into a lever that was disguised as a tooth inside the tiger's mouth. The wall slid open, revealing the doors to a hidden elevator.

Garret eyed Noah. "I'll bring her back for you."

The weakened lawyer nodded. "You better."

As Garret and Abby entered the elevator, there was another round of applause, and more shouts of "Bravo!" came from the guests.

Noah turned around, smiled feebly and bowed.

57

BROKEN HONOR

There were no elevator floor numbers on the panel. It swooshed upward by itself with a mind of its own.

"I hope Olivia's all right," ventured Abby.

"Don't worry. She is," stated Garret confidently.

The elevator halted and opened automatically. A welcoming party of Chin and his henchmen waited. Beside Chin was Olivia, bound in a chair with her mouth taped.

"You certainly are irritating, Garret. I take you; you escape and then you come back on your own," mocked Chin.

"I changed my mind."

"Does that mean you are reconsidering my offer? However, I told Duke you were supposed to come by yourself. Or is Tommy's daughter a present for me?"

"Duke won't be taking orders from you anymore," uttered Garret with chilling undertones.

The meaning was not lost on Chin. He ripped out a dagger and put it to Olivia's neck. "You have taken my son."

"Not me. Duke lost to Noah. Your son broke the code but Noah kept Shaolin honor."

Chin thundered revenge, "Your daughter will see you die!"

"You have never beaten me in a fair fight, Chin." Garret sneered contemptuously.

"What's the saying? All is fair in love and war. You are no match for me now, Garret. A fat cat lawyer's life has made you soft. You have lost the heart of the Tiger."

Marco screamed. "Get the access codes first!"

Garret snickered. "Predicament, isn't it? I'll only give you the numbers if you kill me. But, if I am dead, I won't be able to tell you what they are."

Chin pressed the dagger to the base of Olivia's skull. Garret stopped cold and said softly but firmly, "She's a bystander, Chin. Killing her means you break the code, too. But you and I know that's the only way you can beat me."

The gauntlet was laid down.

Enraged at the taunting, Chin threw the dagger at Garret with the force of a rocket launcher. Garret easily deflected it with a flick of the wrist into the hands of Abby. Abby whipped over to Olivia and slashed the duct tape binding her wrists.

"Bring it on, cowboy," sneered Garret.

His words incited a battle royale; everyone got into the act.

Abby hurled the knife into the forehead of one of Chin's men, causing instant death.

Olivia grabbed a sword as another tough lunged toward her. She stuck it in front of her and impaled her attacker with such force that it went through his stomach and back, severing his spinal cord. He lurched, teetered and slumped to the floor.

Behind her, another aggressor waving knives in each hand like a banshee, screamed as he rushed to the attack.

Garret yelled, "Watch out, Olivia!"

Olivia wheeled around and kicked the knife-waving henchman in the windpipe with such force that it snapped his neck.

"Where did you learn that?" asked her astonished father.

"A girl has to learn to defend herself in New York," answered Olivia.

Abby was a whirling dervish, clawing, kicking and slapping with both hands and feet. A well-placed knee into the groin of a would-be assailant caused him to drop to the ground, helpless. A double hand chop to the neck, followed by a ferocious stomp onto the vertebrae, finished him off.

"Enough of this! Finish them off!" shouted Chin.

Four brutes walked up to Abby and Olivia. The two women were no match for them. Blows deflected off them; kicks hurt them more than they hurt their opponents. The experienced thugs subdued them easily by grabbing their hair and putting them in headlocks.

Chin barked out, "Garret, our audience is ready." He turned to Olivia and leered, "I am the man your father never was."

The girls' captors twisted their bodies so they could watch the main event between Garret and Chin.

A lifetime of hatred, love, jealousy and competition culminated in an intense, dirty, personal mano-a-mano combat.

Evil versus more evil, white versus yellow...power versus power.

Chin charged Garret with circular arm movements, hands formed in the trademark Tiger claw with thumb and fingers spread through his open hands. Garret prepared with the Leopard paw, a half fist that prepared to strike with the second knuckles of his fingers.

Switching on a whim to the Crane's beak, the Snake's hand and the Dragon's hand, these skilled veteran warriors mixed up their stances and moves as they put on a dazzling display of Hung Gar Shaolin martial arts kung fu.

Dancing with precision and control, efficient and lightning fast, power rocked the room for the prize of being king of the lair.

An unexpected snapping kick from Chin propelled Garret against a stone lion statue. His passport flew out. Chin caught it in midair and scanned through it.

"Well, well, Garret." Almost invisible was a tiny set of numbers on the back page prefaced by the letters *KOK*. "The King of Kentucky access codes, I do believe."

The impact broke Garret's leg, and he remained on the ground as Chin tossed the passport to Marco. The computer specialist typed furiously. Then his face filled with horror. "There's only eight million dollars in these accounts."

Garret's firm voice explained, "That's the base salary you've paid me ever since you killed Mary in the plane explosion. And, as I have told you, there is no more. Now let Olivia and Abby go."

Silently, Chin walked to the wall and took down one of the ancient iron swords.

Olivia and Abby tried to break free but were no match for their captors' strength. Chin's hoodlums brought the girls beside Garret.

"Please don't, Chin," pleaded Olivia.

Chin walked to Garret and plunged the sword into him. Garret gurgled in death throes.

Olivia screamed, "No!"

Chin turned to Olivia and Abby and said, "Your fathers not only pronounced their own deaths, but yours as well."

58

DAVID AND GOLIATH

C hin pulled out the sword from Garret's torso and ominously raised it over Olivia's neck, when suddenly an arrow flew through the air. It rocketed with such velocity and the blade so razor sharp that it skewered Chin from back to front. With the arrow's head protruding through the front of his chest, a dumfounded look crossed Chin's face. The henchmen fled as their boss reeled.

All eyes turned in the direction the arrow came from to see Noah dropping the crossbow, then striding confidently and cockily toward Chin. "Say hello to the fat boy for me."

Chin, bleeding profusely and ignoring pain, pulled the arrow out. "My son will be avenged."

"Yeah? Like father, like son, and I'd say you're both going to the same place, so you can have coffee with him there."

Howling like a banshee, Chin charged at Noah and whaled on the younger man. Left uppercut. Right uppercut. Chin's arms rose, forming double claws and attacks with the full force of the Dragon.

He followed up with a double twirl kick to the head,

knocking Noah down. As Noah got up, Chin performed a flying leap with arms outstretched that sent Noah crashing to the floor again. He rose but, just as quickly, Chin kicked his legs out from under him. Rather than a battle between warriors, it looked like a man playing with a boy.

Olivia went to grab a spear, but Noah shouted, "No!"

Totally spent, Noah collapsed under a series of machine-gun blows to the head and midsection.

Chin leered, "I'm not done yet." He pressed a button on the wall and another wall slid out, revealing an enraged Bengal tiger.

As the beast vaulted to the attack, the strangest thought raced to Noah's consciousness. A quote from the immortal philosopher, and one-time catcher for the New York Yankees, Yogi Berra. *It ain't over 'til it's over.*

"It ain't over," stated Noah, as he rose to his feet and leapt in front of the girls.

Mano-a-tiger duel to the death. Noah versus the tiger. Protection of beloved versus unfettered animal fury.

The clash was ruthlessly violent as man and beast tangled and rolled on the floor. No amount of Hung Gar training would help. Noah chopped the beast on the back, but his blow was as effective as swatting a fly. It infuriated the tiger. It roared as it disentangled itself from Noah and circled him...watching...waiting.

At just the right moment, the tiger catapulted itself at Noah, knocking him down like a bowling pin. Noah sprang up, but the animal swung its paw as it tried ferociously to shred him to pieces. The feline knocked Noah down again and jumped on him, scratching and biting Noah's face, arms, torso and legs.

Bleeding and bitten, Noah tried to fend off the feline's relentless assault. In the recesses of his mind, he tried to think of anything that could help. Yogi Berra wasn't gonna help here.

Two things came to mind. One was a Bible verse taught to him by his mother. *Yea, though I walk through the valley of the shadow of death, I will fear no evil for Thou are with me.* The other came from Master Wu's indoctrination of Confucian thinking. *The virtuous man is free from anxiety; he is free from perplexities and he is free from fear.*

Somewhere deep within, from a place he didn't know he had, Noah summoned strength and erupted. "Not this time, not ever!"

The tiger leaped at Noah with open jaws. Noah evaded the feline's teeth and grabbed it by the scruff of its neck. With the strength of Samson pushing away the temple's pillars, Noah tossed the tiger twenty feet away.

Enraged, the feline charged back but, with dazzling speed, Noah sidestepped the tiger's aggression.

Noah went on the attack. He picked up the chair that Olivia sat on and bashed the tiger on the head, stunning the beast to immobility.

He then went after Chin. The two wounded warriors, one with the experience of a thousand battles against the giants of the world, the other driven by the most powerful force in the universe, love.

Noah grabbed Chin by the mouth. Chin bit down hard, causing Noah's fingers to bleed, but the young lawyer refused to let go as he squeezed and tried to rip Chin's jaw out of the socket.

Then, suddenly, Noah let go. Chin was off guard for a split second, just long enough for Noah to leap and double kick the Tiger Master. Once, twice, three times.

Noah was possessed—acrobatic, artistic, awe-inspiring and totally aggressive.

Noah spun and hooked his foot, landing it hard against Chin's shoulder, knocking him to the floor. Chin was down, but then...another problem.

The tiger regained consciousness and raced toward Noah.

Noah rapidly stepped to a computer, picked it up by its cord and whirled it like a modern-day David with his slingshot. He released it, and the projectile smacked the tiger full force in the side of its body. Incensed, the tiger leapt at Noah. The young lawyer dove out of the way of the beast.

As the tiger came back, Noah picked up Chin and threw him directly at the open jaws of the feline.

The tiger caught Chin in his mouth midair. With a bite force of over five hundred pounds, the tiger sank its jaws into Chin's chest. With the sound of crunching bones and Chin's screams filling the air, blood gushed like a river.

Noah maneuvered deftly behind the animal, grabbed it by the nape and gave it a sharp blow to the middle of its head, knocking it unconscious.

The war was over. The blood-drenched Noah had triumphed. He panted at Chin, "You lose, I win."

Olivia and Abby ran to the exhausted Noah, propping him up.

Chin lay on the ground, writhing in tortured agony. Noah's crossbow was beside him, and he slowly put an arrow in it.

Staggering, he rose unsteadily, aimed it at Noah and shot. The arrow sliced the air as it rocketed toward its destination. Noah ducked, but he was not the target. The arrow embedded itself into a wall socket.

Noah heard a short hissing sound, then flicked his head in time to see the flash of the electrical socket flaring ice-cold cobalt blue, igniting everything in its path.

Tongues of flame curled upward, creating frantic strobing shadows. Noah fought his way through the snarling fire, when the overheated floor exploded outward. A piece of flying pipe hit Noah on the head, sending him crumpling to the floor.

Head woozy and his whole body aching in reluctance, Noah tried to orient himself as waves of angry flames leaped up around him.

"Noah!" screamed Olivia.

The sound of her voice jolted Noah to look in her direction. Behind her, Noah saw Chin, with crossbow ready, firing at another wall socket on his left and shot another arrow. It found its target on the other side of the room.

Now, there were two fires on opposite sides of the room, igniting walls and furniture. With the blaze licking the ceiling now on two flanks, black clouds drifted murderously throughout the room.

As a burning hailstorm of plaster and wood pelted him, Noah struggled to his feet and dashed to Olivia and Abby as Chin picked up another arrow and shot it at a socket on his right.

The socket exploded and flames burst out. From left, right and behind, three blazing infernos surrounded Noah, Abby and Olivia. With no place of refuge, Noah picked up a chair hoping to shield the girls but a huge piece of burning ceiling broke off, knocking the chair from Noah's arms.

Chin readied another arrow, aiming at the socket directly behind the trio. If another fire started, holocaust was inevitable.

A bleeding Garret somehow rose to his feet. With a broken leg, he falteringly hopped on his good leg to the staggering Chin, moving so slowly that his clothes ignited.

With howling flames bellowing up his legs and

scorching chunks of ceiling crashing around and on him, Garret embraced Chin in an inescapable tight bear hug. Searing pain ravaged every part of their epidermis, but these two warriors had unfinished business that could still change their destinies.

The younger Chin fought to escape, grabbing Garret's throat, but the lawyer refused to release his grasp. As the two began to burn as one, Chin gasped, "I can still make you wealthy beyond your wildest dreams."

"You just don't get it, do you, Chin?" Garret rasped. "This is not about money. This is not about honor. This is about Mary and Jocelyn. You killed them and Tommy and I planned this for years. Finally, we have redemption."

"Daddy!" screamed his daughter, Olivia.

Daddy! Olivia had not used that affectionate term with him for fifteen years. Was this the time? Had he finally achieved his goal?

Maintaining his hold on Chin, Garret swiveled his head to see his now twenty-six-year old daughter trying to battle through the scorching death trap to reach him. He knew it was more than a rescue attempt. In the past forty-eight hours, she had discovered the hidden truth of who he really was and why he had acted the way he did—Olivia wanted to make amends after years of hating him.

But the conflagration was too intense and there was one final message he wanted, no, he needed to convey to her. If he didn't, he knew that guilt would forever haunt her.

He called out to her. "Don't come, Olivia. Save yourself. It's okay. I have waited until now to avenge your mother. You were always right. It was my fault. My fault, not yours. But I hope I've made it right. I love you, Olivia, absolutely, completely and forever."

"No!" screamed Olivia. She saw the ceiling above Garret

collapse with screeching white hot steel falling on and around him. "I don't hate you! I love you!"

She saw Garret smiling at her as he held Chin tight and burning like a single candle.

"Olivia!" called Noah as he fought through the flames to reach her. Seeing her tear-filled eyes as she stood there, immobile, he picked her up in his arms and re-entered the fire.

As Noah carried her, she watched the flames shoot outward, upward, downward, then finally engulf the two former best friends who had become worst enemies.

It's over.

NOAH PUT OLIVIA DOWN ALONGSIDE ABBY. WITH THE BLAZING maelstrom consuming the room, they desperately tried to find a way to safety.

But no solution appeared in sight. It would be only moments before the scorching embers whipping at their seared bodies and the screeching timbers falling around them would transform them all into human torches.

Suddenly, sunlight broke out from the far side of the fiery wall on the other side of the room. Master Wu had pushed aside the blackout curtains covering the glass doors to the balcony. Standing in its entrance, he beckoned, "Hurry. Come! Now!"

Noah turned to Olivia and Abby. "Trust me." With that he picked up Olivia and hurled her to Master Wu. Olivia shrieked as the flames surrounded her but Noah's idea worked—she was safe.

As soon as Master Wu caught Olivia, he put her beside him. Noah then picked up Abby and threw her to his Sifu.

As soon as Abby was airborne, Noah glared at the hell-fire in front of him. He had thrown Olivia and Abby over and through the flames but the heat was too intense for him to try to run through it.

He spun his head...and heard the answer.

The tiger had regained consciousness and bellowed its displeasure at the prospect of being barbecued. It was standing on a ceiling segment that was not on fire!

Noah quickly stepped to the tiger and stared right into its face. "Okay, boy. Hang in there with me and we'll both get out of here. Okay?"

He pushed the feline off the unburnt fragment. With the tiger following behind him, Noah used the ceiling section as a shield, battling his way through the inferno to join Master Wu and the girls on the balcony.

The only problem was that they were fifty-four floors above ground. But, even here, they couldn't escape the flames, and the fire reached out to touch the balcony.

There was no choice. Noah, Abby and Olivia leapt over the balcony. Screaming, plummeting down, down, down.

All four accelerated to their inevitable end—the deep end of the Tiger Palace's swimming pool. They hit the water, which broke their fall, but the momentum carried them another fifteen feet down. They touched the bottom before rising to the surface.

Gasping for breath, they bobbed up and down in the water.

Eyes searching frantically, Noah saw Abby and Olivia but there was someone not there. He shouted, "Where's Master Wu?"

Olivia pointed to the high rise. Master Wu had gone into the inferno and was tugging the snarling, snapping and freaked-out tiger to safety on the balcony. After evading one vicious chomp of the feline's incisors, one lightning punch by the aged master to the animal's temple knocked it out.

Holding the beast to his chest, Master Wu forced the animal to leap with him off the balcony. Moments later, man and beast joined the waterlogged survivors of war.

Hearing the angry howling of fire engines and police cars, Noah bobbed out of the water and said, "Let's get out of here."

There was no disagreement.

59

REVELATION

HONG KONG - WEDNESDAY EVENING

Exhausted, battered, bruised and burnt, Master Wu led Noah, Abby and Olivia up the stairs and into the upper floor of his studio.

He pointed at the thirty-foot-long rosewood table. Despite their fatigue, Olivia and Abby still marveled at the intricately carved tiger and crane on the tabletop.

"Your fathers gave it to me," explained Master Wu. "Actually, they gave me everything you see...This was our war room, where we planned for what happened today."

Noah shot his mentor a quizzical look. Master Wu acknowledged his unvoiced question with a deliberate, measured nod of his head.

"This is where we planned your future, Noah. Your scholarships to the United States, your job with Pittman Saunders. We had only a sketchy idea and you more than fulfilled what we had hoped for."

He turned his attention to Olivia and Abby. "This was done for the two of you."

Ignoring the baffled looks in the girls' eyes, Master Wu

turned back to Noah as he went to one end of the table. "Noah, go to the other end, please."

"Sure." Noah took the twenty obedient steps.

"Help me lift the top off and we will put it to the side," ordered Master Wu.

He and Noah gripped the edge of the elongated tabletop —it was easily six hundred pounds. "One. Two. Three." They squatted and hoisted the cover and laid it gently to the side.

"Omigod," was the collective comment. Noah, Abby and Olivia gasped at the sight of what was hidden beneath the lid. Billions upon billions in various denominations and currencies were stored below the table.

Noah was stunned. "How many times have I been in this room and not known what was here? There's Chinese RMB, Canadian, Australian, Hong Kong, Singapore and US dollars, Philippine and Mexican pesos, euros, British pounds and I don't know what else."

Master Wu nodded. "And what you see is just the tip. It goes down another eight feet."

He took Olivia and Abby's hands. "Your fathers knew that, if the funds were kept in any bank, sooner or later Chin would find them."

Noah exhaled. "This explains why we couldn't find the money anywhere. No paper trail, bank or computer records. It went directly here...Cash is king."

Olivia's hand trembled as she squeezed Master Wu. "But my father was willing to let me die for the sake of not revealing the hiding place. How could he do that?"

"That was part of our plan. Garret could do that because he never knew the location. Only Tommy and I knew about this. Chin thought Tommy was too much of a buffoon to know anything about money."

Noah nodded in sudden understanding. "That's why Chin killed him. To Chin, Tommy was expendable."

"Exactly," continued Master Wu. "Garret didn't want to know the whereabouts of the money. He knew that if he did, Chin would eventually force it out of him. Tommy chose me because I was the one person Chin would not suspect. I was too stupid and old-fashioned but, most important, I couldn't care less about money. That's why it would never even cross his mind to consider me."

Master Wu paused for a long second, allowing Olivia, and Abby to absorb this revelation that rocked their lives and completely transformed their thinking of who their fathers were... and the resentment that they had harbored against them.

"Abby, Olivia, your fathers had no choice if the two of you were to stay alive. They did not have the kinds of networks Chin had. Your mothers were the loves of your fathers' lives. They tried to stand up to him... They never forgave themselves for what happened to Mary and Jocelyn. But it wasn't simply about them."

A pained melancholy expression crossed his face. "We had to keep you away from Hong Kong until you were of an age that Chin's insatiable appetite for young forbidden fruit would not matter anymore. But, when Noah graduated and came back, it was time for the finale."

"Revenge for our mothers?" queried Olivia.

"No," said Master Wu, shaking his head. "To protect you permanently. It was inevitable that Chin would find out about his stolen funds. Chin would squeeze Garret and Tommy to tell him where his fortune was and, if they wouldn't tell him, he would unleash hell on you girls until your fathers caved. Putting you directly in harm's path now was the only chance to keep you from being Chin's victims.

Terrible odds for success...but the only ones available. This was all about survival."

The sifu shifted his gaze back to the girls and said softly, "Your survival."

Abby and Olivia began crying as the weight of a lifetime of hatred for what their fathers had done to their mothers began evaporating. Noah stepped over and put one arm around Abby and the other around Olivia. Olivia buried her face in Noah's chest.

"But they knew they could not accomplish it alone. I told them about you, Noah, when you were not even twelve, I told them it would take much, much time before you would be ready... and that was just to be given a chance."

Master Wu made the Shaolin hand sign. "You did it, Noah. I'm proud of you. And now you are free. All of you."

Turning to Olivia and Abby again, he put out a straight-forward question, "And you are a few dollars richer than you were at the beginning of the day. What will you do?"

"Give us a moment," said Olivia.

She and Abby got up and stepped outside the room.

Noah looked at the old photo of himself and Master Wu hanging on the wall. "So when did you decide that I was to be the guy?"

"The day that Garret and Tommy arrived at your parents' doorstep. You had a black eye from trying to beat up two boys much bigger than you who stole an old lady's buns from her street cart."

Noah snickered at the recollection. "Boy, that was stupid of me. Jerry and Chuck could have killed me."

"Exactly, Noah. You didn't care about yourself. You only cared about doing what was right."

"Like I just said. Pretty stupid of me."

Olivia and Abby returned to the table and seated themselves.

Abby opened. "Olivia and I were unanimous in deciding that we didn't want any of the money for ourselves. Between our families' homes and savings, we don't need anymore. At first, we thought we should just burn it. It's blood money and we want nothing to do with it. But then, we started thinking what our fathers would have wanted. They could have disposed of it themselves if that's what they really wanted."

Olivia put on a poker face as she stared directly into Noah's eyes. "So these two spoiled rich bitches have decided to give the money to you to do whatever you want. We are washing our hands of it."

You gotta be nuts. Noah steepled his hands with his fingertips. "I've always wanted my own personal volcano and a private jet to take me there."

No one laughed. "You can think about it and let us know later," offered Abby.

"Nope. I know exactly what I'm going to do. I'm going to do what I wanted to do when I came back to Hong Kong—I'm going to play basketball with a bunch of kids. We'll use the money to form the Chad Huang Foundation, an organization dedicated to helping at-risk and underprivileged youth. That is, assuming my conditions are met."

"Which are?" asked Olivia.

"That the two spoiled rich bitches in front of me join the organization for exactly the same pay as me." Noah grinned. "Zero. The same salary as my dad and mom received. I also want to have Sam Xi on as one of our board members. He's fourteen, from a dysfunctional family and he's our target demographic."

Noah's voice softened. "Chad had taken Sam under his

wing. If he's not here to continue, helping and being with him is the least I can do."

"Can we meet him first?" asked Abby.

"You're going to wish you hadn't said that," chuckled Noah.

EPILOGUE

C hin battled to stay conscious. In his severely depleted state, the combination of Garret's vise-like lock on his body and the toxic black plumes of smoke and scorching heat were overwhelming. He knew it would be over in less than two minutes, maybe one.

It was impossible to escape the deathtrap... but...

But Chin was a battle-hardened veteran who had faced death innumerable times and won. He knew the key was to keep calm and watch for or create a break. Fighting through the agony of movement, he slowly tilted his head back, then thrust it forward. His skull hit Garret's forehead. Normally, Garret would have shrugged it off but because of the heat and his weakened condition, the force was enough that Garret hit oblivion. His body dropped to the ground, a victim of his own miscalculation. By wrapping himself around Chin, Garret provided the tiger master a scant protection against the white-hot angry fire, absorbing the brunt of it himself.

I'm not done yet! Chin knelt to the ground and draped Garret's body over his.

Over the blood-curdling roar of the fiery furnace, Chin heard Master Wu's familiar voice shouting, "Hurry, Noah. Come! Now!"

Wu's voice jolted Chin to an even more determined awareness. With the floor beneath him burning, Chin's hands and knees charred as he crawled toward the elevator. As he moved, the inferno scorched his face, arms and hands but his plan was working. Garret's body shielded him from being completely barbecued.

Chin arrived at his private elevator, pain screaming from every pore in his body, his chiseled body replaced with his own cooked flesh.

He pressed the elevator button and miraculously it opened. Bleeding and burnt, Chin stood. He stooped to pick up Garret's body and tossed the corpse into the flames.

Chin stumbled into the elevator and forced himself to pick up its emergency phone. His fingers screamed for mercy as he punched in a number.

"Yes, Chin, what can I do?" asked Wing, one of his faithful staff at the gargantuan Tiger Palace.

"Help," croaked Chin. But before he could utter another word, he dropped the phone and collapsed to the floor.

Wing went into immediate action. He called down the elevator and saw Chin, at death's door, lying on the floor.

He knelt next to his boss and detected faint breathing. He withdrew his cell phone but, before he could punch in a number, Chin rasped, "No."

Stunned, Wing replied, "You need to go to a hospital. Now."

Chin's voice was barely a whisper. "No hospital. I need my own medicine."

Wing knew what Chin wanted but didn't feel there was

adequate time. "The closest tigers are more than four hours away. You won't make it."

The tiger master had never seen a Western physician or a doctor of TCM, but Bengal tigers were more than just Chin's trademark. He revered them, respected them and used them. He regularly ate tiger parts, not simply for their healing or aphrodisiac qualities, but because he believed his spirit would meld with the tiger's. The tiger was his source of strength, his vitality and his power. If he was going to heal, the tiger would be key to his recovery.

Chin was adamant. "No hospitals. Do it, Wing."

"Yes, Chin."

WITHIN AN HOUR, WING RODE WITH CHIN ON A PRIVATE JET to a refuge in the Himalayan foothills where the cool mountain air would help him recuperate. This location was less than an hour away from the Sundarbans mangrove forests where the greatest concentration of Bengal tigers lived. There would be plenty of poachers to provide Chin with enough medicine for his healing.

As Wing gently wiped Chin's body with soothing water, he saw Chin's head moving slightly indicating he wanted to speak. Wing leaned over, "Yes, Chin."

"Find out where my children are," he rasped. Then Chin fell unconscious.

Wing understood. Chin's four other children were each smarter, more creative and more dangerous than the deceased Duke. There was no way that King, Queenie, Prince or Prez would abandon their inheritance.

Noah Reid, you are a dead man.

THE END

Dear Reader,

If you like what you've read, a review would be much appreciated as reviews are critically important in helping readers make a choice about trying a new author and for helping Amazon to take notice and begin marketing on my behalf.

If you are willing, please leave a review in your local Amazon copying and pasting into your browser **http://mybook.to/FuryUnleashed**

Fury Unleashed is the beginning of Noah's adventures .

In the second of the Noah Reid series,*Venomous,* Noah takes Master Wu on a final pilgrimage to his home monastery in the mystical mountains of China.

He discovers unprecedented evil on land, by sea and on air as Chin's son, King, leads the savage charge to recover the family fortune.

He'll do anything and use anyone from his own merciless mercenaries to his specially bred vipers to achieve his goal. If you like adventures like Indiana Jones or Jack Ryan, you'll love Venomous.

Pick it up for a great pre-order price by copying and pasting into your browser **http://mybook.to/Venomous**

ABOUT THE AUTHOR

Wesley "Wes" Robert Lowe began as a keyboard player for rhythm and blues bands and as a jazz pianist. After completing a Master of Music at the University of Toronto, he composed music for internationally acclaimed films, documentaries and television programs.

With storytelling in his blood, Wes expanded to writing and directing films and media projects, many that incorporate his knowledge of the Chinese experience. In addition to exhibitions at film festivals and being broadcast throughout the world, this led to his chairing a Canadian government fund on Chinese Canadian history.

Today, Wes's bestselling action thrillers captivate audiences with stories that infuse the modern with elements of ancient mysticism, where the conflict of yin and yang integrate seamlessly into contemporary tales of relentless, warp-speed action.

When not writing, Wes loves playing his 1908 Steinway grand piano, custom-roasting his own coffee, and being the chaplain for Chinese military vets.

Receive two FREE novellas, exclusive to our subscribers. To join, visit:

www.wesleyrobertlowe.com

BOOKS BY WESLEY ROBERT LOWE

THE NOAH REID ACTION THRILLER SERIES

Fury Unleashed
Venomous
Manipulated (Spring 2020)

THE RAYNA TAN ACTION THRILLER SERIES

American Terrorist
The Mandarin's Vendetta
Unholy Alliance

Visit www.wesleyrobertlowe.com for more info or if you
are a member of KINDLE UNLIMITED, you can borrow
the ebooks for free.

Made in the USA
Monee, IL
12 August 2021

75515373R00180